Becoming
Bernadette

ALSO BY DANIELLE GRAINGER

THE DENTON HEIGHTS SERIES
Under Her Wing (Book 1):
The Shasti and Madison Story

In Her Cage (Book 2):
The Jaleesa and Tina Story

Within Her Grasp (Book 3):
The Marta and Shanice Story

By Her Command (Book 4)
The Rowena and Minjung Story

Toward Her Passion (Book 5)
A Rikki Carmichael Story

THE BERNADETTE SERIES
Wrecking Bernadette (Book One)

(S)mothering Bernadette (Book Two)

Becoming Bernadette (Book Three)

Desiring Bernadette (Book Four)

Loving Bernadette (Book Five)

BECOMING
Bernadette

BOOK THREE IN THE BERNADETTE SERIES

DANIELLE GRAINGER

Paperback ISBN   978-1-953734-12-9

First Edition 2021

9 8 7 6 5 4 3 2 1

Cover design by Sarah (Forcoverservice)

Published by:
Bibi Books Publishing Company, LLC

Dedication

This work is dedicated to those who honor boundaries and play by the agreed-upon rules.

Acknowledgments

Big thanks go out to those who encouraged me to continue the Bernadette Series. Thanks to Miss A, Miss S, Miss M, and GBoo. Special thanks go out to the fans of the Bernadette series. It is affirming when you reach out and make contact. This sort of validation is encouraging and stimulating. And many thanks to reviewers – your feedback is essential.

Table of Contents

Chapter 1
Live in the Present

I am fully covered in my old-lady flannel pajamas and have been for two weeks since my second bad encounter with a stranger. And I do not intend to have a third. I used to love walking around the apartment nude, but now I feel too vulnerable. I haven't even wanted to touch myself or watch porn or read erotica. Lisa says I have post-traumatic stress from my experience with Mama_Luvs. It was abuse, Lisa keeps telling me. She says I'll bounce back to my usual self eventually. I'm not so sure.

I mean, how did I, Dr. Bernadette Garneau, a respected professor of mathematics, end up chained to a hotel bed for over eight hours and abused by a woman who I thought could be *the one*? That shows you how naïve I am. And stupid. Yeah, it was pretty stupid to meet a stranger alone like that. And it was the second time I did it! Apparently, I'm a slow learner. I rub the scars on my wrists caused by the leather cuffs she'd put on me, but it doesn't soothe me at all.

"Hey, listen," I say to myself. "You had your safe calls to Lisa and Miss Olga in place."

Yeah, so what? Didn't do any good, I answer myself in my head.

"And you had safewords set up with Mama_Luvs."

Monster Mama, you mean?

I replay my time with Monster Mama in my head, trying to figure out what I could have done differently. Mistress Ciara told me I must learn to "use my voice." That other Dommes won't know how to take care of me. She said, "You need to speak up, speak out, and fix whatever isn't working for you." She also said I made a glorious submissive and that I was not meant to be anyone's slave. Hindsight, I'm finding, is definitely not 20-20. There are so many ways this second meet-up could have gone worse. I didn't like what Mama was doing to me. She should have known.

"No!" I admonish myself. "Don't think of her as Mama. She is a

1

psychopath. Not the nurturing mommy Domme you wanted so desperately. Give it up, Bernadette."

Okay, fine! Fine! Fine! I know. I could have ended up dead. I reach for another chocolate donut, grateful for a day off from classes. We're only one week into the spring semester, and I'm tired already. I need to get out of the college freshmen game. I just don't know how. Maybe I need to start doing independent research and publish on my own. Maybe then they'll see my worth at the university.

I take a sip of coffee and think I may be on to something. When I moved out of my house after breaking up with Jen, I made sure the boxes of professional journals, articles, and website printouts came with me. Maybe I'll dust those boxes off and have a look today. Wistfully, I think about all the other stuff I own that's still in my house, the house I own, the house my ex is now living in with her new girlfriend, the one she replaced me with. It's mid-January, but I hope to be moving back into my house on June first when the lease is up. Every day, I pray that Jen is late on a rent payment so that I can evict her and move in earlier. I pound a fist in the air, determined to get my life together. I then drain my coffee.

"Taking back my life," I say to no one.

The university is closed today for Martin Luther King, Jr. day. Personally, I think having some events for enlightenment and enrichment would be better than giving everyone a vacation, but it is what it is. I have a little time to kill before heading out to meet Madison and Shasti at the coffee shop – the coffee shop that Rikki owns. Rikki of the penetrating green eyes. The same Rikki who is so obviously in a relationship and so clearly off limits. Oh, well. All the good ones are taken, I guess.

Normally with time to kill, I watch porn or read erotica. And, yes, I know, these are very wholesome amusements for a thirty-two-year-old single woman. Hmm, I have that erotica novel, *The Transformation of Two* by E.J. Dubois, waiting patiently for me on my e-reader. I take a breath and decide, no, I'm not ready. Fully clothed, I head to my favorite spot in the kitchen and kneel on a thin pillow. I put my hands face down on my thighs and lower my head, eyes closed. Kneeling helps me find a submissive mindset. If I were submitting to a Domme right now, pleasing her would be the focus of my mind. But today, I kneel to ground myself. It's almost a form of meditation for me. Sometimes, I only need five minutes to calm myself, but today, it's more like twenty.

Finally feeling better, I get up and get dressed in real clothes, sit down at my desk, and do a very grown-up thing. I pull out my lesson plans and add a brief review of infinite limits since this new batch of calculus students seems to be weak in this regard. As their instructor, I need to meet them where they are. Blaming them or their high school teachers for their lack of preparedness for my course is counterproductive and doesn't help them or me move forward.

"Hmm," I muse out loud. "Maybe that's a good lesson for my own life right now." I slam shut the lesson plan book and proclaim to the empty living room, "Don't dwell in the past, Bernadette. Be present now and keep moving forward."

My phone rings as if on cue.

"Great timing, Lisa," I say to my kinky friend that I have never met. "How's Tennessee?"

"Cold," she says. "How's Ohio?"

"Also cold," I answer and then add, "and lonely."

"Aww, I was calling to check in anyway, so tell me."

I met Lisa on the website *Kinks.com* when I sent her a message about an erotica story she had posted. Since that initial breaking of the ice, she has become a good friend and confidante even though she has never seen what I look like.

"I feel kind of abandoned, Lisa. Like, I mean, besides you, no one is there for me. There is no one to champion my day-to-day stuff. The small stuff, the big stuff, the stuff in-between. No one to guide me."

"You're lonely, B."

"Did you know that none of them listed me as their sub on *Kinks*?"

"No?"

"Nope. Not Mistress Ciara, not Goddess Julie, not Mama_Luvs."

"Did you list them as your Dominant?"

"No-o," I say tentatively, knowing I am about to be schooled.

"Well? Two things. One – maybe you weren't with them long enough to establish that kind of definitive relationship. And two, B, you have to remember that these people were out for sexual encounters. Well, sex and power, that is."

"I thought I had something real with Mama_Luvs."

"I know you did. Unfortunately, that's how she lured you in, B."

"She was very convincing." I cluck my teeth and say, "I can't tell a predator from a donut."

Lisa laughs, which makes me smile.

"You're so funny, B," Lisa said, "And I know it's only been two weeks since that Monster Mama weekend, but how's the local scene?"

"Oh, I forgot to tell you. Remember that former student of mine I was telling you about? The one with the BDSM bracelet?"

"Yeah."

"She stopped by my office the other day and invited me to join her and her Mistress at a coffee shop in the next town over."

"No kidding. Are they looking for a mènage á trois?"

"A threesome?" I blurt. "Oh, God, I hope not. Madison's too young. And she was my student." I hear the panic in my voice.

"Easy there, B. I didn't mean anything by it." Her voice sounds apologetic. "Just, you know, be aware that people have all kinds of kinks."

"I don't get that vibe from them, but I'll be on the lookout for anything weird."

Lisa burst out laughing. "Oh, good luck with that. We're all weird."

"Speak for yourself," I say with a laugh.

"I am," she says and then cackles. I've only known Lisa for about two months, but she has a knack for knowing what will bring me out of an impending funk. "Oops, Rachel is tapping her wrist, meaning I have to go. We're going to the local dungeon this afternoon."

"No kidding?"

"An expert on wax play is giving a demonstration."

"Oh, wow. I've always wanted –" I stop talking as a surge of arousal swirls through me.

"It's incredible, B," she says gleefully. "And listen, don't expect to hear from me later. I think Rachel will be keeping me a bit busy once we get home."

"Oh, I hear that, friend." I'm happy for her. She and her wife have an amazing power exchange relationship. One that I am trying to find for myself. I stand up and tuck my lesson plan book back in my briefcase.

"Oh, oh, oh," Lisa says with glee. "I finally posted another Muriel story."

"No way!"

"Yes, way. Oops, gotta go. Bye, B." She hangs up abruptly. I don't feel slighted by it either because her Domme wife runs a fairly strict ship, according to Lisa. And the last thing I want to do is get in the middle of a relationship and piss off someone else's partner.

Knowing I shouldn't, I click open *Kinks* on my laptop. Ahh, I have seven messages, but I refuse to look at any of them. I don't care who sent them, and what I really mean by that is I'm not ready to read a message from anyone looking for a play partner to abuse. Been there, done that twice. With a sigh, I hit up Lisa's page and find the "new" icon lighting up her latest installment in the "Begging for Discipline" series. She's such a good writer, but she only publishes her stuff here on *Kinks* for some reason. "All right, Muriel," I say to the imaginary character, who I'm sure is in some kind of predicament, "let's see what mischief you've gotten yourself into *this* time."

Muriel Learns a Lesson

The Domme stroked the blonde head nestled between her spread legs. She tapped the crop lackadaisically, almost lovingly, against the naked form in front of her. "What a privilege it is for you to lick me." She tousled the blonde's hair again. "Don't you think, Muriel?"

Muriel did her best to answer, but the ball gag in her mouth precluded this.

"Sounds like you have a lot to say, Muriel," the Domme goaded. "Why don't you come over here and tell me." The Domme's grin was evil. "Oh, that's right, you can't. You're a little tied up right now, aren't you?" The Domme's submissive was draped over a spanking bench. Her mouth was gagged, and her hands were tied behind her back. Her ankles were tied to the legs of the bench, effectively spreading her wide for easy penetration. Ahh, but that would be later. Maybe.

The Domme arched her pelvis into the blonde's face. She thrust her hips rhythmically. Oh, she was close. "She sucks pussy like a champion, Muriel. She's going to make me cum. Oh, no, no, no, no, you bad girl. You don't get to close your eyes. You brought this on yourself."

"Oh, right there, girl." The Domme pressed the blonde's mouth firmly against her clit. The tongue worked feverishly on the distended organ. "See how much pleasure this sub brings me, Muriel?" The Domme moaned. She was going to cum any second now. "Bet you'd like to be where she is." Her head tilted back as the first wave hit her. "Ahhhh," she moaned as she came. "Yes, yes, keep licking, Princess." Her pussy pulsed as Princess kept working. "Show Muriel how it's done." She inhaled deeply and moaned her exhale.

"Did you enjoy that, Princess?" she asked the blonde, still working between her thighs.

"Yes, Ma'am," the blonde said. "Thank you for honoring me today, great lady." Her mouth and chin and cheeks were wet with the Domme's cum.

"Hear that, Muriel? That's respect. Oh, but you don't know anything about that. Do you?" The Domme smiled down at Princess and said, "Your Mistress said you were a good pussy licker. She was right. I'll give her a good report when I return you. Would you like that?"

"Oh, yes, Ma'am. Thank you." She licked the Domme's arousal from her lips.

"Lick me clean, Princess. Muriel is usually the one to

serve me this way, but she's being punished. Do you wish to know why she's being punished?"

"If you wish to tell me, then yes, Ma'am," Princess said.

"She dared to look at another Domme. Your Mistress, in fact. At the party last night. She was on her leash as usual. She had her eyes down like a good girl. But then she didn't. Curious to see what caught her eye, I followed her gaze." The Domme reached down and stilled the head below her. "Kneel back," she instructed Princess, who did as asked. "She was gazing lustfully at your Mistress, who had opened her home to us and fed us and provided entertainment." She scoffed and looked toward Muriel, "Didn't you, bad girl?"

Without waiting for an answer, the Domme leaped to her feet and grabbed Muriel by the chin. "Didn't you?" Muriel nodded and lowered her eyes. The Domme pushed her sub's head away with disgust. "All the training. Out the window. No respect. None." The Domme checked Muriel's bonds to make sure there was adequate blood circulation. She wanted to punish her sub, not harm her. Satisfied all was well, she reached down and stroked Muriel's freshly shaved mons. Normally the Domme would have praised her submissive for such good grooming, but not today. There would be no praise today. Well, at least not for Muriel.

Muriel's breathing labored as her Domme continued to touch her intimately. She moaned when a finger pressed against her clit briefly and then entered her. She tilted her pelvis, trying to make better contact. Her Domme allowed this for some reason and swirled her middle finger around and over her growing clit. Muriel's moans came fast and furious. She was so aroused. She knew not to question her Domme's motives, but she was surprised her Domme was stroking her pleasurably. If only her Mistress would penetrate her again. If only. Muriel bucked her hips against the working finger. She couldn't bring her legs together to get more friction because they were tied wide open.

And then the finger went away. "No, no, no," Muriel groaned behind the gag. She sounded desperate, even to her own ears.

"What's wrong, Muriel?" the Domme asked. "Didn't get to cum?" She leaned down and put her face inches from her submissive's. "Too bad. We don't always get what we want, do we?"

Muriel shook her head.

"But sometimes we do. Like me, for instance. I want to fuck Princess now. And I'm going to. And I also want you to hear her moan as I give her pleasure. I want you to watch as she orgasms right in front of you."

Muriel groaned, clearly in agony.

"Bring the flesh-colored strap on, Princess. Yes, that one. And the harness." Princess did as bidden. "Put it on me, please."

Princess seemed used to this sort of work and fell to her knees. She strapped the harness and dildo on her temporary Mistress in no time. The Domme checked the fit and patted the sub on her head. "Nicely done. Good girl."

"Watch this trick, Muriel," the Domme said as she handed Princess a wrapped condom. Princess tore open the foil packet and then put the condom in her mouth, forming an O with her lips. She leaned forward and maneuvered so the tip of the dildo pressed against the condom she held in her mouth. She leaned forward slowly, and the Domme watched as the entire dildo disappeared into the sub's mouth. Princess pulled back and sat on her haunches. The Domme beamed. "See that, Muriel?" She lifted the condom-encased dildo toward her bound sub. "You can't do this, can you?" Muriel didn't react, but she also didn't look away. The condom was perfectly rolled over the entire dildo.

"On your hands and knees now, Princess," the Domme commanded softly. "Good girl. Reach back and open up your pussy lips. Show Muriel how wet you are." The Domme moaned appreciatively as she watched. "Mmm, I can't wait to thrust into you. I want to make you moan. I want to make you cum loud and proud. Would you like that?"

"Oh, yes, Ma'am." Princess's voice was thick with arousal. "Please, Ma'am. Please."

"Hear that, Muriel? She's begging me to fuck her."

Muriel groaned, and it wasn't in pleasure.

I groaned right along with Muriel. I was so aroused but couldn't bring myself to relieve the tension. It would seem like a betrayal to Muriel somehow. God, it would be absolute torture to watch my Domme use another sub right in front of me. I would never survive it. I remember being in

Mistress Ciara's townhouse for all of ten minutes and getting jealous of all the subs who had come before me. I feel for Muriel, and I can't stop reading.

"See how she presents herself to me? She wants me." The Domme made sure Muriel watched as she slowly entered the sub in front of her. Princess moaned in appreciation and anticipation all rolled into one. "Hear that, Muriel? She likes it. She likes the attention I'm giving her."

Muriel's brow bunched up in worry.

The Domme gripped Princess's hips and thrust in. "Oh, Ma'am," Princess said as she inhaled sharply.

The Domme responded by pulling out slowly and then ramming the dildo back home, causing Princess's breasts to bounce. "You cum whenever you want, dear. You have permission." The Domme thrust in and out. Her breathing labored as she also became aroused. For her, penetration was the ultimate power. It made her feel strong and invincible. She also felt that power keenly when a submissive allowed her to be in command and in control. She could cum again, but she wasn't going to, not with Princess. No, she had something much better planned.

Princess whimpered as soft cries accompanied her orgasm. She fell forward on her elbows, ass up in the air. "Thank you, Ma'am," she gasped out of breath. "Thank you."

The Domme rubbed the ass in front of her and then pulled out. "Take this off me and clean it. Then clean yourself up." She pointed to the bathroom door. "Wait for me in the kitchen."

"Yes, Ma'am," Princess said. "Thank you, Ma'am." She scurried away to do the Domme's bidding.

The Domme silently walked over to Muriel, who was now crying. The Domme undid the ball gag and then walked around to undo the ankle bonds. She pulled her submissive up by her still-bound hands and walked her over to the same spot where she had just rewarded Princess. She pushed Muriel down to her knees, and Muriel looked up at her Domme towering over her. The sadness in her eyes almost made the Domme cave, but she stayed strong. She spread her legs in invitation. A small smile lit Muriel's lips, and she looked up expectantly. The Domme nodded, a similar smile reaching her own lips. Muriel shimmied forward as tears fell down her cheeks.

With her hands still bound behind her, she eagerly kissed her Domme's center over and over as if asking for forgiveness. The Domme reached down and grabbed the head with both hands, guiding her sub in her mission. Muriel licked and sucked and nibbled until her Domme bucked against her face and came in her mouth. Muriel continued to lick and swallow every ounce of nectar she could until her Domme stepped back out of reach. Muriel looked up.

The Domme reached behind and undid Muriel's wrist restraints. She guided her to a laying position on the padded mat, flat on her back. Muriel instinctively opened her legs as she had been trained. Always be available to your Dominant.

A fresh strap-on acquired, and the Domme pushed

inside her sub using the intimate missionary position. Muriel wrapped her legs around her Domme, pulling her in deep. It didn't take long. Muriel moaned in pleasure as her Domme thrust inside. Her orgasm came quickly. Once Muriel's moans subsided, the Domme pulled out and rolled to Muriel's side. She pulled her sub close and stroked her face soothingly.

"I hope you've learned your lesson, Muriel."

"Oh, yes, Ma'am. I have." There was genuine contrite in her voice. "It won't ever, ever happen again."

"Good," the Domme said. "You are forgiven and have been punished sufficiently. This whole incident is now in the past and is forgotten. Let's focus on the present, shall we?"

"Oh, yes, please, Ma'am," Muriel said, snuggling against her strong Domme, who pulled her close and rocked her gently. She lived for this and had almost lost it. But the past was in the past now, and she would live in the present from now on.

Chapter 2
Yes

I find a parking spot on the street about a block away from the coffee shop and consider myself lucky. This part of Denton Heights is popular, and parking spaces are at a premium. I've walked past the coffee shop before but never gone inside. Jen had taken me to this bedroom suburb of Cincinnati when we had first gotten together, and I remember how inviting the shop looked with its hanging Edison lights crisscrossing the interior. The green plants framing the shop's sign in the big front picture window made it look homey and inviting. It looked like a great hangout, but Jen isn't a coffee fan, so although I wanted to go in all those years ago, we didn't. Ah, but Jen is in the past, isn't she?

I take a couple of deep breaths to slow my pounding heart before going in. The outside of the shop looks just as I remembered it – inviting and cozy, but why in the world am I so freakin' nervous? I'm just here to meet new friends. That's it. Friendship and friendship only. Lisa got in my head about that three-way. I groan and pretend to read the drink specials on the A-frame placard on the sidewalk and construct an imaginary shield around myself, proclaiming to everyone that I am not a kinky pervert and I am not here for a threesome.

The bell jingles on the door as I stand outside, and someone says to me, "It's cold out there, Professor. Come on in."

I turn to find Rikki, the owner of the coffee shop, holding the door open for me.

I bite down a "Yes, Ma'am" and say, "Thank you" instead.

"Hang your coat up here or take it with you," Rikki says with a smile and gestures to a row of coat hooks.

Oh, my God. Why does she make me so nervous? Her dark copper hair is pulled back into a low ponytail and is a style that suits her, as do her clothes. She is wearing a long dark brown skirt that goes well below the knee, a festive green button-down shirt, and a vest that matches the skirt. And her boots——I almost blow out a sigh of arousal but don't because she is looking at me. I quickly turn away, take off my coat, and hang it up on one of the empty hooks by the front door.

"Professor," Madison calls from across the shop, "over here." She beckons me with a wave to a cozy area of the shop that almost looks like a living room set up in a rectangular configuration of furniture. Two couches face each other, creating the rectangle's longer sides, while two high-back, overstuffed chairs make up the two shorter sides. My mathematician's heart soars when I see that the coffee table inside the rectangle is a perfect match size-wise for the setup. Madison is sitting on one end of a long couch, and her mistress, Shasti, is sitting in one of the comfy-looking chairs next to her.

I wave back and turn to Rikki. "You have a lovely shop. I've never been inside before today, I'm sorry to say."

Her smile is genuine and threatens to unravel me when she says, "Well, that changed today, didn't it?" She is looking directly at me. Into my soul. Oh, my God.

"Uh, yes. Indeed, it did." Oh, yeesh. Did I just say, "indeed"? Yes, yes, I did. I chide myself to get it together. Rikki has a girlfriend, and I will not be that person who breaks up a couple unlike Jen's new toy that broke us up.

"Go get comfortable," Rikki says and gestures toward Madison and Shasti. "I'll send Brittany over to get your order." She turns to go but then swivels her head to look back at me and says, "On the house."

"Oh, you don't have to –" I start to say.

"No arguments," she says with a shake of her head, and I melt inside. She oozes authority. She is an unmistakable Dominant alpha-type personality. The way she speaks. The way she moves. The way she looks directly at you. My face gets warm, and it's got nothing to do with the temperature of the shop.

I head over to Madison and Shasti, becoming more aware of my awful clothing choices the closer I get to them. Why did I think faded jeans and a flannel shirt were fashionable? And the fact that I desperately need a haircut has now become uber obvious. I must look like a slob. But you know what?

Whatever. I'm not here to find a partner or a girlfriend or anything like that. Friends. That's what I'm after. That's it. And they will have to take me as I am.

"Hi, Madison," I say and wave even though we are only three feet from each other now. I make no move to hug her. It still feels weird to be hanging out with a former student.

"Hi, Professor," Madison says in a breathy way that betrays the fact that she is excited that I am here. I see that she has a Calculus Two problem set in her lap and must be doing homework. I am one hundred percent positive that I will be helping her with some of those problems before our visit is over. Oh, no. Did they ask me here to help Madison with her Calc homework? That would suck. But I choose to think that they want my friendship above that.

"Glad you came out today, Professor," Shasti says, lowering the book she is reading. "Join us. She gestures to the other couch on her left, opposite Madison.

I sit, grateful that my back is to the wall and I can drink in the atmosphere of Rikki's shop. "Thanks for inviting me. I probably need to get out of the house more often." The coffee shop is a little cold, and I wish I had a scarf or something to wrap up in. Maybe it's just nerves. I can't tell. These people know my awful secret. The secret that I am a pervert. But so are they, so there you go.

"This is our little oasis," Shasti says. "We talk freely with each other here, just so you know."

"Good to know," I say and look up to find Brittany heading toward me.

Madison notices her, too, and says, "Everything they have is good here. You should try a chocolate croissant." She rolls her eyes in ecstasy, and I can't help chuckling out loud.

"Ahh, I don't want to spoil my dinner," I say. That's not the real reason I don't want to order one. It's because I know Rikki is treating me, and I don't want to take advantage.

"See, peanut?" Shasti says to Madison. "That's how grownups act."

"Mistress," Madison says seriously, her eyes narrowed, "I am *not* grown up."

Shasti burst out laughing. "No, decidedly not."

I chuckle along with them. Yes, despite being around twenty-five years old, Madison is a *little*. A *little* who takes Calculus. Still smiling, I turn to greet Brittany. She is wearing a forest green apron with the emblem "Rikki's Coffee Shop" emblazoned across the front. The apron does nothing to hide the tight white t-shirt underneath, and I wonder if Rikki picks out Brittany's clothing every day. Many Dominants do that for their submissives. I wonder if Brittany is also a *little* because she is wearing her dark blonde hair in a ponytail high on her head, making her look younger than her age which I estimate to be early twenties.

"Hey, Professor, what can I get for you?" Her smile seems genuine, and I feel a pang of guilt for the attraction I have for her Domme.

"I saw you had a cinnamon vanilla latte on special today?"

"Perfect," she says with that same endearing smile. I can see now what Rikki sees in her. Despite her bratty attitude the first time we'd met, she seems quite charming now. "Whipped cream?"

"Ooh, yes, yes, yes," Madison says. "Get that."

I chuckle and say, "Okay."

I turn down the chocolate croissant offer and watch Brittany cheerily walk away.

"She seems different than the Brittany I met two weeks ago," I say quietly to Shasti.

"It's all Rikki," Shasti says.

"Oh?"

Madison leans closer as if she doesn't want to be overheard, so I do, too. "Rikki is a brat tamer."

"Oh, I see," I say and nod my head. "That explains it, then."

Madison nods her head knowingly.

"How are those, er, abrasions healing, Professor?" Shasti asks.

Involuntarily, I rub my left wrist. "Oh, fine. I think I'll have a scar on this left wrist, though."

"Not quite the souvenir you wanted from that weekend, is it?"

"No, not at all. Seriously, though? Parts of the weekend were good, but I thought it would go in a different direction. I was so stupid. Meeting a stranger four hours away from home was not a good idea."

"Probably not," Shasti says. There is no reprimand in her voice, only sympathy. "Rub some vitamin E oil on those areas once the scabs are gone, okay? That'll provide moisture, and you'll be less likely to scar."

"Thank you," I say. That is excellent advice, and I make a mental note to stop at a pharmacy on the way home. I hadn't thought about trying to prevent the scarring. Do I secretly want the scars as a reminder of the bad choices I've made? I don't think so, but the jury is still kind of out on that.

"May I ask a personal question?" Shasti places her book gently on the coffee table.

"I suppose," I say, not sure where she is going. I hope this isn't her segue into asking me to join their two-some.

"Were you raped?"

"Oh," I say, surprised by the question. Madison lays her calculus book on the couch. "I'm not sure. I know that sounds crazy."

"It doesn't," Shasti reassures me.

"I've gone over that in my mind so many times that I'm confused about what happened." I fold my hands in my lap and take a moment to gather my thoughts. "I mean, I consider myself a feminist who has the right to do whatever I want with my own body, right?"

"Agreed," Shasti says with a nod.

"And I also have the freedom to tell my partner what I want out of the sexual partnership, right?"

"Yes, as it should be."

"Mama_Luvs seemed to understand what I needed, but after a while, I could tell that she –"

"She was a Mommy Domme?" Madison interrupts.

"Supposedly, but she turned into something else."

Brittany interrupts us by delivering my coffee. It's in a glass double-wall mug, and I hold it up to examine the geometry of it. I thank her, and then she plops down on the couch next to Madison, Madison's calculus book in between them. "I am officially on break," she says and pulls her phone from her apron pocket. She rests the bottoms of her feet on the edge of the coffee table, which I'm sure Rikki would frown on. She buries her face in her phone. I wasn't sure if I should continue or if the thread of the discussion has been broken.

In true Domme fashion, Shasti takes charge. She nods her head toward Brittany and says quietly, "Only if you're comfortable."

"It's okay." I take a few sips of the cinnamon vanilla latte and moan my appreciation.

"That good, huh?" Brittany grins and peers over her phone.

"It's fantastic. Thank you." I take another sip and sigh. I needed that. I think Rikki's Coffee Shop is going to become a regular stop for me from now on. "So, about Mama_Luvs –"

"The turd whose ass Rikki wants to kick?" Brittany asks this time without looking up.

I chuckle. "Uh, yep. That would be the one." Brittany has a definite way about her, and I regret forming such a negative opinion the first time we'd met. I look back at Shasti and say, "Look, I was there that weekend under my own volition. I was a willing participant. We discussed safewords, but I never used one."

"Why not, Professor?" Madison asks. Poor thing, she looks so sad and concerned for me. Maybe I shouldn't give details. Madison is a *little*, after all, and she might not be ready for such grown-up things.

"Well, long story short. I wanted to use my safeword. I mean, I was awake and lucid most of the time, but what if she didn't honor it? What if she didn't stop? Then the real nightmare would have begun. And I guess this way, I felt like I still had some control."

"Oh, Professor," Madison says, "I'm so sorry."

"I'm doing okay, though. I think. I'm totally going to play it cool for a while. No more meeting strangers." I hold up my right hand and say, "Promise."

"That would be the wise thing to do," Shasti says.

Brittany bursts out laughing. "Oh, my God. Look what she wants to do to me." She hands her phone to Madison, whose eyes grow wide. She covers her mouth with her hand.

"That looks, um, painful," Madison says finally. "I don't know if I could stand that."

I am curious but don't want to ask. I look up to see Rikki behind the counter, holding her phone, grinning like a Cheshire cat. How cute that they are teasing each other at work like this.

Brittany holds up the phone so Shasti and I can see the picture. I almost choke at the shock of it. On the screen is a close-up image of someone's pussy.

Oh, my God. The pussy has been sewn shut.

"Oh, my," is all I can say. I can't wrap my head around that. Wow. People are into some weird shit, but I have learned that what goes on between consenting adults is their own business.

Shasti shrugs and says to Brittany, "If that's what you two want to do, then go for it."

Brittany nods once and buries her face back in her phone, her thumbs flying furiously as she types in a response.

Shasti motions for me to continue.

"Well," I say, "I guess by not using my safewords with Mama_Luvs, I gave her my consent, didn't I?"

"You did." Shasti sighs and pats my forearm. "But I know how hard it is for submissives to use their voices sometimes. However, Professor, you must do so if you feel you're in danger. And it sounds like you were in danger. Promise me you'll do that from now on?"

I nod and reach for my coffee. "I promise." I hope it's true. "Shasti, can I ask you a question?"

"Sure, Professor. Anything."

"What exactly is power exchange? I keep hearing about it, but I can't quite put my finger on what it means." I reach for my latte and decide to hold the mug in my hands. I want to put on my coat, but I don't want Rikki to think I'm accusing her of not making sure her customers are comfortable.

"That's a good question," Shasti says. "It sounds like you didn't have an equal power exchange with that woman. Tell me more about your weekend with her."

I smile at her. She is using her Mommy Domme power on me. "Okay, uh, well, at first, everything was good. She made me feel subordinate by making me strip and then kneel in front of her."

"And you did so happily because you knew that she would make you feel good things, correct?"

"Yes, Ma'am." I cringe. "Oops, I'm sorry. I meant no disrespect."

Shasti chuckles. "None taken. It's a compliment." She patted my forearm again. "Go on."

"I felt like she would take care of me and nurture me. And in turn, I would take care of her. And I did." I look up and realize that I now have everyone's attention, including Rikki, who is standing directly behind Brittany. "I, uh," I clear my throat, "took care of her needs immediately."

Heads nod in understanding.

"And then you hoped she would take care of you in the same way?" Shasti asked.

"Oh, no. Not sexually. Not yet, anyway. Later, I hoped, but, no, I wanted her to, um, nurture me. And she did. She took me to an art museum, and I really liked that. See? She wanted me to grow."

"That sounds wonderful," Shasti says. "Your journey that weekend started well then?"

"It did, but then she ordered food I didn't like at the restaurant."

"Welcome to my world," Madison blurts and then pouts.

I lean forward and whisper, even though everyone can hear, "Bigs just don't understand that vegetables are disgusting. Do they?"

Madison bursts out laughing and screeches, "No, they do not!" She bugs out her eyes at her Mistress, who wags a finger back but then shakes her head and smiles. This is clearly a common point of contention between them.

"But exploring new foods is part of helping a person grow," Rikki says.

"Yes, yes," I say, knowing she's right. "So up until the madness the next day, we were kind of fulfilling each other's expectations, I guess."

"Sounds like it," Shasti says. "There seemed to be a continual give and take. Each getting her needs met. Power exchange in a limited fashion."

"Where does the 'power' part of that come in, though?"

"Not everyone would strip and kneel before another person on command, Professor," Brittany says. "You gave her power over your free will."

I nod my understanding.

"Initially, I think," Madison says. "But with Mistress and me, I take a lot from her. I need her. She takes care of me." She shoots her Mistress a grateful look, which is returned.

"She needs me," Shasti adds. "And that fulfills me. But I also make sure she understands that I need her. I want her to feel that deep in her bones."

"I do," Madison mouths soundlessly.

"So, it's like a give and take? Take and give?" I am more confused than ever.

"Yeah, sorta," Brittany says. "When she tells me to clean the kitchen, I do it. When she tells me to secure myself to the St. Andrew's cross and wait for her, I do it, even if I'm waiting for over an hour." Rikki laughs behind her. This playfulness must be part of their relationship. "And then when she uses my body for anything she wants, I am there – present and in the moment."

"Sounds like she has the power over you, though," I say, not daring to look up at Rikki. "But what power do you have over her?"

Brittany blushes to the roots of her hair. I haven't known her for long, but it's odd to see her this uncomfortable. She clears her throat and says, "I get the most amazing orgasms I've ever experienced. She sends me into endorphin-fueled subspace." She closes her eyes as if remembering. "And it's exactly what I want. She fulfills her need for Dominance, and I get to cum."

The group chuckles quietly, and I sneak a peek at Rikki. Her smile is an amused one. Her sub makes her happy. That is clear.

"And, Professor," Shasti says, "don't forget that in a healthy D/s power exchange relationship, subs have a lot of power. One utterance of their safe word and everything stops."

"I never thought about it that way," I say. "I guess I was afraid she wouldn't stop."

"You'll never know," Rikki says. "But it sounds like she wasn't respectful of you or your body." She sighs and adds, "It sounds like there ceased to be any exchanges in power, and she took it all. And that is totally unacceptable."

I nod. "Thanks for letting me ask questions like this. I don't have…" I feel myself tearing up and reach for my empty coffee cup.

Shasti reaches over and pats my arm again. "It's okay, Dr. Garneau. You have us now."

"Yeah," Madison adds quietly.

"Thank you," I say to both of them. Then, I look over at Brittany and Rikki and say the same to them.

"All right," Rikki says authoritatively and pushes back off the couch. "It's back to work for both of us. Brittany, please get the professor a refill."

"Yes, Ma'am," Brittany says and tucks her phone into her apron. She turns to me and says, "Stick with us, Professor. You're in good hands."

"Thank you. I think I will."

For the next half hour or so, we chat amiably, and as predicted, I do end up sitting on the other couch with Madison, helping her with calculus. The integration-by-parts technique can be pretty frustrating and confusing for beginners, but she seems to get it after a while. I even throw a few classic problems at her that I know Professor Yang will try to trip them up with. It's not that I have insider knowledge about that; it's just what I would do.

"Oh, no," Shasti groans.

"What, Mistress?" Madison says, and we both turn to look where Shasti's gaze has landed.

Walking in the front door and heading for the counter is the most gorgeous androgynous creature I have ever seen. She is tall, and her short, sandy brown hair is styled perfectly to suit her chiseled features. Her high cheekbones and pouty lips are drawing me in. Oh, my God. I have never seen such a handsome butch before. Look how authoritatively she walks. Shit, why did I choose this day to look like a bum?

"Who is that?" I whisper to Madison, whose fawning expression must mirror mine.

"That's Daddy Vic," she whispers back. She sits up taller and, in full voice, says, "Hi, D—"

Shasti clears her throat, which cuts Madison off, but the dreamy woman who goes by Daddy Vic hears her and turns.

"Hey, squirt," Daddy Vic calls over to us. "How you doin'?" Daddy Vic's black leather jacket hugs her body and throws my imagination into overdrive. And her black boots. It is becoming very warm in Rikki's coffee shop.

"I'm good," Madison says with a giggle.

"I'll be right over," Daddy Vic says and then looks at me. Her overlong gaze hits me in all kinds of lovely places.

Daddy Vic pays for her coffee and sits in the chair opposite Shasti. "And who is this lovely vision?" She looks me over from head to toe, and I should be offended, but I am not—quite the opposite.

"Victoria," Shasti says, "this is Madison's teacher."

"Ahh," Daddy Vic says knowingly. "So, *this* is the math professor you keep going on and on about."

I am embarrassed by this revelation. Does Madison have a crush on me? Oh, my God. I never led her on in any way. I hope Shasti knows that. Shoot, I hope Madison knows that.

"Um," I say, totally disarmed, "I'm Bernadette. Nice to meet you."

Daddy Vic puts her hand out, and I find myself reaching for it with my own. She grasps my hand and holds it without saying anything for a few overlong moments. Her eyes have locked onto mine, and I find that I am breathing heavily.

"Are you collared?" Daddy Vic asks me softly.

"Um, no." I feel my cheeks reach incineration temperature.

"Have dinner with me." Daddy Vic's piercing brown eyes urge me to say yes.

"Yes," I hear myself say.

Chapter 3
So Much Fun

We are seated at a secluded corner table at Mamma Mia's Italian Restaurant. It's the kind of table with a curved bench going three-quarters of the way around. Daddy Vic has these smoldering brown eyes that melt me with every look. She has positioned us out of the eye line of most of the other diners. She is sitting so close to me that our legs are touching, and I can feel her body warmth.

I wish I'd had a chance to go home and change, shower maybe, but she insisted we didn't delay after Shasti and Madison said their goodbyes and left the coffee shop. And here we are.

"Did you enjoy your chicken parmesan?" she asks as a hand rests on my thigh, which sends a roll of excitement directly to my sex.

I don't answer her for a moment, but then I clear my throat and say, "Yes. Thank you. That was a good suggestion." I drain my wineglass, and she refills it for me instantly with her one free hand.

She fills her own glass, and we've now officially killed the bottle. She takes a sip, so I do as well. The hand on my thigh makes slow circles. My body is responding. I can't help it. And somehow, I know she can tell.

"I, um, think it's neat that you're a chief high school security officer," I say. I'm trying to distract myself from the hand that is making its way up my leg. "It sounds like you do a lot of behind-the-scenes stuff that the students and teachers don't even know about."

"Exactly," she says. "And we don't want them to know. We want them to feel safe and secure. Of course, they freaked out when we had that active shooter drill last fall."

"That sounds terrible," I say, the hand momentarily forgotten. I can't imagine the university making us go through one of those drills.

"Better to be prepared. Don't you think?"

"Yes, it is." All evening, I've desperately wanted to ask her how she wants to be addressed. Daddy Vic? Vic? Shasti called her Victoria. Ma'am, maybe? Oh, or maybe she wants to be called Sir. I don't know. I'll let her bring it up. She's definitely running this show so far, and that's fine by me.

"You look good in these jeans," she says and leans close. "But you'll look better out of them."

"Here?" I panic. Oh, God.

"No, I would never do that to a sub without discussing it first," she says.

"Oh, okay." I blow out a sigh. "You had me worried there for a minute."

"Come home with me?"

"I have to teach in the morning."

"I have to work." The hand has moved to my crotch, and my legs separate a little in invitation. She rubs me up and down, applying just the right amount of pressure. I buck my hips gently in encouragement. "You like this," she says, stating the obvious.

"Yes." I turn to face her. Her lips are so close. I want her to kiss me. But she does not.

She holds my gaze and says, "Let's go back to my place."

"Okay," I say.

She calls for the check and pays the server. She gives me the address and apartment number in case we get separated as I follow behind her. Once we're out in the parking lot, she looks up at the sky and mentions how cold winter nights can be in January. "But the stars are out," she says.

"It's so pretty out here," I say with a shiver.

"C'mon, let's get going." She chivalrously walks me to my car.

Once I'm alone, I wonder if I shouldn't just drive home. I can't believe I'm going to her apartment. Oh, my God. I just met her a couple of hours ago. Okay, first of all, we have to discuss safe words. I'll insist if she doesn't bring it up. And and and I won't let her tie me up. Not tonight, anyway. And since Shasti and Madison seem to know her, I'll take that as a vote of Daddy Vic's trustworthiness.

Her apartment complex is one of the newer ones in Denton Heights. I'd checked it out when I searched for apartments after my breakup with Jen, but it was a bit too pricey for me. Before I get out of the car, I text Lisa to let her know that I am on a date and will text her later when I'm leaving. She doesn't get back to me immediately, so I text her Daddy Vic's address and Shasti's phone number, just in case.

She parks her pickup and waits for me to walk up from visitor parking. She doesn't reach for my hand, but that's okay. We hardly know each other. We head inside the lobby and take the elevator up to the third and highest floor. Her apartment is at the farthest end of the hall. She doesn't speak as we make our way, so I don't either.

Her apartment is magnificent. From the third floor, you can see Cincinnati's downtown lights in the distance and the downtown lights of Denton Heights close up. "This is a beautiful view," I say. Not having a name to call her is hard for me. I wish she would tell me.

"It is," she says. "Hang up your coat by the front door. Would you like water?"

"Yes, please." I head to the kitchen after hanging up my coat as instructed. The kitchen is wonderfully clean, bright, and uncluttered. Although, to be honest, it doesn't look like she uses it much.

She hands me a bottle of water from the fridge and takes one for herself. "Restroom?"

"Uh, yes, please," I say and follow her directions down the hall. I genuinely do have to use the bathroom, but I also need a minute to regroup. Am I doing this? Really doing this? What is it I'm doing, anyway? I am about to have sex with an extremely attractive butch lesbian. Yes, I'm about to do this. After freshening up and rinsing my mouth, I head back to the living room. The lights are low, and soft music plays in the background. She's making it romantic. That's so nice.

"All good?" she says and stands up.

"Yes," I say and stand near the doorway to the kitchen.

"You want something to call me, don't you?" The look in her eye tells me this amuses her.

"Yes."

"What do you think is appropriate for the evening?"

Oh, no, she's making me decide. She's momentarily giving me control. That is so gentlemanly. And as a gentleman, I should call her Sir.

"May I call you Sir?"

"Yes, that works," she says. "Take your shoes off."

I do so and tuck them out of the way near a bookshelf.

She moves closer, so close that I involuntarily take a step back. She puts both hands on my shoulders and pushes me up against the wall. I gasp at the suddenness of it, but then her lips are on mine, and I melt into them. Her thigh insinuates itself between mine, and she presses hard against my center. I moan. I can't help it. A bulge in her pants presses up against me. Adrenaline spikes when I realize what it is. She is packing. Her lips travel from my mouth to my chin to my neck and then to the sensitive spot behind my earlobe. I shiver.

"Oh, Sir," I say, trying out her honorific.

She answers by leaning back and unbuttoning my flannel shirt. Her thigh still claims me. She kisses the newly exposed skin above my bra line, and I reach for her head with both hands to encourage her. She has other ideas, though, and grabs both wrists. She pushes my arms back, pinning them to the wall. She goes back to kissing my bra line and says huskily, "Take this off." She pulls at my sports bra with her teeth and releases my arms.

I know my face is tinging red as I take off the flannel shirt and then shrug off the sports bra – not the sexiest thing to wear on a date, but I didn't know I'd be on a date this evening, so it's not my fault. It doesn't matter, I tell myself. I'm so wet for Daddy Vic right now, so it just doesn't matter. Once my breasts are freed, I think she will continue her trail of kisses, but she doesn't. She leaves me standing up against the wall topless and moves to sit in a chair in the living room.

"Come here," she says quietly, but the tone in her voice makes it clear that she is in command. I move to stand in front of her. She reaches up and rubs her middle fingers over my nipples, hardening them instantly. She smiles and looks into my eyes. "Strip for me, please."

Oh, God. Does she want a striptease or something? There's no way. I'll just, I don't know, take off my jeans. I watch her face and reach down to undo the button of my pants. Her gaze follows my hands. I pull down the zipper, hook my thumbs into the sides, and push them down my thighs. They fall to the ground, and I step out of them. I kick them to the side, watching to see if she maybe wants me to fold them up carefully like Mama_Luvs did. She doesn't.

"Panties," she says simply. Her focus is directly on my crotch.

"Yes, Sir," I say.

I whisk my boi shorts down and kick them over toward the jeans.

"Masturbate for me," she says simply.

I was not expecting this.

"Masturbate, Sir?"

"Lay down on the hassock." She points to a huge flat-top hassock behind me that almost looks like a coffee table but isn't. And it's uber clear what this hassock is used for. I sit down, and she motions for me to scoot back. When I am in the right spot, she nods. "Open your legs for me, baby."

I shudder. A wave of arousal hits me as I do as she asks. Oh, God, I feel so dirty. "Touch yourself," she commands and leans forward.

I dare not kid around and touch my knee or something. I don't know how she'll react, especially because she looks so serious right now. My stomach fills with butterflies as I reach down with my right hand and rub my inner thigh. My other hand joins in, and then my right hand slakes through my wetness.

"Show me," she says.

I hold up wet fingers.

"Beautiful, baby." She nods for me to keep going.

I swirl the fingers of my right hand through my wetness, coating my outer labia and inner. I trace a path between inner and outer lips and then plunge my middle finger inside. I thrust in and out for a while and then rake my fingers up and over my clit. I involuntarily buck my hips at the contact.

"Spread your lips. Let me see that hard clit."

I moan at her words and spread my legs wider. I open my labia, revealing my growing nub.

"Stroke yourself," she says. Her breathing is labored. This is clearly turning her on. She sits back and pulls the zipper down on her black pants. She reaches inside and pulls out a dildo. It is lifelike - fleshy colored with veins and everything. My hips buck slightly as my thoughts turn to what I hope is coming next.

Daddy Vic strokes the phallus with her right hand, her hips undulating slightly. She is as turned on as I am.

"Don't cum yet, baby."

"No, Sir." My voice is breathless. I open my legs wider and spread my lips in invitation. "Fuck me, Sir. Please fuck me." Oh, God. Who am I saying these things?

Daddy Vic pulls something out of a jar on the side table. She uses her teeth to rip open the foil packet. It is a condom. She pushes the condom down over her phallus, and I wish it had been me doing it with my mouth.

She leaps up and, within seconds, impales me on her dildo.

"Oh, yes, Sir. Yes, yes, yes."

She thrusts fast and furiously. I wrap my legs around her body, keeping her in place. She grunts her approval. My fingers work my clit. "Sir –" A pre-orgasmic wave hits me. "Sir, can I –" She lifts her body to get a better angle to drive in deeper. I can't help it. My insides clench, and she can't move in or out for a moment.

"Fuck," she says. "Your cunt is like fucking iron."

I can't respond. My pussy spasms, and my hips buck up and down to her rhythm. I moan my release, hoping the neighbors won't hear me, but I don't care. She continues to thrust inside me as wave after wave washes over me. I am flying. And she keeps on pumping.

It isn't long before her thrusts change, and she moans her own release. It's low and long and is music to my ears. "Fuck, baby," she says. "I knew I had to have you."

"Thank you, Sir." Her breathing is heavy as she lets her body weight fall on me. Her hard phallus remains inside me, keeping me filled. I like it. Very much. "I've never been fucked like that, Sir."

She leans up on her elbows, taking the weight off of me. "No? Interesting. Let's rest. I want to fuck you again. Would that be all right, baby? Can I fuck you again? In a little while?"

"Oh, yes, Sir. Please, Sir," I say, hoping she'll stay inside me for a while longer.

I teasingly tighten my pussy muscles as she tries to pull out.

She chuckles and says, "That's some talent you've got there." It's a talent I didn't even know I had until tonight. She climbs off me and stumbles back to her chair. "Normally, I'd make you lick your essence off my dick, but you don't want to lick a condom. I'll buy a new dildo just for using in you."

"Yes, please, Sir. I'd like that very much," I say calmly, but inside, I am screaming, Oh, my God. She wants me to come back. My heart soars while my wetness oozes down my thighs. I close my legs as I sit up and just know that my cum is soaking the hassock's covering.

She seems to know what I'm worried about and says, "It's washable."

"Okay. Thank you, Sir." I scootch forward so that I'm sitting on the edge of the hassock.

"Would you like a tour?" She pulls the condom off and tosses it in a small trash can next to her chair. She stands up, fixes the phallus back inside her pants, and zips up. She is fully clothed, and I am fully naked. And I like it. I don't know why, but I like this imbalance of power.

I hope she reaches for my hand as she leads me down the hall, but I am wrong. She opens a closed door opposite the bathroom. I assume it is her bedroom, but I am wrong again. There are so many things that I can't take them all in at once. She has a playroom in her apartment.

I must have had a stricken look on my face because she laughs and says, "We're not playing in here tonight, baby. Next time. It depends on what you'd like to explore with me and what your limits are. But not tonight."

I chuckle and shiver a little. I'm not sure if it's from the cold or all the possibilities. She shows me the St. Andrew's Cross with its tie-downs and padding. I'd never seen one up close. She shows me a spanking sawhorse, which I hope she'll drape me across one day. There are a bunch of floggers and paddles and a couple of canes. The whips are displayed at the end of the long line, but she says she isn't good enough to use the biggest one on anyone yet. That gives me hope that she is a caring Domme and will look out for my best interests.

"We should have discussed safe words," she says. "But I was so hot for you; I couldn't wait."

"Uh, same goes for me, Sir," I say and stroke the leather collars hanging on the wall near the cross. "I like the stoplight system."

"Red and green are obvious, but what does yellow mean to you?"

"Slow down, please, Sir. Or pause for a moment until I can regroup. That's what yellow means to me." Oh, God, how I want her to push me up against the wall again and kiss me. I am so vulnerable right now.

"Got it. And you will use your safewords." She looks directly at me. "Is that understood?"

"Yes. Yes, Sir. And I, um…" I hem and haw for a while until I finally show her the scars from my last encounter, explaining my anxiety about bondage. She nods her understanding and shows me a set of Velcro restraints. She puts one on my wrist and shows me how I can easily break the bond. "Thank you, Sir. I can deal with that, I think."

Have I died and gone to heaven? She is so thoughtful and seems to understand my needs. Not to mention drop-dead gorgeously hot. And she took me home to play with. *Me!*

"Let's sit for a few minutes and recharge," she says, leading me out of the playroom. "I want to know more about your experiences."

We sit back in the living room and drink some water. My wine buzz is dissipating, and I'm suddenly very thirsty. She sits in her chair while I sit on the hassock. I feel like I'm on display. Maybe I am. In broad strokes, I tell her about my experiences with Mistress Ciara and Mama_Luvs. I thought she would tell me more about herself, but she doesn't. Instead, she says that she requires her subs to get tested for STDs and STIs regularly and suggests I go to the Planned Parenthood right in town. I tell her there's one near the university that I can go to on my lunch break tomorrow. She rummages in the side table drawer and flashes me a printout showing me she is clean and disease/infection-free. I hope to have a similar printout to show her soon. I'm not sure how long it takes to get results.

While we talk, she makes me lie down with a pillow under my head. From her command chair, she asks me to spread my legs and open up my pussy with my fingers again. I don't think I am an exhibitionist, but this turns me on immensely.

"You have a beautiful pussy, baby." Before I can answer, she says, "And I'm going to fuck it again. Right now." She unzips and pulls out her dildo. She rolls another condom over it and says, "I'm going to teach you how to ride me."

She gestures for me to move off the hassock and lays down in my place; her phallus sticks straight up in the air. She shimmies close to one side.

"Sir, I've never –"

"That's okay. Most lesbians haven't." She pats her right side. "Stand here facing me." I move to her side. "Swing your right leg over me and settle your knee near my hip. Yes, yes, that's it." I miscalculate a little, and her phallus is

31

in front of me and not anywhere near the place we both want it. "Your left leg is going to stay on the floor to give you leverage and keep you from tiring out." She runs her hands up and down my inner thighs, and I sigh. "Move up a bit. Yes. Lift your pelvis." Her phallus touches my sex. "You're in control right now. You will set the pace. Do what makes you feel good. Don't worry about me." She reaches up and kneads my breasts. "I'll be fine."

I chuckle, but that is short-lived as I lower myself. Her cock keeps sliding away from the goal, and I am getting frustrated.

"Use your hand to guide me inside."

I reach beneath me and grab her phallus to guide it to the goal. I slowly lower myself until it bottoms out against my cervix. I moan and lift up and then slowly drop back down. "Oh, Sir," I say and rise up and down. I establish a nice rhythm and feel the instant stirrings of an orgasm in the distance. "This is…" Daddy Vic plays with my breasts and rubs her fingers over my nipples so I lose my train of thought. If I lean forward, will she suck them?

I have no chance to find out because she places a hand strategically near our combined centers so that when I raise and lower myself, she strokes my clit. "Oh, Sir," I say breathlessly. "I'm going to cum, Sir. May I cum, Sir?"

"Yes, of course, you can cum, baby. Cum all over my dick."

Her words ignite me, and I ride her fast and furiously. It feels so fucking good to cum this way. She's so deep inside. Holy fuck. There is no pre-orgasm this time. My pussy tightens and shoots me to the moon and back. I continue to ride Daddy Vic's dick until she wraps her arms around me and pulls me to her chest. I hold my weight on my hands on either side of her head. She takes over the thrusting, and now it's me being fucked by this incredible woman that miraculously walked into my life today. She positively pounds me until she clenches her muscles and then cums underneath me.

"You're a good fuck," she says breathlessly and rolls me off of her gently. The hassock is so vast that there is plenty of room for both of us to lie side by side.

"Um, thank you, Sir," I say. "As are you."

"Go," she says. "Go stand on that platform by the front door. Face me. See the straps? Reach up and hold on to them. Put your feet on the marks so your legs are spread. Yes, that's it. I want to look at you."

The straps are like the ones I'd used on the subway when I went to New

York City one time. They are safe, and I am not worried that she'll abuse me while I stand here. Besides, my clothes are right there. I can grab them and run if things get dicey. But I'm not feeling that at all. In fact, my entire body flushes under her steady gaze. Oh, shit. I am being inspected, aren't I? Impossibly, arousal spikes through my core. She stands and moves close to me. I feel her breath on my skin. It is intoxicating.

"I love exploring a new woman. Turn around."

Once I am situated looking at the wall, she strokes my ass with her hands. She separates my cheeks and says, "You like anal, don't you, baby? Do you like a dick thrusting in and out of your ass?" I don't answer for a moment because I can't. I'm too turned on imagining it. She smacks my ass cheek lightly. "Do you?"

"Mmm, yes, Sir." I practically purr the words.

"Good. I like fucking women in the ass." She pulls my ass cheeks even wider. "We are going to have so much fun, you and me. So much fun."

Chapter 4
Pretty Sore, Sir

Even though I didn't get much sleep last night, I feel rejuvenated and energized as I stand in front of my Elementary Functions class in the large lecture hall. I project another composition of functions problem on the overlarge screen and chuckle as they groan. I am unphased. This is a new concept for them, but no worries, we will prevail. I've chosen and honed tried-and-true examples over the past five years of teaching this course just so these non-math majors can fulfill their math credits.

The lecture ultimately goes well, and I tease them by saying, "See? Math isn't hard." Their laughter is peppered with groans, which makes us all laugh. They are a good-natured group, and I am grateful for that, but they are not the group I want to be teaching. I guess the upper-level courses are out of my reach for now.

I gather my notes and supplies, pack them into my rolling cart, and head out the door, intending to go to my office. I step into the wide hallway, and the smell of coffee changes my mind. "Oh, yes," I say out loud. I turn away from the direction of my office and head toward the coffee shop in the lobby of the Mathematics building. I order a hot cinnamon vanilla latte for comparison purposes and find a reasonably secluded spot in the sea of tables and chairs. I have a few minutes to relax before my official office hours.

I grimace as the first sip goes down. "This is not Rikki's coffee. That's for sure." But I will drink it anyway because I paid for it, and I am not a coffee snob. If I hang around Rikki's shop much longer, I might become one.

I pull out my phone to see if Daddy Vic texted me. Damn. There's nothing. I try not to be disappointed, but I can't help it. I gave her my number, right? Yes, at the coffee shop right before we left for dinner. She said my name would look good in her list of contacts. Should I text her? No, I don't want to seem needy. Maybe she got busy with her job. Being head of security at a school sounds involved. She'll text me later, I'm sure. And besides, I'm planning on getting tested at Planned Parenthood on my lunch hour, and it would be great if I could tell her it was already done.

I decide to hit up the *Kinks* app on my phone and message Lisa. Last night, I sent her a message when I got home to let her know I was safe. Amazingly, she was still up at two a.m. and wanted "details, details, details" of my time with Daddy Vic. As much as I wanted to relive every moment, I told her I'd send a message after my class this morning. I give her the barest of details, and I know she's going to yell at me later. But that's okay. She'll get all the details she wants later this evening when I call her.

Heat rises to my cheeks as I remember Daddy Vic's strong, calloused hands on my skin. How naïve I was to think she was done with me after those two amazing orgasms on the hassock. After another brief rest, Daddy Vic brought me over to the big picture window overlooking the city. She had me press my breasts against the glass, my hips coming to rest on the handrail. Again, I'm not an exhibitionist, but it turned me on knowing someone could glance up and see my naked body. She had already turned the lights out, but I'm sure someone could have seen me.

She maneuvered my body and entered me from behind. It was a long slow fuck this time, both of us being tired and all. But her rhythm was intoxicating. She reached around front and touched me – lazily at first. She coaxed my clit to rise and was impressed by its size. While her right hand stroked my clit and mons, she grabbed my hip with her free hand and increased the speed and depth of her thrusts. She rammed me so hard and buzzed my clit so fast that I came within seconds. Daddy Vic kept thrusting, which intensified my orgasm.

I squirm a little in my seat at the café and feel my cheeks get warm. What a night that was.

I don't think she came that third time, but after I came, she wrapped her arms around me from behind, my back to her front. She held me close and whispered, "Who made you cum?"

"You did, Sir. You did. Daddy Vic made me cum three times tonight."

"Daddy Vic," she echoed. "That's right. Good girl."

"Thank you, Sir."

"Your pussy will be sore tomorrow from the beating I've given it tonight," she said confidently.

"Yes, I think it will be, Sir. No, I *know* it will be."

"You like being fucked this way? Vanilla style?"

"Yes, Sir, but …"

"But you want more."

"Yes, Sir."

"Another time," she said. "For now, you need to go. I have to sleep. So do you."

I washed up, got dressed, and then she walked me out to my car. There was no goodnight kiss, which disappointed me greatly. I had really been anticipating one. But Daddy Vic is in charge. And she was right. My pussy is sore this morning, making me very aware of the poundings she gave me.

A loud group of students move into the large table next to me and broke me out of my reverie. That's okay. I was getting a bit turned on. Not a good thing to do at work.

"It's ridiculous," a young woman wearing a Cincinnati Reds t-shirt and hat says. She and her two friends look to be in their early twenties. "How does Professor Baxter expect us to learn Noetherian Rings when we don't understand what rings are, to begin with?"

"He's clueless," one of the young men says and plops down hard in a chair. "I thought this course was an introduction to groups and fields and rings."

I keep my head down, extremely uncomfortable overhearing comments about my colleague. To stand up now would bring attention to me, so I stay still and drink my quickly cooling coffee.

"I mean," the third student, another young man, says, "last semester we briefly got the basics of group theory, which is abstract enough, and I kind of know what rings are, but not really."

"Maybe we need to complain," the young woman says.

The first young man scoffs. "Complain to Wainwright? He won't do anything. He'll blame us for being lazy or unprepared. Believe me; it won't go anywhere."

The second young man says, "Study group tonight? Library?"

The other two students groan but agree.

"Oh, shit," the first young man says under his breath but loud enough for me to hear. He gestures toward me.

"Good morning, Dr. Garneau," the young woman says sheepishly.

I look over, an embarrassed smile growing on my face. "I'd be lying if I said I didn't overhear your conversation."

"Sorry," the young woman says. "We're just frustrated."

"I can tell," I say. "It sounds like you're missing some fundamentals. You're in Professor Baxter's 8000-level course?"

They all nod. "If you have a few minutes, I can explain a few things to you."

"Oh, please," the second young man says and starts the migration to my table.

The young woman hands me a piece of notebook paper, and I proceed to give them a fundamental definition of rings using integers. They are like hungry baby birds inhaling the information. They seem to understand the integer example well enough, so I move on to polynomials. They ask questions, and I clarify their thinking. When I finish, they seem to truly understand ring theory enough to tackle the Noetherian rings, which, in my opinion, are elegant. I understand why Professor Baxter wanted to get to them so early in the semester.

"Listen," I say to my newborn clutch of birds, "I have to go. Office hours."

"Thank you so much," the young woman gushes. "This was so helpful." The two young men agree and also thank me. They pull out their phones and take pictures of my hastily written notes.

I head toward my office, and just as I get to the door, I hear a familiar voice behind me.

"Professor Garneau, do you have a minute?"

"Madison." I turn to see her eager face. "Of course, I have a minute for you. Maybe even two," I tease her. "C'mon," I say and usher her into my office. I close the door tightly behind us. "Sit. Sit." I point to the lone chair on the opposite side of my desk. She looks about to topple over from her overly full backpack.

"So, so, so?" she asks as she sits and then leans toward me.

"What do you mean?" I ask innocently, knowing the blush on my cheeks betrays me.

She bugs out her eyes. "You're so mean."

"I know," I say with a laugh. "We went out to dinner."

"Where?"

"Mamma Mia's."

"With the white tablecloths and the warm Italian bread with butter?"

I nod.

"I love that place. It's so romantic." She falls back in the chair as if swooning but then bolts upright. "And then?"

"I went to her apartment."

"Oh, wow." More swooning.

"Does your Mistress know about your crush on Daddy Vic?" I hope maybe this question will steer the conversation to another place.

"Yes, of course," Madison says matter-of-factly. "I tell her everything. Now quit stalling. Spill it, Professor." I raise an eyebrow. I'm not used to students speaking to me so colloquially. "Oh, no, Professor. I didn't mean to be disrespectful. I'm sorry."

"No, no, you're fine," I say. "I think I'm just not used to having a former student as a friend. That's all."

"We don't have to talk about it." Her dejected tone almost breaks my heart. "It's okay." She stands to go.

"Sit," I say simply.

She sits, and it makes me wonder if there are varying degrees of Dominance and submission. Like, am I dominant in some parts of my life and submissive in others? "You want info? The intel? The 411?"

Her face brightens. "Yes, please."

"I got home at 2:00 in the morning."

She yelps and punches a fist in the air. "Yes! Oh, my goodness, Professor. It happened so fast for you. Is she going to collar you? Are you going to move in?"

"Whoa, whoa, whoa," I say. "It's been less than twenty-four hours since I met her." And now I desperately want to check and see if she's texted me yet.

"Was it amazing?"

I bite my lower lip and nod.

"I knew it. I knew it." She bounces in the chair like the little that she is.

"Now, listen, kiddo," I say, acknowledging her littleness. "I have office hours now, and you need to skedaddle."

"Yes, Ma'am," she says. Her grin is wide.

"Don't be a blabbermouth, okay?"

"Can I tell Mistress?"

"Of course. You tell her everything, don't you?"

She nods. "Thanks, Professor. I'm so happy for you." She leaps out of the chair, slings her heavy backpack on, and puts her hand on the doorknob. She looks back and says, "I hope it lasts forever and ever."

"Thanks, kiddo." I make a motion with my hand for her to leave.

Once she's gone, I blow out a sigh and pull my phone out of my front pocket. Still no text. Oh, God, maybe she's waiting for me to text first, just like Mistress Ciara wanted me to be early for all of our online chats. Okay, fine. I'll volley first. But, shit, what do I say? Thanks for last night? I roll my eyes. Oh, oh, oh, I have it.

> BERNADETTE: Thank you for dinner last night. I'd never been to that restaurant. I had an amazing time with you at your place afterward.

What else? What else? I want to know so many things about her. I mean, I know she's thirty-six years old. I got that out of her at dinner, but, like, did she grow up in Cincinnati, does she have siblings, where do her parents live, did she go to college? And if so, where and what was her major? All of those things will come with time, I guess. Maybe I should ask if she bought my personal dildo yet? No, that's just stupid. Should I ask if I can see her again? No, no. Not *if*, but *when* I can see her again. Wait, seeing her again is a given, isn't it?

Before I head down my infamous rabbit hole of doubt, I send the three-line text and put the phone away. I have work to do. And an STD test to go take in about an hour.

On the way home from the university, I stop at one of those mega supermarkets where no one will know me and buy a few things I need. One of those things is a box of condoms. Happily, I find a box that doesn't look like it's a box of condoms. A subtle tingle of arousal settles low in my belly as I picture myself practicing putting a condom on a dildo using only my mouth. I love new hobbies.

Once in the apartment, I put my meager groceries away, hit the bathroom, and then take off my clothes. I have been so patient. I haven't looked at my phone since I sent the text from my office. I open it, hopeful. I sigh in disappointment. She must still be at school. It's only five o'clock, after all.

"Be patient, Bernadette," I scold myself. "It'll happen." Well, I'm glad you're so sure, I think sarcastically.

I need a moment to gather myself and kneel down nude on my pillow. Head down, eyes closed, hands linked behind my back this time. I like the way this pose makes my breasts thrust forward as if I'm offering myself to my Domme. I imagine Daddy Vic working at her desk while I sit like this at her feet, waiting to be used, waiting for her to need my body to relieve her tension. These thoughts ratchet up my arousal, and, in my mind, she calls for me, so I get up.

I don't have a hassock, so I pull one of my armless kitchen chairs into the living room and set it down, facing the couch. I sit down, imagining Daddy Vic on the couch, stroking her erect phallus as she watches me. She tells me to open my legs, so I do. I have been perpetually wet all day, and the proof is displayed on the two fingers my imaginary Sir asks me to show her. She tells me to masturbate on the chair for her, and I do, although it's physically not comfortable. I scooch forward and spread my legs out even further.

As I stroke myself in my imaginary scenario, my mind wonders how many other women have sat on display like this for Daddy Vic, naked on her hassock. But no, I'm not going to go there. I can't because imaginary Daddy Vic reaches for a condom.

"Let me put that on you, Sir," I say softly to my empty living room.

Dang it, I should have practiced this part before my imaginary Sir took shape in my living room. I dig through my desk and finally find it – the suction cup dildo. Now, where to position it. What if Daddy Vic is standing? Okay, okay, I know. I hurry to the kitchen and affix the dildo to the fridge. Yes, it stays. Perfect. Wait, is it the right height? I gauge the height of my own crotch and see that the dildo is way too high. I move it. I get down on my knees and am about to get down and dirty on the dildo, but the hard vinyl flooring is already crunching my kneecaps. I grab a couple of dishtowels and fold them under my knees. Maybe I should get knee pads. Do they make knee pads, especially for sex? I'll have to explore that later.

I grab the black box of condoms and read the outside packaging. Oh, cool, they don't contain parabens. How environmentally friendly is that? And they're made of latex. I don't have a latex allergy, do I? I don't think so. Well, I'm about to find out.

I can't find a place to tear it open with my fingers, so I use my teeth and rip off the top. I pull out my prize and am surprised at how small it seems. Oh, wait, they come in different sizes, don't they? I look at the box and see that I bought the large size. Oh, they stretch. Right, right.

It's lubricated, and I give it a sniff. It's odorless, thank goodness, which hopefully also means tasteless. I see the engineering of the condom and realize that the protruding tip must go inside my mouth first.

I position myself in front of the dildo protruding from my refrigerator. I put the condom in my mouth. It slides out, but I catch it before it hits the floor. Okay, that was a fail. I try again, but this time, I tuck the bottom edge between my teeth and lower lip. The top edge sits comfortably against my upper lip. I lean forward toward the phallus and imagine Daddy Vic standing before me. Her hands are on my head, urging me forward. I lean into the dildo and place the condom over the bulbous tip. So far, so good. I push forward, but the condom threatens to go into my mouth. A quick rethink, and I use my teeth to guide the latex and roll it up the dildo. Wait! Teeth might hurt her. I almost choke as I laugh. Dildos don't feel teeth. I adjust anyway and use my lips. I push in as far as my gag reflex allows. I pull back out, applying pressure on the shaft, and am amazed that the condom stays put.

"Shit," I say, disappointed with my handiwork. "Three inches? What a wuss." This will not impress Daddy Vic. I wrap my lips around the shaft again and push forward, determined to gain ground. I try to breathe around my pushes and do, indeed, gain another inch. Knowing that's the best I can do with my mouth, I push the condom down the rest of the way with my fingers. Oh, well, Rome wasn't built in a day, and putting a condom on Daddy Vic's dick won't be mastered in a day, either.

I close my eyes and pump the phallus into my mouth several times, imagining Daddy Vic guiding me back and forth. Her breathing is getting heavier, or is that mine? A surge of arousal courses through my veins, and I can't believe I'm about to do this, but why waste a good condom, right? The curtains are perpetually closed, and who cares if I'm in the kitchen? Damn, why was I doing this with the lights on? I leap up and flick them off.

I should move my kitchen table, but there isn't time. I turn away from Daddy Vic and get on my knees, presenting my sex to her. Daddy Vic moves up behind me. I reach back and spread my pussy lips in open invitation. Her condom-covered dick pokes at the entrance to my pussy. She teases me for a while and then asks in her low butch voice, "Do you want to be fucked, baby?"

"Yes, Sir," I say out loud and push back against her.

"Let it be so," she proclaims and pushes into me slowly. I can't exactly feel the condom inside me, but I know it's there, keeping germs and STDs away. She pumps me slowly. She fills me. I move back and forth, impaling myself on the large phallus. She reaches around and strokes me. "Tighten your pussy, baby," she commands. I squeeze my inner muscles, and the phallus has a hard time moving one way or the other. I can't hold it, and she slams into me, rocking my cervix. I cry out.

"Again, Sir," I plead. "Again." She slams me six ways to Sunday, and my fast and furious fingers beat my clit into submission. The stirrings are there. I'm going to cum. She pistons inside me with her cock.

"Cum, baby," she says. "Cum for Daddy."

I explode. My cries are high-pitched as the waves hit me. Daddy Vic has a hard time thrusting in my spasming pussy.

"You have an iron cunt, baby. Holy shit," she says. She pumps me a few more times and moans her own release.

I stop thrusting and rock forward so the dildo falls out of me.

"Take the condom off me, baby," Daddy Vic says. She wants me to demonstrate my submission to her. I spin around, and she lifts the phallus to my mouth. I know I can't get the whole thing in, so I cheat and use my finger to roll it up until my lips find the edge of it. I taste myself on the latex sheath. I taste good this evening. Pulling off a condom is more difficult than rolling it on, I discover, so I enlist my teeth, and it's off in no time. Careful not to swallow the thing, I use my fingers to dig it out of my mouth.

I hold the condom up and examine it. I've never had a lover use one before Daddy Vic. Obviously, pregnancy isn't a concern, but sharing toys is like sharing needles. Bodily fluids linger everywhere, so I should insist on condoms from now on. But Daddy Vic is way ahead of me. She's taking care of me already.

My wetness coats my inner thighs when I stand up—my tribute to Daddy Vic. I roll the used condom into a paper towel and shove it deep into my kitchen garbage.

I take a big swig of water. Getting fucked makes a sub thirsty, that's for sure. I sigh. I managed to kill a whole half hour. Maybe she texted me in that time. A girl can dream.

Just as I reach for my phone, it dings. Is it her? Oh, my God. It is. It is.

> DADDY VIC: Can you walk? Tell me how sore I made
> your pussy, baby.

I can't help the grin splitting my face. She's thinking of me. I send her a return text.

> BERNADETTE: Pretty sore, Sir. But, yes, I can still walk.
> I got my STD/STI tests done for you, Sir.

> DADDY VIC: As expected.

> BERNADETTE: When can I see you again, Sir?

I hold my phone out, waiting for her reply, but get none. I can clean up my fridge and the dildo while I wait. When she doesn't reply in that time, I figure she's getting dinner or something, so I do the same. One frozen pizza later, and I'm reading porn at my kitchen table, checking for a text from her every minute or so.

When ten o'clock arrives, I give up. She probably fell asleep in her chair or something. I hit the shower and go to bed. I'm confident I'll find a wake-up text in the morning.

Chapter 5
IC

It's Wednesday morning, and before I open my eyes, anticipation jumpstarts me fully awake. There has to be a text from Daddy Vic waiting for me. There just has to be. I sit up. I am naked. She has not commanded me to sleep nude—I just like how it makes me feel a little vulnerable and submissive. Like the way she made me feel Monday night.

My brain isn't quite awake, and I fumble with my phone in the dark. But after a few frustrating moments, I finally get the text app open. Yes, yes, yes! She texted me.

> DADDY VIC: Good Morning. You have work to do today. Work to get ready for my playroom Friday evening. You have an iron cunt – let's keep it that way. Every half hour on the half-hour, you are to do muscle-clenching Kegel exercises for your pussy to keep it strong for me. Even if you're in the middle of a lecture in front of students. Do your Kegels in front of them. Don't cheat. That would be disrespectful.

> DADDY VIC: I also want to see the results of your STD/STI tests. Bring them.

I leap out of bed, my adrenaline surging. I am both ecstatic and disappointed at the same time. I'm excited that I'll get to see her on Friday and disappointed that I have to wait two whole days. I'm also excited because she nailed it. This is precisely what I want from a Domme. Assignments, attention, affection. Wait, I'm not sure her text was affectionate, but I'm going to take it like that anyway. I think about my answer as I get ready for school. Okay, I've got it.

> BERNADETTE: Yes, Sir. Whatever pleases you, Sir. I look forward to satisfying you on Friday. Shall I drive directly to your apartment, or will we have dinner together first?

I receive no return text before leaving my apartment, but I didn't expect one. She's busy getting ready for her day. Or maybe she's already there at her school. I should ask her what school she works at. She knows I teach at the university.

I dutifully do my Kegels as instructed all morning. The ones I did in front of my Calculus 1 class embarrassed me, but I think that's what Daddy Vic wanted. By the time I get to my office for office hours late in the morning, my inner muscles are fatigued, and they don't want to work anymore. Doing the Kegels, though, has also had me in a low-grade state of arousal. Is this what she intended?

I want to ask her, but I've checked my phone for the thousandth time that morning, and there has been no response. She must be terribly busy.

Feeling antsy, I wish I could leave and go home, but I can't. I have too much paperwork to do. The first wave of student assignments was due today, and I need to get a jump on them. I don't dare take them home because I won't do them. I've already planned to practice my burgeoning condom skills, and since I won't be seeing Daddy Vic until Friday, I'll start reading *The Transformation of Two*. I can't wait to see what kind of submissive Two is and how Mistress Diandra handles her. And it'll be interesting to see how she handles two subs at one time. I would hate sharing my Domme with anyone. Is that selfish of me? Maybe so, but I can't help it.

My phone vibrates. It's Kegel time. I have it set to go off every half hour. Just as I reach the tenth one, my phone dings an incoming text. Is it Daddy Vic? I grab my phone and look.

It's not her, but I'm not disappointed because it's Shasti inviting me to meet them at Rikki's Coffee Shop this afternoon after school. What a great idea. Having friends makes me feel good. Oh, shoot. I'll have to do my Kegels in front of them. Oh, well. I send her a quick reply that I'm looking forward to seeing them and that I will be there at 5:00 or so.

Just as I open my computer to grade *Elementary Functions* problem sets, my phone dings again. My adrenaline surges again. This time, it *is* her.

> DADDY VIC: Hope the Kegels are going well, Iron Cunt.

Wait, did she just refer to me as "iron cunt"? Is this a nickname for me? I'm not sure I like it, but, well, at least I have a pet name now.

> DADDY VIC: Next time you are alone in your office, I want you to reach under your shirt and caress your nipples. Make them hard for me, baby. Hard enough to put clamps on. Keep stroking until you feel it in your pussy. Once that happens, go to the restroom. Touch yourself. Put your fingers inside your pussy and then pull them out. Taste yourself. Tell me how you taste today. Keep doing those Kegels. On Friday, you're going to get the fucking of your life.

I am swooning much the same way Madison swooned in my office yesterday. Daddy Vic has that effect on both of us and knows how to push my buttons. That's for sure. And I certainly don't need to stroke my nipples to get turned on. Her text already did that.

> BERNADETTE: (AKA IC). Thank you for the instructions, Sir. I am alone now and will do as you command. I will report how I taste in a little while once I hit the restroom.

There is no immediate return message, but I'm learning not to expect one. Expectations only lead to heartache. I have no idea where I heard that, but it's kind of fitting right now. I peek at the window in my office door and don't see or hear anyone in the hallway. I unbutton one button in my shirt and then lean forward and face away from the door. I reach in as if scratching an itch and then pull my bra down, freeing one nipple. I stroke it gently. The only thing I feel at the moment is apprehension and fear that I will get caught. Maybe that's what Daddy Vic wanted. When I frame it that way in my mind, I relax a little and let myself feel good.

My left nipple hardens as I stroke it. Oh, this is so relaxing. Who knew? I switch hands, recheck the door, and work at my other nipple. This one also hardens but sends a direct message south to my already soaked center. I stroke a few more times and find myself lifting my hips. This is what she wanted, exactly what she wanted.

I button up my shirt and head to the nearest restroom. It's pretty secluded here on the third floor. I enter the farthest stall and yank down my pants. The boi shorts are next. Yeesh, I've soaked through them. She has me so freakin' aroused today. I dip my fingers into my pussy and pump a few times. I purposely avoid my clit, because if I touch myself, I'll cum in no time. Not that she has forbidden me to cum; it's just that touching myself like this at work is bad enough. I pull my fingers out and thrust them into my mouth. I taste good, as usual. I know Daddy Vic won't go down on me. Dommes, apparently, don't lower themselves to suck pussy. That's the job of the sub, I guess.

Oh, God, will she let me go down on her Friday? I want to taste her so bad. Without my permission, my fingers stray to my clit and circle furiously. Oh, fuck. My orgasm is right there. I listen for signs of other people. I hear nothing. I give in. It's right there, speeding toward me.

The door to the restroom opens. Fuck, I can't stop myself. I clamp a hand over my mouth. Three more strokes, and I erupt. "Mmmph," I moan behind my hand and continue stroking. My eyes roll back as ecstasy washes over me. The students are deep in conversation and are not paying me any attention. Thank God. I struggle to get my breathing under control and grab some bathroom tissue. I am dripping cum. Oh, my God. I can't believe I just did this. I clean myself up, which causes delightful aftershocks. This is torture. After tossing the paper in the toilet, I flush and then pull my pants back up.

I open the latch with my elbow because my hands are covered with drying cum, and bolt to the sink. Thankfully, both students are now in stalls. They are still talking. I wash my hands quickly and bolt out of there. They have no idea who was in that far stall making weird noises.

"Oh, my God," I say under my breath. "Who am I? Who does that? Who the hell am I becoming?"

I text Daddy Vic that I taste wonderful today but get no reply. I didn't expect one.

The coffee shop is getting busy when I arrive. I am refused when I try to pay Rikki for my cinnamon vanilla latte. I insist, but she insists more firmly. You can't beat an authoritative Domme, can you? I hope she doesn't think I am taking advantage of her. I leave a generous tip in the tip jar, and she notices, acknowledging me with a smile. When she hands me my drink, I take a sip and sigh. It is just as wonderful as the last one, and I tell her so. She beams her appreciation, but I'm disappointed she doesn't have time to chat. She has a business to run.

That's okay because my phone vibrates, telling me it's time for another set of Kegels. Shasti and Madison aren't here yet, so I claim the seats we had last time and pretend to read something on my phone as I do my Kegels. Kegels in public. What has come over me?

"Daddy Vic has come over you," I mumble under my breath. By the twentieth Kegel, I can barely hold it. I blow out a sigh, hoping no one was watching me do my IC Olympics.

I sip my coffee and watch the way the shop operates. Rikki's employees banter good-naturedly with each other and with the customers, and it seems like a fun and happy place to work. Each employee also appears to take a turn bussing the tables, keeping the whole place running like a well-oiled machine. From what I can tell, Rikki is a good leader, and her employees not only respect her but they seem to like her, too.

"Hi, Professor," Madison calls from the front door. She tosses her coat and scarf unceremoniously on a hook and practically skips over to me.

"Hi, kiddo," I say. "How was school today?"

"Okay."

"That's it? Just 'okay'?"

"Yeah."

"Sometimes that's all you can get out of her," Shasti says. There is mirth in her eyes, and it is clear that she is smitten with her sub. "Peanut," she says to Madison, "go get our coffees, please."

"Can I..." Madison has an expectant look on her face.

Shasti sighs. "Yes, yes. Get a full-blast sugary frappuccino with whipped cream."

"Yay." Madison skips toward the line at the counter.

Shasti shakes her head. "She is a handful sometimes."

"I'm sure, but you love it."

Shasti rolls her eyes and nods. "Listen, I don't mean to be nosy or anything," she says, "but Madison tells me you're seeing Victoria."

"I, um, yes. Just the one date so far," I say. "We're having a second on Friday."

"Second dates are fun. So full of possibilities." Her smile grows. "I just want to make sure you're ready to get out there so soon after your recent ordeal."

"I think I'm okay." I take a sip of coffee. "To be honest, I haven't thought about Mama_Luvs in a while. I lived. I learned." I shrug.

Shasti looks toward the counter. Madison is rocking back and forth on her feet, waiting not-so-patiently for their coffee drinks. "Okay, I don't know how to say this, but I want you to be careful. Make smart decisions. If at any time you feel uncomfortable, use your safe words."

"Yes, Ma'am," I say. "I will."

"And if at any time it ceases to be fun, then stop and leave."

"Is there something I should know, Ma'am?"

"No, it's just that you went through a lot last time, and I want to make sure you use your head and, more importantly, your voice."

"I will. Thank you, Ma'am."

Before I get too deep in thought about her concerns, she says, "And you don't have to call me Ma'am, Professor."

"Oh, shoot. Did I?" I feel my face flush. "Natural instinct, I'm afraid."

"That's okay. You're submissive. I feel the pull to nurture you as a Domme. That's why I wanted to make sure you were okay."

Madison makes her way over carefully with the drinks. I chuckle at the concentration on her face. She is determined not to spill a drop.

"Professor?" Madison says once the coffees are delivered safely and she's situated on the couch.

"Yes, kiddo?"

"What do you think about slaves?"

I laugh out loud, not because the subject of slaves is humorous; it was just not what I expected Madison to say. I look at Shasti, who rolls her eyes and shakes her head. Rikki must have overheard us laughing because she looks over, smiling.

"Um, what brings this up?" I ask her. I nestle my coffee cup between both hands for warmth.

"Oh, my goodness," Shasti says, "she's in this I-want-to-be-a-slave phase." She shakes her head again. "Maybe you can talk some sense into her."

"Kiddo, no one truly *wants* to be a slave."

"Why not? There are a lot of slaves in our community."

"Do you want all of your rights taken away? Your free will? Maybe when you envision BDSM slavery, you're thinking about something different."

"How so?" Madison cozies into her couch and takes a sip of her sugary caffeine concoction.

"I'm not that experienced, as you know, but I've done a lot of reading and soul searching. We all have desires, but slaves don't get to voice their desires, do they? They may have them, but they don't get to act on them. You desired a Frappuccino, right?"

"Mm hmm." She takes another long sip and then grimaces. She clutches her head. "Shit. Brain freeze."

"Language, young lady," Shasti scolds.

"Sorry, Mistress." She groans again as her brain thaws. She finally blinks her eyes open.

"You okay?" I ask her.

"Yes. That was not fun at all."

"That curse word will be dealt with when we get home, young lady," Shasti says, and I can tell that she means it.

"Oh, c'mon," Madison pleads. "You curse sometimes."

"I most certainly do not," Shasti says, looking offended.

"Oh, yes, you do." Madison leans closer and whispers, "When you cum."

I inhale my coffee and instantly start choking. I cough to get the liquid out of my lungs. A steady hand pounds my back, and a voice tells me to keep coughing. Amazingly, the pounding is helping.

"I'm okay," I say, which causes a new cascade of coughing. The hand alternately rubs and pats my back. I focus on breathing instead of talking this time and turn to see who came to my rescue.

"Are you okay?" Rikki asks me. Her striking green eyes search mine. Her concern pulls me in, and I want to lay my head on her shoulder and close my eyes.

"Green." Oh. My. God. Did I just say her eye color out loud? I look down at my feet, completely embarrassed.

Rikki bursts out laughing. "She's okay, everybody." A collective cheer goes up in the coffee shop.

"What did she say?" Madison asks.

"Stoplight system," Rikki says. "She called green."

Madison and Shasti laugh.

"Way to almost kill the professor, peanut," Shasti teases.

Madison's face is stricken.

I take a deep breath and accept a water bottle from Mark, one of Rikki's assistant managers. I nod my thanks and take a tentative sip. It goes down well. I clear my throat, look right at Madison, and say, "Holy moly, that was funny, kiddo."

"You almost dying?" She looks baffled.

"No, no, no." I take another sip of water. "What you said about your Mistress cursing."

"Oh, no." She buries her head in her hands. "You heard that?"

I nod, and she looks devastated.

"I don't even want to know," Rikki says. "Do I?"

Shasti shakes her head and says, "No, no, no, no, no."

"Okay," Rikki says and stands up. I'm not sure if she realizes that her hand is still resting on my back.

"Hey, Madison, listen," I say. "It's okay. Your Mistress told me that we speak freely here. Right?"

"I guess," she says glumly. "You're not mad?"

"Me?" I point to myself. "No, I'm not mad."

"Okay, well, I'm sorry for almost making you die."

A good-natured chuckle goes up in our intimate circle. Rikki pats me on the back one last time and says, "Glad you're okay, Professor."

"I'm fine. Thanks for the rescue. And the water." I hold up the bottle.

"Of course." Rikki takes her leave and heads back toward the counter, and I am ashamed to say that I watch her every step. Her dress pants hug her body so well that I can't look away. And her authoritative walk. Oh, my God.

Shasti clears her throat.

Shit. I'm caught. A blush creeps up my face, and I suddenly get interested in my coffee.

"It's okay, Bernadette," Shasti says. "She's an attractive woman."

I press my lips together, look up at her, and nod once as I'm dying of embarrassment.

"What were you saying about my frappuccino, Professor?" Madison asks.

"Right, right." I come back to the present. "Slaves may desire frappuccinos, but slaves don't necessarily get them."

"I guess not."

"Think of it this way. You want affection, to be taken care of, to be protected, and to have a sense of self-worth, right?"

"Right."

"And your Mistress gives you all of these things, I'm sure."

"Oh, yes." Madison looks at her Mistress with bedroom eyes.

"Slaves might desire these things but are not guaranteed any of them."

"No?" Madison's face falls.

"They may not get *any* attention from their Dominant."

"I wouldn't like that." Madison pouts and it is the cutest thing ever.

"Do you still want to be a slave?" I ask her.

"Maybe not, but ..."

Shasti clears her throat and says, "She wants me to put her in a cage and lock the door."

"Where will you go to the bathroom?" I ask. Hey, it's a fair question.

"Yes, Madison," Shasti says, "what if you have to poop?"

"Aww, you guys are ganging up on me." Madison sits back on the couch with her arms folded across her chest. "Not fair."

"Your cage will be in the garage with no heat," Shasti says. "There will be no internet. No TV. No Trolls movies."

Madison works her mouth back and forth as if weighing things. "Well, maybe you could put me in my cage for a little while? I mean, not as a slave, but as, like, I don't know, a reward or something?"

I chuckle, and Shasti says, "You want me to lock you up in a cage in the cold garage as a reward?"

"Mm hmm," Madison says, all smiles. "And you can leave a bucket in case I have to, you know."

Shasti doesn't respond to her sub but looks at me and says, "Last month, she wanted to be a puppy, tail and all. That lasted two days. The month before that, it was degradation and name-calling."

"Oh, I don't like that," I say. "I would internalize too much of it, I think."

"That only lasted a couple of hours," Shasti says. "But, hey, at least she's trying out new things."

"As am I," I say.

"Which is a good thing, but you still need to be careful and take care of yourself," Shasti says.

"Yes, Ma'am." This time I hear myself use her honorific. "Oh, sorry."

"No worries," she says, and then she engages Madison in a quiet discussion about what to share and what not to share about their private relationship.

I do my best not to eavesdrop and go back to people watching. My phone vibrates. Oh, good. Kegel time. Kegels get my focus back on the tall butch woman with the chiseled features and amazing hair whose strong hands will be all over my body in three days.

Chapter 6
Desire

Back in my apartment Wednesday evening, I nuke a frozen Salisbury steak with mac-n-cheese meal and try to figure out what to do with myself. I don't feel like grading papers. That can wait until the weekend. Ooh, the weekend. Friday evening at Daddy Vic's. Maybe an overnight stay? And Shasti mentioned they might have a movie night on Saturday unless I'm still at Daddy Vic's, of course. Oh, the possibilities.

Oh, oh, oh. I know what to do. My e-books are waiting. Yes, yes, yes. That's the ticket. I'm a bit surprised that I didn't feel the need to kneel this evening. Maybe that's a good sign that I'm recovering from my traumatic Mama_Luvs disaster. Feeling better about myself, I head in for a shower and do my Kegels in there, but I have to admit I'm getting tired of them. Maybe my princess parts aren't as iron as Daddy Vic claims. I chuckle out loud. She gave me such a weird nickname. Iron Cunt. There are worse things she could call me, I guess. I spend a few minutes shaving and feel neat and clean. Shaving always turns me on a little bit, so that's a plus.

Shower and Kegels complete, I snuggle into bed on top of a layer of towels. My bedroom stash of toys is cleaned and ready for use. Who knows what I'll use tonight? Maybe just my fingers. That makes it easier for cleanup. And, hey, since Daddy Vic hasn't taken control of my orgasms yet, I'm going to take advantage of the situation. I have a few condoms in the drawer so I could practice my fancy condom trick. Maybe. I don't know yet.

I turn the electronic pages in my new book until I find the first page of Chapter One in *The Transformation of Two* by E.J. Dubois.

> Angel threw her body on the cot and groaned. "One, how the hell do you stand the silence rule?" Before One

could answer, she added, "It's stupid. Why can't I talk whenever I want? Like, we can't even respond when Mistress gives us commands. We can't say, 'Yes, Ma'am' or 'Yes, your exalted highness.'"

One frowned at her Mistress's new slave. "When she asks us a direct question, we answer, Two."

"Angel," she spat. "My name is Angel. I've been telling you that for two weeks now." She threw One a look that usually withered people to their cores, but One seemed utterly unaffected. Instead, One finished putting lotion on her skin, turned out her light, and lay down on her cot as if the conversation were finished.

But Angel continued. "And, like, we never wear clothes. Ever. I should at least get to wear an apron when I cook for her. And pajamas in bed. My old Mistress dressed me in silk." There was no response from the cot across the slaves' quarters, so Angel kept going. "Why doesn't she touch me? And why can't I touch her? I mean, she makes me watch you go down on her, and then she fucks you until you orgasm –"

"It's called a stimulus-response," One said from her darkened side of the large room.

Angel scoffed. "Yeah, right. I remember the lecture. 'Slaves don't cum. They may respond to stimulus, but orgasms are for Dommes.' Do I have that right?" She scoffed again. "I mean, my last Mistress tried me out at the auction house. She liked the way I gave lady-head. I got her off in, like, ten minutes. And she was a squirter. Ho-ly, what a mess that was. She told me to clean up and get in her car. She'd bought me."

"You need to have more respect for your new Mistress, Two," One said from behind closed eyes. "She took you in. And you don't have to stay, you know. You're a slave of your own volition. You can go back to your old life anytime."

"No," Angel said simply. She couldn't handle her old life then, and there was no way she could handle it now. Having someone make the decisions for her and guide her – that's what felt right. Being owned felt right. Angel sighed. She hated to admit it, but One was right. She was here as Mistress Diandra's new property because her last Mistress didn't want her anymore. Whatever. Angel turned off her light and pulled the sheet over her naked body. She knew better than to stroke herself. She'd tried the first night she was there and got caught somehow. Standing in the corner naked had been humiliating. That lesson learned, she never tried to masturbate under Mistress Diandra's roof again. Her pussy, she was told, belonged to Mistress now. Except for the initial inspection before agreeing to take her on, Mistress hadn't touched her since.

I roll onto my side and turn the electronic page. "Oh, Angel," I say, "just go with the flow because the flow is going to be amazing." My phone buzzes for me to do Kegels, but I turn it off. If E.J. Dubois stays true to form, I will be doing some involuntary Kegels soon. I turn the screen a little brighter and read on.

The following day, after Angel made them all breakfast, Mistress made her kneel on a mat on the kitchen floor. She was instructed to keep her eyes focused on the tile. It was expensive porcelain tile, Angel noted. One, meanwhile, stood for inspection by their Mistress. One held her hands behind her head while Mistress ran the business end of a crop over her torso. She teased One's nipples until they hardened. She ran the crop up One's inner thighs and then through her labia. When it came back wet, Mistress was pleased. Angel snuck peeks but didn't dare watch openly. This had gotten her into trouble the second day she was there, and she'd had to stand in that stupid corner again.

"Who do you belong to, One?" Mistress Diandra asked.

"You, Ma'am," One said.

"Make sure Mistress Flavia remembers that while you're on loan this weekend. I am not giving you to her permanently, but it's time you had some new experiences."

Angel didn't hear a response. One must have nodded or genuflected or something. But just as Angel had the thought, she realized what One's leaving would mean. She was going to have Mistress all to herself for two whole days. That realization frightened her. She hated to admit it, but One had made her transition to the house a little easier. And, no, she was never going to admit that to One. Ever.

"I'll put out your traveling clothes tomorrow," Mistress said. "Oh, now, why the tears, One?"

"I don't want to put on clothes, Mistress." The emotion in her voice was unmistakable.

"That may be true," Mistress Diandra said, "but there's clearly something else bothering you."

"I ... I will miss you, Mistress." One wasn't quite sobbing, but it was clear that she was upset.

"You'll be back in two days," Mistress Diandra said evenly. "If you're back any sooner, it will mean that Mistress Flavia was displeased with you. And that, as you know, won't go well for you at all."

Again, Angel didn't hear a response. She finally understood that this was a 'speak only when asked a direct question' house.

"Go get the media center queued up as I instructed earlier," Mistress Diandra commanded. One left the room to do as bidden. "Two, look up." Angel did as she was told. "Good girl. I reward obedience. You've had a bit of a rocky start here in my house. But you seem to be making progress. Begrudgingly, perhaps, but progress nonetheless."

Angel nodded.

"Stand to be inspected."

Angel's eyes opened wide. Maybe Mistress would touch her. Finally. She assumed the same inspection stance One had used and separated her legs a bit wider than shoulder-width apart. Maybe Mistress would take the hint and touch her there.

Mistress Diandra left the room momentarily and came back with a large tray filled with items for discipline and sex. "These will be used on or in you exclusively. The flogger I used for One's maintenance this morning belongs to her body only. It will never be used on you or yours on her."

Angel's ears perked up at the word flogger. Yes, please.

Mistress Diandra pulled out a crop, almost identical to the one she had inspected One with earlier, except this crop had the number two emblazoned on the handle. Mistress Diandra ran the crop over Angel's calves and outer thighs, up her torso, around to her back, and across her shoulder blades. Her new Mistress was touching her, but it wasn't the skin-on-skin contact she craved. She hadn't realized how much she missed being touched.

The crop ran over her breasts, but her nipples didn't harden. The crop traveled lower and through her labia and did not come out wet. Angel wasn't surprised. Cooking breakfast and genuflecting to a Mistress were not sexy things. A good flogging got her wet. Being tied up and fucked got her wet. Shit, she'd even take a vanilla spanking at this point, for fuck's sake.

"We'll work on this," Mistress Diandra said, holding up the dry crop. "Go use the restroom, clean up, and meet me in the media room upstairs. Don't dawdle. Oh, and get that mop of hair tamed and tied back."

"Yes –" Angel clamped her lips shut. She hadn't been asked a direct question. But ho-ly, they were going to the playroom. Finally.

"I'll overlook that slip," Mistress Diandra said. "Now, go."

Yes, Ma'am, Angel thought and headed back to the slave

wing. She hoped Mistress was timing her because she made it to the playroom in record time.

"Punctual," Mistress said. "That will be rewarded."

Angel smiled and then sat on a mat to the left side of Mistress's chair in front of a wide movie screen. One sat on the other side. Mistress Diandra clicked a button on the remote control in her hand. Porn? No way. They were going to watch porn together. That was both amazing and confusing. Angel simply could not figure out her new Mistress's methods.

Her old Mistress used her mouth daily for oral ministrations. Her old Mistress used her back, buttocks, and thighs for regular stress-releasing beatings and used her holes for penetration with all manner of things. Angel had almost lost her composure the day the condom-covered bananas came out. So far, there had been nothing like that from Mistress Diandra. But maybe that was about to change.

"Let's watch this scene together," Mistress Diandra said from her padded chair, "And then we'll discuss it." She hit a button on the remote, and the scene started playing.

The blonde femme's long hair cascaded over her shoulders as if she were in a shampoo commercial and not about to sink her strap-on dildo into the brunette on her hands and knees in front of her. The blonde reached down for the protruding dildo and lifted it tentatively toward her target. The brunette looked back at her with an odd expression. Angel couldn't tell if the expression said, "Impale me already" or "Do we really have to do this?" The blonde inserted the dildo into the brunette's pussy and rhythmically moved her whole body back and forth in order to thrust in and out. If she had been allowed to speak, Angel would have said, "Use your hips, asshole."

The thrusting continued at the same boring pace until it made Angel sigh out of boredom. And why was the sound off? Half the fun of porn was hearing the girls cry out in fake ecstasy.

Mistress Diandra stopped the action - if you could even call it action. "What did you see, Two?"

"Two chicks fucking," Angel said, keeping her eyes on the paused scene.

"Look at me directly when you answer me." When Angel looked up, Mistress Diandra asked, "Did either one desire the other?"

"Pfft. Not at all. It was shitty acting if you ask me."

"Very true." She smiled at Angel, which frightened her a little because the smile seemed genuine. She wasn't used to a Domme doing that. "I think you're quite astute behind that gruff exterior."

Angel puffed up visibly at the compliment and felt her cheeks get warm.

Without leaving her seat, Mistress Diandra ran the crop through Angel's nether lips. It was not wet when she showed Angel. She said nothing about it but said, "Let's watch another." Mistress Diandra skipped ahead past several other scenes to another set of chicks. And, again, one of them sported a strap-on.

The redhead licked and kissed the breasts of the raven-haired woman beneath her on the couch. The woman's nipples hardened, and her head fell back. The redhead threw her counterpart a devilish smile and proceeded to leave a trail of kisses down her body until finally stopping to feast on the woman's pussy. The woman on the couch reached down and stroked the redhead's hair in encouragement and spread her legs wider. Angel was envious of the woman's flexibility. Maybe Mistress was going to work them on flexibility today.

After a few more moments, the redhead sat up on her knees and shimmied forward so that the strap-on dildo rested on the raven-haired woman's pussy. Without inserting it, she thrust forward and back, rubbing the dildo over the clit. Without much warning, she pulled back and thrust inside the woman beneath her. She thrust slowly at first but then gradually increased the speed. The woman on the couch arched her pelvis, inviting the redhead to dive in deeper.

Mistress Diandra paused the playback. "What did you see, Two? Did either one desire the other?"

"Absolutely," Angel said. "I think the dark-haired chick's ready to cum any second now."

"And the top? Did she show desire for her bottom?"

"Yes, of course," Angel said, not sure what Mistress was getting at. "She, uh, couldn't wait to slam it into the other one."

"When you serve me and my household, Two, I need you to feel that kind of desire. In all things you do. Not just sexual acts required of you." She ran the crop through Angel's labia again, and this time it came back wet. "You sensed the desire between these two women, and it affected you physically."

Angel nodded. There was no denying it.

Mistress Diandra kicked off her shoes and pulled up her skirt, revealing that she wore no panties. She slid to the edge of the seat. "One?" One looked up at her Mistress expectantly.

"Service me, please," Mistress Diandra commanded.

A look of pure adoration fell across One's face. She placed herself on her knees in front of her Mistress and kissed her feet repeatedly. Angel was amazed to see tears in One's eyes as if servicing their Mistress was the greatest gift in the world. One kissed her way up one leg to Mistress's knee and then started along the other leg, this time going higher.

"Clearly," Mistress Diandra said, "you can see that One desires to please me." Angel nodded. "I want you to watch me, Two. Not One." Angel nodded her understanding. "When I ask you, I want you to be able to tell me what clues you see about *my* desires, okay?"

"Yes, Ma'am," Angel said. Wow. This was different. She had never gotten a chance to watch a Mistress's reaction while being serviced.

Mistress Diandra opened her legs wider, signaling to

One that she was ready. One stroked her Mistress's center with her tongue. Angel wasn't sure, but it sounded like One sighed at the first taste. Mistress Diandra reached down and stroked One's head as if rewarding her. One moaned and then doubled down by picking up the pace between her Mistress's legs.

"Good girl," Mistress Diandra said and exhaled in a low moan. "That's my girl." Her hips moved up and down, and One stilled her tongue and head. Mistress rubbed herself against One's chin, lips, tongue, and nose. Her breathing got heavy, and her eyes became heavy-lidded. She fixed her gaze on One. "Now," she commanded, and One dove in, latching her lips onto Mistress's clit. She sucked and must have been using her tongue on the hardened clit, too, because Mistress grabbed One's head to hold her in place. Her pelvis arched and bucked against the still-working mouth.

Fierce jealousy overcame Angel. She wanted to push One out of the way. She wanted to be the one to taste their Mistress and make her cum. It was so frustrating. She swallowed hard and watched her Mistress's face to see what it looked like when she came.

Mistress Diandra's moans increased. She was about to cum. Angel held her breath as her Mistress's eyes rolled up behind closed lids, her back arched, and her whole body bucked. Angel finally remembered to breathe and watched One continue working until their Mistress stilled her with a hand to her head. One sat back on her heels. Mistress Diandra gazed at One while she caught her breath and basked in the afterglow of orgasm. A smile crept up her face. "Good job, One." She breathed deeply for a few moments and reached for the crop with the number one on the handle. She ran it through One's labia, and it came back soaked. "Well done, One." She held up the dripping crop. She gestured that One should kneel in her usual spot at her side.

"Kneel in front of me, Two," Mistress Diandra said and reached for the crop numbered Two.

Angel couldn't help herself. She threw herself at her Mistress's feet and kissed them over and over and over. Tears streamed from her face.

"Thank you, Two," Mistress Diandra said. "That was a lovely gesture. Now sit up." She smiled at her slave and said, "Open your legs, please." Angel was not surprised when the crop came back wet. Witnessing the reciprocal desires between both Mistress and slave was something she had never seen, and she wanted it for herself. "This is excellent, Two." She reached down and tousled Angel's hair. Angel felt her whole torso flush. "Would you like to clean me –"

"Yes, Ma'am," Angel interrupted.

"Never, ever, interrupt your Mistress, Two." Mistress Diandra reached down, grabbed Angel roughly by the hair, and pulled her face to her pussy. "Clean me."

I threw my tablet down and pushed Two out of the way so that I could be the one to clean up our Mistress. My name is Six, after all. I spread my legs wide, wider than is comfortable, trying to be more flexible than I am. My fingers fly to my thighs, and I imagine this is my tongue on my Mistress's thighs. I move up to her labia and vaginal entrance. I stick my tongue inside and swirl it around. Oh, how I wish she had fucked me, but slaves take what they can get. My fingers find my clit and stay there until my hips buck like

Mistress Diandra's, and I cum as silently as possible. Since I have not been commanded to close my legs, I fall asleep with them wide open.

Chapter 7
I've Got You, Baby

I open my phone Thursday morning and find another text from Daddy Vic. I don't know why, but I'm relieved to get any kind of communication from her. I hadn't realized the extent of my anxiety about that. Maybe I'm heading into what Lisa called sub frenzy. I don't know, but even though I have to pee, I sit on the side of my bed and read her text. Wow. It's long.

DADDY VIC: Iron Cunt - Arrive at my apartment at 8 p.m. Friday. No sooner. No later. Do not speak upon entering. Take off your clothes and then grab the straps where I inspected you last time. Do not move from there.

DADDY VIC: Thursday Instructions - You are NOT allowed to cum on Thursday. Continue your Kegels every half hour. Stop at 6 p.m. You need to rest those muscles for Friday. Also, you are no longer allowed to wear panties. I only allow at most one layer of fabric between your cunt and me. Wear pants to work on Thursday, and whenever you are at your desk alone, open your legs as wide as you can. Use the desk itself to stretch and hold them open. I require flexibility in my subs, so you might as well start working on that. Rub your nipples. Make them hard. With your legs wide open, reach down and press the heel of your palm over your clit and your cunt. Press hard enough to make yourself wet. I want a picture of your wet cunt by 5 p.m.

Thursday. Remember, you are NOT allowed to cum on Thursday.

DADDY VIC: Friday Instructions - You are not allowed to cum before you see me on Friday. No more Kegels. You are to wear a skirt to work but no panties. I require my femmes to wear skirts, so you'd better get used to that. This time when you spread your legs at your desk, you'll insert two or more fingers into your cunt and push them in as far as you can and then pull them out. Fuck yourself for a full minute. Pull your fingers out and lick them clean while you rest for thirty seconds. Do this routine at least ten times. Do NOT touch your clit. Do NOT cum. I require another picture of your wet cunt. This time, with your fingers inserted. I want this picture by 5 p.m. Friday.

"I own one skirt," I say out loud with a laugh. I stand up and get ready for work, trying to make sense of her instructions. As I get in the car, panty-less, of course, I realize something. "Oh, my God. She called me a femme." I'm floored. I have never been called a femme in my life. Maybe I need to get that haircut. It's already spilling over the collar of my shirt. Perhaps I'll ask Daddy Vic on Friday for advice on what to do with it.

I get through Thursday easily enough with my instructions from Daddy Vic. I brought in a scented wax warmer from home to cover up the scent of my arousal. This way, I'd feel semi-comfortable, spreading my legs and rubbing myself in my office. It's weird not feeling the weight of boi shorts under my pants, but I kind of like it. It's freeing. Luckily, I had the foresight to wear dark pants because the pressing of my palm against my center makes the fabric soak up my arousal. Daddy Vic knew that, didn't she? That was sneaky. Naturally, I became a hot, wet mess. I sneak out during my office hours to take the required picture in the same restroom stall where I masturbated yesterday. This time, no one comes in to overhear the kinky professor in stall number four.

By Thursday evening at six p.m., I am ecstatic that Kegels training is finished. As far as flexibility goes, I discover that I am not very. That's why, instead of my usual nighttime masturbation session, I search for a YouTube video to show me how to increase flexibility. It can't hurt, right? I am horny but exhausted by the time I go to bed. I go to sleep thinking about Friday's instructions. I don't let my mind conjure up possibilities of what will happen at Daddy Vic's Friday evening because I don't want to have any preconceptions before getting there. Daddy Vic will do to me what she wants to do. She's in charge, and I like it that way.

When I wake Friday morning, I'm disappointed that she didn't send a follow-up text or a reply about the pussy picture I sent her the day before. Oh, well. It doesn't matter, right? I'll be seeing her in about fourteen hours and counting. I check my personal emails using my phone and brighten when I see that my test results are in. Clean. Perfect. I'll print out a copy for her when I get home.

The hardest part about my Friday instructions is the damn skirt. I don't even know why I have it. Maybe it's because my mother always expected me to wear a skirt to certain events, like the last event we attended as a family before she passed. It was the Alameda County Choir Concert at Ridgeline Hall. It was right before her diagnosis with cancer. That was the very last time I'd worn that skirt.

A flush of shame overcomes me as I sit at my desk and slide my fingers under my skirt. What am I doing? I'm at work. What kind of person slides her ass to the edge of her office chair and then deliberately reaches underneath the only skirt she owns and pushes two fingers inside her pussy? Who does that? Apparently, I do. I watch the timer on my phone, plunge in and out for an entire minute, and then pull them out to lick clean for thirty seconds. I keep an eye on the window in my office door, hoping no one comes by to chat. Once thirty seconds is up, I plunge again. Oh, God, my legs have opened themselves wider, all on their own. I stretch my legs so far apart that my groin hurts. I use the desk to spread myself wide. I rake my fingers across my G-spot and pull out, feeling the stirrings of an orgasm.

"Do not touch your clit," I whisper under my breath. "You are not allowed to cum."

When I've done all ten sets, I bolt out of my chair to the restroom and dive into my favorite stall. I tuck the hem of the skirt into the waistband. I'm not surprised to see my arousal dripping down my thighs. I take several pictures trying to capture the best shot for Daddy Vic.

I wish I could touch my clit. I want to cum so badly. Just as I'm about to make a bad decision, the door to the restroom opens. I grab some toilet paper and clean myself up. It takes a lot of paper, and I hope beyond hope that my scent isn't permeating the room. I flush the toilet, right my skirt, and wait for the person to enter a stall so that I can sneak out. She doesn't. Damn it. What do I do? I have no choice. I have to wash my hands. Just as I'm opening the door to the stall, I hear the outside door open and close. Did she leave? I step out, and the restroom is blessedly empty. Thank God. I wash my hands using a liberal amount of scented institutional soap.

~~~

I am showered, freshly shaved, and excited as hell as I pull into Daddy Vic's apartment complex. I even tried to dress provocatively in a low-cut shirt, which is way sexier than the flannel shirt I had on the first day we met. I walk up to her door but don't knock until the time on my phone says it is precisely 8:00 p.m.

"Come in," says a voice from inside.

The door is unlocked, so I walk in to find Daddy Vic in her command chair. She is as striking as I remember, and a nervous flush runs through me. Her lips are full, and her features strong and sharp. She looks like she stepped out of a menswear magazine. Although she is butch, she is not manly. She may look hard, but she has soft and feminine undertones as well. Everything about her is perfect, including the one lock of hair that curls down over her forehead. I want to sit in her lap and brush it away, but that is not allowed right now.

The lights are dimmed, and the music is soft. She has set the tone perfectly. I grin shyly at her and silently step to the spot where she inspected me last time. She gives me the barest of nods as if acknowledging my obedience to her instructions. I hang up my coat and wordlessly show her the printout of my test results. She nods and gestures for me to continue disrobing. I take off my shoes and then my socks. I feel like I'm playing strip poker, trying to remove the least revealing items of clothing first. I don't dawdle in my task, nor do I hurry. I try to stay calm and cool on the outside, but inside, I am a mass of anxious energy. I mean, I've only known her for about a week, and I really don't know her at all.

Daddy Vic leans forward when I remove my bra and then my pants. There are no boi shorts underneath, of course, as per her rules. She smiles. She is obviously pleased that I obeyed her instructions. I reach up for the straps and wrap my hands through them. I spread my legs so my feet hit the marks on the floor.

She sits back and steeples her fingers. Her gaze rakes over my body. I stand quietly, watching her. She twirls a finger, indicating I should turn to face the wall so she can look at me from behind. It isn't long before I feel the warmth of her body behind me. She picks up my test results and examines them. She places the printout back on my clothes.

"Face me," she says simply. I turn to meet her hungry gaze. Apparently, I am about to be her feast. I shiver, and my nipples harden. She notices and grins. "Are you happy to be here?"

"Yes, Sir," I say, grateful to be able to speak. "Very excited." She steps closer, and I think she's going to kiss me, but she leans down, sticks out her tongue, and flicks one of my nipples. This makes me shiver again, hardening my nipples deeper. Without warning, she latches on and sucks my nipple hard. I arch toward her, trying to increase the pressure, but there isn't much I can do while holding onto these straps. Daddy Vic moves to the other nipple and sucks it as hard as the first. This direct contact is affecting me, and I gush with wetness down below.

She reaches down with her right hand and cups my mons as she continues sucking my breasts, alternating between them. I arch into her hand to increase the pressure. She slips two fingers inside me and gives a satisfying grunt at my wetness. She grips my pubic bone and pulls me toward her. I haven't got much room to move, so I end up on my tiptoes trying to accommodate her silent request.

She presses the heel of her hand hard against my pubic bone, and I wince a little.

"Do you like pain?" she asks huskily.

"Yes, Sir," I say. My breathing betrays how turned on I am. "To a point, Sir. I'm not sure how much I can take."

"We're about to find out," she says gleefully and releases my crotch. She sticks her wet fingers in my mouth, and I know what to do. I lick my essence off of them. "I want to show you some of your presents before we go to the playroom."

"Presents?"

She reaches behind me and pulls down a black duffel bag from the shelf. It looks high-end. She opens it, and I can tell it is full of toys. She pulls out three items. They look like open-ended test tubes with screwtops. I am confused.

"Just the start," she says and leans forward to harden one of my nipples by licking it several times. She places the open end of one of the test-tubey things over my nipple, presses it, and then turns the screw top.

"Oh," I say as it gets tight around my nipple. The contraption has created a vacuum, and it hurts but also feels amazing. She does the same thing to the other nipple, and I am in heaven. It's odd to see the tubes dangling off my breasts like elongated pasties.

"I want big nipples," Daddy Vic says simply. "You'll take these home and use them every day. Every chance you get."

"Yes, Sir," I say, wondering if these contraptions really work.

She tightens one of them. I grunt a little. The sensation is fantastic. She smiles back at me, but the smile turns devilish when she holds up the third tube. Is that a backup, I wonder?

She reaches between my spread legs and strokes my clit. I buck my hips a bit, and she swats me on the thigh. "Stop." I obey. "Reach down and spread your lips. I want to see your clit."

Once again, I obey, and then she does the impossible. She places the open tube over my clit, presses, and turns the knob. My clit is caught in a vacuum. "Sir, Sir, Sir," I say, not sure what I want. The sensation is so strange.

"Yes, IC?"

"What are you –? Is that safe?"

She chuckles. "Yes, it's safe. Color, please?"

"Green, I guess."

"Good." She twists the knob a bit more, and my clit pulses as it's sucked further into the tube. "I want a big clit. Wear this every day. Whenever you can."

"Okay."

She swats me on the thigh and looks up at me, her brow furrowed. I feel like I have somehow angered her, and I don't know why.

"I demand respect from all my subs."

"Yes, Sir," I say, although I'm still not sure what I did wrong. "I understand, Sir."

"Make sure that you do."

She adjusts my tubes, grabs my bag of toys, and then heads down the hallway toward her playroom. She leaves me standing there thinking my own private thoughts. Thoughts like, "Is she sane? Can I trust her? What have I gotten myself into?" I realize just now that I didn't tell anyone that I was coming here tonight. Wait, wait. Yes, I did. I told Shasti at the coffee house the other day. But she won't think to check on me. I didn't set that up with her. I glance over at my pile of clothes. My cell phone is in the pants pocket. Do I dare?

"Tighten the suction," Daddy Vic commands from the other room, and I jump. It's as if she can read my mind.

I sneak a peek at my nipples, and they are grotesquely huge. I can only imagine what my clit looks like. I can't quite make it out over my larger-than-it-should-be stomach. To do her bidding, I have to let go of the straps. I am grateful to be able to shake out my arms. I tentatively twist the one on my right breast. Oh, it's delicious. I bask in the pain. It radiates straight down to my incredibly wet pussy. I twist the one on the other breast and ride that wave as well. I am afraid to tighten the one on my clit. Before I do, I suck in my stomach, bend over at the waist and look. Holy crap. This tube thing has sucked my clit inside. It's huge. How long will it stay that way once Daddy Vic releases it? I reach down and tentatively turn the knob. My clit grows. There is pain, but it is weird pain. It's both pleasurable and not. I ride this new sensation and then hear Daddy Vic's hard-souled shoes on the wood floors heading toward me. I straighten back up and grab the straps. The vacuum tubes bounce as a result and bring me another wave of pleasure.

"Sir, may I speak?"

She doesn't say anything for a moment, as if weighing whether she should let me, and then acquiesces. "Speak," she says.

"I am to use these vacuum tubes every day?"

"Every day. You have average nipples. I want them bigger."

"And my clit?"

"Above average," she says matter-of-factly. "But I want it even bigger."

"Oh," is all I can think to say.

"Follow me," Daddy Vic says and heads back to the playroom.

The tubes on my breasts bounce as I walk, but the one capturing my clit works itself loose, and I catch it in my hand before it hits the floor. Once inside, I wordlessly show Daddy Vic my plight. She reaches low, separates my lips, and inspects my clit. I feel like a piece of meat, but I am strangely okay with that. "Put it back on," she commands. It takes me a moment to figure out the device's mechanics, but I do, and soon my clit is recaptured in its vacuum of torture.

"Go to the cross," Daddy Vic says.

I notice the restraints for wrists above and ankles below. I inhale sharply. Restraints. I rub my wrist. I told her about my anxiety about restraints. I know I did. Does she remember? I head to the cross and stand in front of it, not knowing where she wants me exactly.

"Turn," she says. She is a woman of few words this evening. I turn and face the cross. My back is now to her. "Normally, you'd be shackled with these." She shows me the leather straps with locks hanging off them. "But I will honor your needs and use these. She lifts my right wrist and slips it into a Velcro restraint. "Pull like you want to get out." I pull, and it takes some finesse to get just the right angle, but I finally pull free. "Will this suit your needs, IC?"

"Yes, Sir," I say. I know there is mirth in my eyes. She keeps calling me IC – Iron Cunt. "This suits my needs."

"Stoplight safe words?"

"Correct, Sir. Thank you for honoring that as well."

"Always." Daddy Vic gives each of my vacuum tubes a twist, causing waves of pain that turn to pleasure. I am so wet that I'm sure she can detect my arousal with her sense of smell. She attaches my other wrist and then my ankles. I am now standing with my arms up, and my legs spread like the letter X. I am not smashed up against the X, thank goodness, and have plenty of room to move. Well, not a ton of room, but at least I'm not strapped down tight.

She moves behind me and presses her clothed body against my naked one. I feel the bulge of her dildo against my buttocks. She reaches around me and splays her right hand against my stomach—her left splays across my chest above my breasts. I feel totally possessed, owned, and helpless. And that is precisely how I want it.

Daddy Vic's right hand makes slow circles on my stomach and then moves lower and lower until it bumps up against the tube, vacuuming my clit. With one hand, she deftly removes the device, and it clatters to the wooden platform. She swirls her fingers in my arousal and then grabs the tiny stalk of my enlarged clit with her thumb and middle finger. She moves them up and down together as if jerking off a tiny penis. I tilt my pelvis so she has better access.

"IC likes being jerked off," Daddy Vic whispers in my ear. "Doesn't she?"

My breathing is labored, and there is a slight buzz in my ears. Adrenaline maybe. Oh, God, she could make me cum this way. "Yessss," I hiss, finally answering her question.

She swats my ass with her left hand. I jump. I wasn't expecting it. What the hell?

"I demand respect," she says again.

"I respect you, Sir," I say in my defense. I hear the confused pleading in my voice.

"Show it."

"Yes, Sir," I say. "How?"

"Always remember that I am the giver of pleasure. Every sentence you utter must show me respect. Every. Single. Sentence."

"I understand, Sir," I say but don't.

She jams the tube back on my clit and twists. I gasp at the sensation. She takes the tubes off my nipples, reaches around me to kiss and suck each one in turn, and then puts the tubes back on. I love how big my nipples look inside them. But I'm pretty sure they won't stay that way permanently.

She steps away, and now I feel cold. She fumbles in my new bag, and then a new sensation trails over my ass cheeks. It moves up my torso and over my shoulder blades and back.

"This is deerskin," she says. "Very soft. You'll graduate to tougher materials as our relationship progresses."

The softness disappears. Thwack! I gasp and jump. I was more surprised than hurt by whatever it was she hit me with. "Look in the mirror in front of you," she says and thwacks me again on the other ass cheek. "You can watch what I'm doing." I find the mirror she's referring to, and it reflects the full-length mirror on the far wall. I watch as she pulls her arm back slightly and flings the stranded implement at me. It's a flogger. Oh, my God. I'm being flogged for the very first time. And it kind of hurts, but it kind of doesn't. Not yet, anyway.

She continues her motions, and I get lost in the cadence of her blows. The continual thwack, thwack, thwack feels and sounds amazing. I know she is taking it relatively easy on me this go-around and is trying to gauge how much I can take. "Still green?"

"Yes, Sir," I say. "This is lovely."

"It's about to get harder." She wasn't wrong. She flicks the flogger, and it hits me hard, and I screech in pain. She flicks it at me again and again. I cry out with each blow but absorb the pain into my body and let it flow through me.

"Color," she calls, continually flicking the flogger at me.

"Green," I grunt, even though my body is saturated with pain and can't absorb much more. But I don't want to stop now.

The flogger triples in cadence on my ass and back and thighs. My stoicism has long left the building, and I can't help squealing with each hit.

"Respect!" she roars and strikes me.

"Sir! Yes, Sir," I bellow, finally understanding what she wants. I keep forgetting to address her as Sir.

"Better," she says and moves to flog my back gently. My ass, on the other hand, is freakin' on fire. It pulses, and I wish she would run her strong hands over it to soothe me, but she doesn't. I use the mirror to watch her work and am enthralled by her rhythm and technique. I can't stay focused on her, though. I have to focus on soaking in the pain. Her strokes get faster, harder.

"Yellow," I screech. It's too much. She stops. I realize that she wasn't going to stop until I called a color.

"You are a beautiful shade of deep red, IC. Deep red," she says from where she stands a few feet behind me. She is clearly proud of her work.

"Will you touch my skin, Sir?" I hear the pleading in my voice. "Please,

Sir? I need relief." My back and buttocks are pulsing and burning.

"Ride it," she says and sits on a bench to my right. "Close your eyes and feel it."

I feel like I can't make sense of what's up or down with my eyes closed. I'm flying. Logically, I know it's just my body flooding with endorphins, but I feel drugged in an oh-so-good way. When I focus, I feel the pulsating pain more acutely. "Sir," I say breathlessly. "I ... thank you, Sir." The throbbing sensation seems to travel throughout my torso, trying to find a home. And find a home it does. Right where I want her to touch me the most.

"I'm going to fuck you now," she says matter-of-factly.

I can't answer her. My breathing is too difficult. I am keenly aware of her body close to mine. "Touch me, Sir," I whimper. Something is happening in my body. My pussy is burning. I want these vacuum tubes off me. I want her to suck my nipples. No, I want her to fuck me. Both. Anything. All of it.

As if answering my prayer, she takes all the tubes off and then tweaks both of my nipples. "Nice," she sucks air in between her teeth. "This might work," she mutters cryptically and flicks one of my nipples again.

"Please, Sir. I'm dying." Oh, God, I am pathetic. "I need—"

"Open your legs wider," she says, even though the restraints already have me spread pretty far. I open them wider as instructed. I hear her fumbling with her clothes, and then without warning, impales me on her cock. She pushes me up against the cross and starts thrusting. I've never been fucked up against a wall before. I feel overpowered and possessed by her. It is amazing.

Her clothes are rough against my tender and burning ass, though, making the sensations confusing.

Daddy Vic reaches around my hip and swirls her finger through my wet folds. She strokes my enlarged clit like a little cock. It's so sexy, and I cum without warning. "Fuck," I cry out and buck against the cross. "Fuck, Daddy. Fuck."

She doesn't stop stroking my clit, and I continue cumming. My legs turn to jelly. "Help," I cry. I can't hold myself up. My weight falls back against her.

"Okay, okay, okay," she says and wraps both arms around me. She undoes the restraints on one wrist and then the other. She lowers me to the ground. She lays on the floor with me and spoons me from behind. "You're okay, IC," she says. "A little sensory overloaded, that's all."

I shudder as another aftershock hits me. "Daddy," I say, "hold me."

"I've got you, baby. I've got you."

Chapter 8
Take It All

A dildo is thrust inside me. "Hold it in, Iron Cunt," Daddy Vic says. I am draped face down over the spanking horse but not restrained in any way. She instructed me to hold onto the handles in the front and helped my feet find the footrests in the back. She says I can push against them when she fucks me in a little while. God, I am so turned on. Daddy Vic is so good-looking, and she takes charge like my dream Domme.

After I gloriously lost all control of my muscles following the mind-blowing orgasm from her floggings, I thought maybe we were done for the night. But no. She held me for a while and then got me some water and a protein drink full of "essential nutrients." I didn't ask what that meant, but I trust her and felt much better after a while. While I was resting, she scolded me for not hydrating before coming to play and grilled me about whether I was on medications or hormones or taking herbs. I answered truthfully, no, to each one. Satisfied with my answers, she added a water protocol to my growing list of requirements.

Daddy Vic walks up behind me, and I hear her adjusting some kind of mechanical crank. Oh, shit, the footrests and, consequently, my legs are opening wider. She tugs at the dildo. "You're doing a great job holding this inside you, IC. Resist me. Keep it inside." I clamp down my vaginal muscles and do my best to win the battle. "Nice. Nice." The compliment is genuine. She pulls it out and then jams it back inside me and tells me to keep it in again.

She walks around the horse and shows me a second dildo. This one is bigger. It's as big as Mistress Ciara's BBC that she fucked me with over Thanksgiving. "Open," Daddy Vic says to me, and I open my mouth wide. She slides the monster inside. "Lick the head and suck." I do as she asks. She pulses the dildo in and out of my mouth, never going too far. But then she does. She pushes in further, and I abandon licking the tip to focus on breathing when she pulls it out. Mistress Ciara helped me understand the art and finesse of silicone cock sucking, and I am doing fine until she hits the back of my throat, and I gag. The gagging reflex causes me to clench my core, which causes the dildo to slide out of my vagina.

"You have a lot of work to do, Iron Cunt," she says to me. "You barely took four inches in your mouth. That is kind of pitiful. By the time I'm done with you, baby, you'll be swallowing my entire lineup of cocks and begging for more."

I sigh. I cannot foresee that particular future. But okay.

She moves behind me and says, "Look at your legs spread wide open like a slut. And you're not even restrained. Are you a slutty girl?"

I don't know what to say, so I keep quiet. I yelp when her hand hits my raw ass cheek, and I jump at the impact. "Answer me!" she roars.

"Yes, Sir. I am a slutty girl."

"You're *my* slutty girl, aren't you? Don't you forget it." This is a weird headspace she's putting me into right now, but I will play along. I have no choice. And, besides, she may be right. I just might be a slut. Is that a bad thing?

She slides her hand between me and the horse. She rubs my clit with her strong fingers. "Say it," she says.

I'm not exactly sure what she means, so I improvise, "I am Daddy Vic's slut. I am her fucking slut. I want her to fuck me with her cock until I pass out again."

She moans. Those must have been the right words. "Good girl," she whispers, causing me to shiver. I don't know what it is about those two words, but it has a visceral effect. She pulls her hand away from my clit, and I mourn its absence.

"You're in training," she says abruptly. She wheels something toward me. "You will work on blow jobs while I discipline you."

"Sir? Discipline me for what?"

"Not taking care of your body. Not hydrating. Your body belongs to me now," she says evenly. "I thought you knew that."

"Yes, Sir. I understand now."

I look up to see her screwing a dildo onto a movable board. It looks like a smaller version of the portable white eraser board we had in the women's locker room in college. The coaches would wheel it over and write motivational sayings or game strategy or whatever.

Daddy Vic wheels it closer and adjusts the height so the dildo is right at my mouth. "This is a four-inch dildo—a tiny thing. But you're in training and need to get used to your mouth being filled. When the cock meets resistance, keep pushing. The cock head will slide into your throat if you relax enough. You will open your throat and take it all. It'll get easier over time and with practice. You will continue to fuck your mouth with this dildo until I tell you to stop. Meanwhile," she picks up a riding crop, "I will be reddening your body with this baby. Do you want me to leave long-lasting marks?"

"Uh, Sir, I don't know, Sir," I say. My ass and back are already kind of raw from the flogging. "Maybe not this first time? I have been hit with a crop before, but it wasn't pleasurable." Mama_Luvs beat me with the crop for her own enjoyment. I was a piece of living meat to her. And that was not fun.

"I'll take that as a no. This time. Eventually, Daddy Vic leaves her mark on everyone." She moves behind me and rubs my ass, thighs, and back. I understand what she is doing. She is silently telling me the places she will be hitting me. I'm not sure how much I can take after being flogged less than an hour before, but I have to trust that Daddy Vic knows what she is doing.

"Do your work, little girl," Daddy Vic says. I pull my head back a little in order to put the head of the dildo in my mouth. It's not big at all, so I should be able to do this. "I want your nose pressing up against the foam surrounding the base of the phallus. Think of it as my cock fucking your mouth. You want to put enough pressure on my cock to press against my clit and make me cum. You want me to cum, little slut, don't you?"

"Yesh, Shir," I say as best I can. There's a cock in my mouth at the moment.

"Devour it," Daddy Vic says.

I push my head forward and pull out. I'm trying to gauge how big it is. I yelp when she hits me with the crop on my ass. I push forward and almost have all of it in. A little further, and I'll have it all. She hits me again, and I gasp. I can't see her in the mirror to know when she's going to strike me. But she knows that, doesn't she? I push forward on the cock, and it's almost all

81

the way in. It's right at the back of my throat, but I breathe, and I'm okay. My nose almost touches the foam.

"Ungh," I cry at another hit. And another and another. She is in a steady rhythm now, so I move my head to match her strokes. That's the best way to help my body make sense of this new level of pain. I bob my head back and forth fucking my mouth with the cock.

"All. The. Way. In," she commands, hitting me with every word.

I don't answer her. The cock is pushing against my throat. I know I need to relax and let the cock head push my throat open, but Daddy Vic is smacking away at me, and it's hard to relax. My ass is heating up from her ministrations. Please move to another spot, I will her, but she does not. I will be bruised for sure. Deeply.

I push forward and stop when the cock is at my throat. I'm afraid, but I press on and let it push my throat open. Okay, that wasn't too bad. Daddy Vic smacks me on the back of the leg with the crop. Thank God she moved on. Now, I can semi-focus on opening my throat. I pull my head off the cock, take a big sighing breath, and then go back to work. The head pushes at my throat. Stay relaxed, open, let it go in. It's in again. It's in. I pull out and breathe. I keep this up and notice that Daddy Vic has moved on to beat me on my back now. I hadn't even noticed.

"Good fucking, cock sucker," she growls at me. "You'll be sucking down my ten-incher in no time."

I beam at her praise and double my pace. The cock head opens my throat with every thrust. I am going to have a sore throat tomorrow, that's for sure.

"Will you drink water tomorrow, slut?" Whack, whack, whack, she hits my back.

I pull off the cock. "Yes, Sir," I say and then get back to work.

"Will you take my special supplements?" Whack, whack, whack, she hits the back of my legs again.

"Yes, Sir."

"Will you deep-throat my cock?" Whack, whack, whack, she hits my ass cheeks again.

"Yes, Sir. One day, I'll do it." I redouble my efforts and am amazed at how easy it seems to be now. I don't know what I was so afraid of.

"Good girl. Good little slut."

She continues to hit me with her crop, making moaning noises as she does so. She is getting turned on. I feel dizzy and pull off the cock in my mouth and say, "Yellow, Sir."

She stops and comes up to my head. She moves the cock out of the way. "What's up?"

"Red, Sir. Sorry. I feel light-headed."

"Let's rest then. Take your water and go sit on the hassock in the living room."

She helps me up, but then I find my way to the hassock on my own.

"Once you feel better, lie on your back," she calls to me. "Let me see your gaping pussy between your wide-open legs inviting me to fuck you. It will be your invitation to me."

"Yes, Sir."

My ass, thighs, and back hurt from being beaten, but I pay them no mind and feel better after a while. I think it was the odd angle my head was in. Or her constant smacks from the crop. It was intense. I take a deep breath and lay back on the hassock. I let my legs fall to the sides in the sex doll pose that Mistress Ciara taught me. She told me that Dommes might not have my best interests in mind, but I think Daddy Vic does. She calls me "little slut" now. It's kind of endearing, and I like it.

Daddy Vic walks into the living room, holding a small canvas bag that zips up one side. It looks like some of the pencil cases that my students use. "This is twice now that you've interrupted our play because your body isn't in tiptop shape. I'm severely disappointed."

"I'm sorry, Sir."

"This is a week's worth of supplements. I'm putting them on your clothes by the front door so that you won't forget them. Instructions are inside. You'll take them three times a day. Is that understood?"

"Yes, Sir." I look up at her through my open legs.

"Sit up," she says and walks over to the jar containing a million condoms. "I like obedient subs. Are you an obedient sub, IC?"

"Yes, Sir." I am hurt that she would question that. "Always."

She rushes over, grabs my chin, and looks into my eyes, searching for what I don't know. She must have seen whatever she was looking for because she nods and breaks eye contact. She unzips her pants and pulls out her cock.

She strokes it a few times as if it is the real thing. She rips the condom package open with her teeth, and I blurt, "Sir, may I put that on you?"

She looks surprised but then says, "Sure," and hands me the condom.

I pull the condom out of the package and put it in my mouth, tucking the lower bit between my bottom lip and teeth, and accidentally blow out a puff of air, inflating the thing a little. She chuckles. "Nice party trick, IC." I smile and lean toward the cock. I push against it and unroll the condom. The head of her cock hits the back of my throat, but I push on and let my throat take it in. Before I gag, I have to pull back out, but I see that I've gained at least five whole inches when I do. Whoa. That's a new record for me. I push the condom down her cock the rest of the way with my fingers. One day, I hope to do that with only my mouth.

"Impressive," Daddy Vic says succinctly. "Lay back." With her condom-covered cock dangling in front of her, she reaches down and pulls up restraints attached to the hassock legs or something. She puts my wrists in restraints and then does the same for my ankles. I am spread-eagled before her. I am aroused and squirm for her to mount me.

She doesn't. Instead, she dips her head down between my legs. I feel something laid over my center, and then her tongue flicks my clit causing me to jump. "Daddy," I say, bucking my hips slightly. I wasn't expecting her to touch me this way. She pulls my thin inner labia into her mouth and sucks hard. It hurts, but in a good way. I feel her lips, but there is a barrier between her skin and mine. Dental dam. That must be it. Daddy Vic is uber-cautious about being safe. And that is a good thing and is a big part of the reason I trust her so much.

Daddy Vic licks my clit, but then moves to the other side. Her mouth is warm, even through the barrier, and feels so fucking good. I can cum from this. She thrusts her tongue into my pussy and swirls her tongue around. I'd forgotten how good it feels to have someone suck my pussy. It's been so long. She pulls her tongue out and puts her entire mouth around my clit, and goes to town. She sucks as if milking me. My pelvis rises, and I start shaking.

"Daddy," I shriek, "I'm cumming." I buck my hips against her face as I release. She rides me the whole way like I'm a bucking bronco. I am still cumming when she buries her cock inside me. Her thrusts spark a second orgasm. "Oh, God," I moan. "Daddy, again." I lift my pelvis to the ceiling so she can drive her cock deep inside, and I cum again. "Fuck, Daddy. Fuck." My entire body clenches, and I can tell she has difficulty pulling her cock out and getting it back in.

"Fucking iron cunt," she growls. She continues to pummel me even as my aftershocks wane, and then she cries out herself. Her head tilts back, and her eyes close. She grimaces and then cums with a long low moan that arouses my entire body again. Her thrusts slow, and then she falls on top of me, spent. I wish I could use my arms to hold her or stroke her back, but I can't. I am restrained.

"Oh, fuck, little slut. I love that iron cunt of yours," she says breathlessly into my neck. I want her to kiss me. But she does not. She is quiet for a while, and her body weight becomes increasingly heavy on me. I think she might be falling asleep. I am helpless. I know I can get out of these restraints if I need to, but I kind of like her weight on me. It's like she has possessed my body. Her cock is still buried deep inside, possessing me from the inside.

"Daddy?" I say softly. She is getting a little too heavy.

"Mmm," she moans and then lifts her weight off me. "So good, fucking slut. So good." She moves off the hassock and loosens the restraints on my ankles. "Feet on the hassock." I obey. "Knees up. We're not going full in tonight, but soon." I don't know what she means until she kneels between my open legs and lifts my ass off the hassock onto her thighs. She pushes her cock back inside me and pumps a few times. "You're a good fuck, IC. There is so much we're going to do together." She lifts my ass even higher and presses the tip of her cock at my backdoor entrance. "Color, IC?"

"Green light, Sir."

"Excellent. That's Daddy's little slut." She pushes her cock against my entrance and gains no ground. She dips her fingers into my pussy and slathers my wetness all over and in my tiny hole. She massages the area with her fingers. "Loosen up, slut."

"Yes, Sir." As soon as she commands this, I realize I have been clenching my muscles down there. I do my best to relax.

"Ahh," she murmurs, "here we are." She pulls my ass cheeks apart and pushes the head of her cock against me again. This time, I feel she has just the right spot and pressure and tell her so. She nods and keeps pressing. I wish I could help her by spreading my ass cheeks for her, but my hands are still restrained.

"Ungh," I groan as the tip of her cock breaks through the strong ring of muscles.

"Good slut. Take my cock in your ass." Her voice is thick with lust. "All of them are mine, slut. All of your holes are mine to use whenever I want to. The next time we go to Mamma Mia's, you're going to wear a skirt, and I'm going to finger you during our meal. Maybe I'll let you cum. Maybe not."

"Oh, Sir." Although the thought of public sex scares me to death, it also turns me on like crazy.

She pushes her cock into my ass about an inch and then pulls back. She pulls out, lubes me up again with my own spendings, and then pushes in again. She does this several times. "When is your next period?"

I'm not expecting the question. "Um, what, Sir?"

"Your menstrual cycle. Your period. When are you due next?"

"Umm, let me think." I am fairly regular, but it's hard to do the math with Daddy Vic micro-fucking me in the ass. "Umm, oh, shit. Tomorrow or Sunday, Sir."

"Excellent," she says. There is joy in her voice. "In your bag are ass plugs. I'm sure you know how to use them. Stretch yourself out tomorrow—all day. Meet me at the coffee shop at noon. You'll show me your big nipples in the restroom. I'll suck them there. And I'll personally check to make sure one of the plugs is inserted in your ass. After that, give yourself enough time to prepare for our big evening. You know what I mean by 'prepare yourself,' right?"

"Stay hydrated, Sir?"

"Well, yes," she says, but she clearly expected me to say something else. It dawns on me that we're talking about butt plugs, and that means anal sex.

"Cleaned out with an enema, Sir?"

"They told me you were smart. Use several until the solution comes out clear. Have a light breakfast, meaning no meat and no fried foods. Eat nothing after that except protein shakes with the supplements. And be back here at eight p.m. No sooner. No later. I want the biggest plug in your ass when you arrive. I want a tampon in your cunt and tuck the damn string. No one wants to see that shit."

"Umm, okay," I say tentatively. "Yes, Sir."

"Your nipples are to be hard and full. Use your suction tubes all day and have them in place when you knock on my door. So that means a loose shirt and no bra. I want to suck on your tits as soon as your clothes are off. I also what that clitty of yours large and full. Have that tube in place there as well. And obviously, you are no longer wearing panties. Even during menstrual cycles." Her eyes fill with glee at this announcement.

"Yes, Sir. I understand." But that makes me incredibly nervous. Sometimes, my cycles can be pretty heavy.

"Do you know what starts tomorrow, IC?"

"Umm, no, Sir, I do not."

A devilish smile creeps up her face as she says, "It's anal week, of course. All anal, all the time. Just because your pussy is out of commission doesn't mean I can't use the rest of your body for my personal pleasure."

Chapter 9
Anal Week

I walk into the coffee shop Saturday morning a little before noon, the time Daddy Vic said I should arrive. My heart smiles when I see that she's already here and sitting in the section where Shasti, Madison, and I have hung out a couple of times. The butt plug is snug and, so far, isn't too annoying. I'm wearing my good black jeans and a loose shirt since she wanted me to use the suction tubes on my nipples before entering the shop. I purposely parked at the far end of the street so no one would see me suctioning my breasts in the car.

I debate whether to get my coffee at the counter first but decide Daddy Vic would want me to greet her immediately, so I change direction. She's not great at communicating protocols, so I make an educated guess. She hasn't looked up from her phone yet, so she must not know I'm here. Anybody looking at me can see by the shit-eating grin on my face that I am totally smitten with this strong butch Domme. That's right, bitches. She's mine!

"You look handsome this morning, Sir," I say and plop down on the couch next to her chair. She looks like a prince on a throne. *My* prince. "Are you as tired as I am? Not that I'm complaining –" I cut my sentence short because she shoots me a glare that clamps my mouth shut instantly. She looks back down at her phone. I don't know what to do, so I sit with my eyes down, waiting for her to acknowledge me. Even silent, she has a commanding presence that one part excites me, and one part scares me.

Several long and silent minutes go by. I want to pull out my phone, but I don't want to annoy her any further. I have my back to the counter and have no idea if Rikki or Brittany are watching my awkward obedience to Daddy Vic. It's kind of confusing and kind of embarrassing.

"You're not wearing a skirt," Daddy Vic says without looking up.

"I didn't know I was supposed to, Sir," I say quietly. "I don't usually wear them, like, ever."

"Get used to it. I like my girls in skirts and dresses. Your pussy is mine now. I should be able to touch you without fuss. Did you take your supplements this morning?"

"Yes, Sir," I say.

"Did you pump up your nipples?"

"Yes, Sir."

"Go to the restroom. Pump them some more. I'll be there in a few minutes to suck them."

I get up, hoping no one overheard her commands. Thank goodness this restroom is a single-serving one. I lock the door and unbutton my shirt. I pull my bra up over my breasts, releasing them. They are a little sore because of my period, which did, indeed, start this morning. I mean, I'm not flowing heavily or anything, but the hormones are definitely flowing.

I unbutton my shirt and pull the vacuum tubes out of my front pocket. I latch them on and tweak the screws to tighten the suction. Oh, God, if Rikki or Brittany or any of them knew what I was doing in here, I'd die.

There is a light knock on the door. "Let me in." It's Daddy Vic. I close my shirt over the tubes and unlock the door. I turn away from the door as it's opening just in case someone is outside. I don't want to flash Rikki's customers. Daddy Vic shuts the door quietly and throws the lock home. She places one hand on the small of my back, the other on my chest, and guides me to the wall. My back hits the wall softly, but her aggressiveness has my heart pounding.

"Offer them to me," she says.

I move my open shirt out of the way and then cup my breasts from below to lift and squeeze them. I point the nipples toward her. She moans, yanks the tube off my right nipple, and dives in. The seal she makes around the nipple is incredible. Her sucking is like nothing I've ever felt before. It hurts a little but turns me on, too. I reach up, run my fingers through her hair, and pull her tighter to my chest.

She lifts her head and says, "Don't touch the hair," and dives onto my left breast. She pauses for a moment and says, "Pump the right one again." She puts a tube in my hand. It's hard to place the tube over my breast and turn the screw with just one hand, but amazingly I manage it. She sucks my breasts alternately for a few minutes. I wonder if she will require me to take my pants off. I mean, why else mention the whole skirt thing?

Abruptly she finishes by pulling back and raking her fingernails over my nipples which are incredibly sore from her sucking. "You can stay here until one o'clock. Then you will go to the Freeme Boutique and buy enough skirts and dresses to satisfy me."

"Yes, Sir," I say. I guess I am going to turn into a skirt-wearing soft butch now. I'm not sure how I got here.

"And this hair," she pulls one of my out-of-control locks. "Do not cut it. Do you understand me?"

"Um, yes, Sir."

"I like my girls to have long hair. I need something to pull."

"Oh," I say, surprised. "Okay, I can let it grow, Sir."

"Once your hair is long enough, we'll find someone to style it properly for you."

She spins me around and smashes me face-first against the wall. I turn my head in time so my nose doesn't take the hit. She presses against me, and I feel the bulge of her strap-on pressing against the butt plug. She feels around my ass and grunts when she feels the plug through my pants.

"Good, girl." She dry humps me from behind. "Stick out your ass." She grabs hold of my hips and humps me from behind. "Nothing more to eat today, and take your supplements this afternoon in a protein shake."

"Yes, Sir."

Her pace increases. I manage to get my shoulder against the wall to take the force. She moans low. Oh, God, is she going to cum from this? She slams me and then cries out quietly. She continues to hump but with less fervor. "Fucking good girl," she says, her voice thick with lust. She clears her throat and adds, "Don't forget to clean out this ass of yours. I'll be fucking you for real later. All night. I want to see how much you can take."

I can't answer her. Her bulge grinding against my ass has me turned on so much that I can't speak.

She swats me on the hip.

"Answer me, slut."

"Yes," I answer breathlessly. "Yes, Sir."

"Don't be late tonight."

"No, Sir."

She pushes off me, and I have to use my hands to break my momentum against the wall. Without another word, she backs away, unlocks the door, and leaves just like that.

I am stunned. What just happened? Without warning, the door opens, and I jump. I turn away to button up my shirt.

"Oh," Rikki says, "are you okay, Professor?"

I feel myself turning beet red. I turn back around, knowing she'll know what just happened in here.

"Someone said the women's room was out of order." She points to the "Out of Order" sign taped to the door.

"I ..." I am so embarrassed that I can't find words.

"Professor," Rikki says, genuine concern on her face. "Are you okay? Did she hurt you?"

"No, Sir," I say. "She didn't hurt me."

She laughs. "I am most definitely not a 'Sir.'"

"Oh," I say with a chuckle. "Ma'am. No, Ma'am, she did not hurt me. She just..."

Rikki put a hand up. "It's okay. You don't have to tell me. Your private life is your private life. Just remember to use your safewords during a scene or any time you're uncomfortable." She sighs and looks at the sign in her hand. "I just wish Victoria wouldn't use my restroom for her liaisons."

My face burns with embarrassment. "I'm sorry, Ma'am. It's as much my fault as it –"

"Oh, please," she says with a shake of her head. "This was not your doing. But tell me. What was your color in here? With her. Just now."

"Honestly?"

Her expression is serious. "I expect nothing else."

I look down. "It was yellow, Sir."

"Did you voice it? Did you say it out loud?"

"No, Sir. I mean, Ma'am."

She inhales deeply, and I can sense anger or exasperation or maybe both. She is holding back. "You must, Professor." She grabs my wrist and holds it up to showcase the scar from my liaison with Mama_Luvs when I didn't use

91

my safewords.

I haven't yet made eye contact with her, but I find her green eyes overpowering when I do. "I, um, yes. Yes, I will, Ma'am."

"Good girl," she says and pushes a stray lock of hair off my forehead. My knees grow weak, and I grip the edge of the sink. I wash my hands to cover up my nerves. Rikki praised me as if I were her submissive. I am clearly not. She knows I belong to Daddy Vic.

"I think it's time for a coffee," I say, drying my hands on a paper towel.

We leave the restroom, and she chatters on about different types of coffees, and I end up agreeing to a nitro cold brew something or other. She makes it herself and brings it to me on the couch, refusing to accept payment. It's almost like she feels sorry for me or something, and it's kind of weird. Although I'm still embarrassed, I wish she could stay and talk, but she can't. She has to work.

Brittany bops over and plops down, her nose glued to her phone. "Is it true that Victoria has a wall of pussies?"

"What?" I ask. She's taken me off-guard.

"I heard she takes pictures of her conquests' pussies and frames them. I heard she has, like, over fifty or something hanging in her apartment."

"I've been in her apartment," I say, "but have not seen anything like that, Brittany."

"Oh, too bad," she says and finally looks up from her phone. "I guess it's one of those urban myths." She puts her phone down on the coffee table and asks, "So, what's it like being with Daddy Vic? Is she as good as they say?"

I burst out laughing. "I'm a happy customer," I say and then add. "We've made pretty good use of her playroom." I know I shouldn't talk about it, but I'm kind of bursting to tell someone about Daddy Vic and me.

"Ooh," Brittany says. "Tell me more." She leans forward.

"Brittany," Rikki calls from behind the counter, "get back to work." With a shake of her head, Rikki heads into a back room behind the counter.

"Oops." Brittany leaps to her feet. "Thought she wouldn't notice. Gotta go." She zips behind the counter in record time and takes the next customer's order.

I also shake my head but then notice Brittany's phone on the table. It dings an incoming text, and I know I shouldn't, but curiosity gets the best of me, and I glance at the message.

> MISTRESS: And then once you've licked my asshole for a while, I will open my sphincter muscles and give you my offering right into your mouth. You'll chew and swallow every last slimy morsel. And you will hunger for it because you will be literally starving. I will not have fed you for three days. You'll take everything I give you happily. Of course, you'll wash it all down when I pee into your mouth. You'll swallow it all, brat, especially if you want me to feed you the next day.

I shudder. I can't help it. That is so disgusting. I mean, I know toilet slavery is a *thing*, but I would never do anything like that with Daddy Vic or anyone. Ever. I mean, on my first date with Daddy Vic at Mamma Mia's, she asked me about my hard limits, and that was the first thing out of my mouth. No scat. But God, I can't believe someone as sweet and nice as Rikki is into that kind of thing. Double yuck.

I blow out a breath, refusing to read the new texts pouring onto Brittany's screen. This may not be my kink, but I philosophically know Rikki and Brittany have a right to theirs. Daddy Vic sucking on my nipples and then dry humping me in a public restroom seems tame compared to that.

Ugh, I have to get out of here. The vibe has turned weird for me. I down my cold nitro drink and decide that I like my coffee hot. That settled, I carefully pick up Brittany's phone, click the display closed, and return it to her. When she sees it, panic overcomes her, and she pats her pockets as if looking for her phone. She thanks me profusely. I wave her off and tell her to thank Rikki for the coffee. I kind of don't want to see Rikki right now, knowing what I know. And, besides, I really do have to go. I have clothes shopping to do.

Two hours, three salespeople, and almost two hundred dollars later, I am the proud owner of five new skirts, shirts to match, and one dress that doesn't quite fit. Not yet, anyway. Once I lose a little bit of weight and shape up, then, fingers crossed, my little black number will fit well, and Daddy Vic's jaw will drop open when she sees me. I can't believe that I, a self-proclaimed butch ever since I can remember, will be wearing skirts now.

It is 8:01 p.m., and I am standing in Daddy Vic's entryway, taking off one of those new skirt and shirt combos. Before I started stripping, she nodded her approval of my outfit and then asked me to twirl. I have never twirled in my life, and I wish I could say that I felt like a princess, but really, it just felt weird.

I remove all my clothing, ensuring all three vacuum tubes stay secure, and I move to my inspection spot. I am a bit uncomfortable spreading my legs so far when I have a tampon inside, but she knows it's there, and it will have to be okay. I have extras in my coat pocket, just in case.

From her command chair, Daddy Vic asks, "Is it tucked?"

She means my tampon string. "Yes, Sir. I just checked."

"Good. Turn. Bend over with soft knees and grab your ankles."

I do as I'm told, but as I do, the oddest thought runs through my brain. I wish she would open up and tell me more about herself. Like, tell me how her day went or just anything. I know practically nothing about her. I stifle a giggle because to ask her how her day went while I am bent over presenting my ass to her is simply wrong somehow.

Her warm hands stroke my ass cheeks. I wish she had kissed me first or something, but her contact on my skin is comforting. I hear her putting on latex gloves, and then she spreads my ass cheeks apart. She rubs warm lube around the butt plug I was required to wear and then turns it slowly right and left and then eases it out of my body. I groan in relief. She lathers more lube in and around my tiny hole. How did she get the lube so warm, I wonder? That was considerate. Even though she may not be warm and fuzzy, she is considerate and attentive when touching my body.

Her finger breaches my barrier, and I lose my train of thought. "Ohhh," I moan.

"Slut likes anal."

"Yes, Sir." I moan again as she gently pushes in and out. "Your slut likes anal."

One finger turns to two, and I can't help but lean back into her. This earns me a swat on my ass. I stop moving. She widens her fingers, stretches me, and circles her fingers around. Her fingers go away, and I groan in frustration. I feel something at my back entrance and have no idea what she is about to insert. A dildo? She's not standing behind me about to fuck me, so what can it be? She pushes against my knot of muscles, and it gives in to her quickly. Whatever it is, it is small. She tugs, and I feel it move out a little. Maybe she's letting me know that whatever she's got in there won't get lost. She pushes in again, and then I feel another object hit my muscle ring. This one is bigger. She persists, and it moves inside.

"Anal beads, Sir?" I ask.

"Yes."

I've never used anal beads before. They're interesting. A third bead goes in. This one feels so much bigger than the other two.

"We're going for three more, slut," Daddy Vic says and pushes the fourth, fifth, and sixth beads inside me. Oh, God, I feel so full. "At some point tonight, you'll take all eight. Tighten your vacuum tubes." I'm reeling from the sensations in my ass but do as I'm told. "Stand up," she commands coldly. "Slowly. Use the shelves in front of you if you're dizzy."

I manage to stand without help, even though I do feel a little woozy from having my head hanging down for so long. The remaining anal beads swing freely against my ass cheeks. I cannot imagine being able to take all of them, like, ever.

"Turn," she says, and as soon as I do, she is on me. She pulls both vacuum tubes off my nipples and latches on to my right one. Just like in the restroom at Rikki's, she sucks and sucks my nipples so hard that it hurts. It's almost like she's trying to get milk out of them. I desperately want to hold her head, but apparently, I'm not allowed to touch her hair. Bummer. I really want to run my fingers through it.

She switches to my left breast, and I gasp. She is so forceful. It's not enough to call yellow or anything; I'm just surprised. I guess nipple-sucking is a big turn on for her. She alternates breasts, and I wish I could say it was arousing, but it kind of hurts now, mainly because I'm menstruating, and my breasts are sometimes sore during that time.

She pulls back and yanks the vacuum tube off my clit. I grunt at the suddenness of it.

"Into the kitchen," she says and points to the doorway.

"Yes, Sir," I say and lead the way. I notice my discarded butt plug has been placed in a bag near the inspection platform. I make a mental note not to forget it. Walking with anal beads inserted is odd. The dangling end bounces back and forth.

"Stand there." She points to a spot near the dishwasher and then reaches into a cupboard and pulls out a box. Are we eating? Does she want me to cook that rice for her? Unbelievably, she pours the entire box into two large piles on the floor.

"Sir?"

"Kneel," she says. The expression on her face challenges me to defy her.

"Yes, Sir." I kneel on the hard grains, and I grunt at the instant pain that hits me. Oh, this sucks. What did I do to deserve this? "Why, Sir?"

"Keep your mouth shut," she says. "When I tell you to tuck that goddamn string, I mean tuck it up your cunt and out of sight."

I look down. I messed up. I thought I had tucked it well enough. Damn it. Now she's pissed.

She scoops some of the rice up and makes two more piles. "Lean forward. Hands on the rice in front of you, ass in the air."

The rice on the palms of my hands doesn't hurt nearly as much, but the change in pressure kills my knees. I'm missing Saturday movie night at Shasti and Madison's for this? I clench my body.

"Relax," she says and pulls a stool behind me. She adds warm lube around my tiny hole. She pulls steadily on the beads, and I gasp when the first bead opens my ring of muscles. She pauses at the apex, my ring wide, and then pulls the bead out. I sigh in relief until she pulls the next one out. She does this for all six beads until they're all out. "Going for seven," she says gleefully. I barely hear her because I'm trying not to tear up at the stinging pain in my knees. I wonder if all I am to her is another piece of meat in a long line of meats. I have no time to think about it because the anal bead parade has begun again.

"Count," she says.

This time, the beads go in more smoothly. When she successfully shoves number six in my ass, I'm not sure I can take a seventh. She pushes. My knot of muscles resists. It's too much. I fall to my elbows, and she pushes hard. It goes in.

"Fucking seven," I say, earning a swat on my ass for some unknown reason.

"When you can take all eight, slut, then you can get up off the rice." She smacks my ass again. I feel the beads inside absorb the impact, and it feels wonderful. She must know this. "But if I see that string again, you'll be eating the rice right off the floor."

"Oh, God. Yes, Sir," I say.

"Sit up. Stay kneeling right where you are."

I grunt as the pressure points of the tiny bits of rice change again. I officially hate rice at this moment. She leaves the kitchen. Maybe she's gone to get the playroom ready for the continuation of anal week. Who knows? All I know is that it is agony to move.

Chapter 10
You're Going to Love It

My knees are numb from kneeling on this ridiculous rice. When will this torture be over? Daddy Vic is currently pulling the seven beads out of my ass, but somehow, and I have no idea how, but I must take all eight to get my knees off these tiny torture devices. Who knew rice could be so nefarious?

"Head up," Daddy Vic says and moves in front of me. She places a blindfold over my eyes, and I can't see a darn thing. Great. Now, what is she up to? "Lean forward with your forearms on the floor. Put your forehead on the floor as well. Yes, that's it. Good, slut."

She moves behind me, and more lube is poured over and into my tiny hole. It drips down through my labia and probably onto her kitchen floor. Guess who will be cleaning that up later?

"Adjust so you can hold the weight of your body with your forehead and reach both hands back to offer your ass to me."

"Yes, Sir." I remember how I had to do the same thing for Mama_Luvs when she gave me that enema in the hotel room. Oh God, I'm not getting another enema, am I? I won't be able to find the bathroom with this damn blindfold on. But I do as I'm told and reach back and spread my ass cheeks for her, offering her my body.

"Relax," she says.

"Yes, Sir." I must have been tensing up.

One hand grips my left hip, and I feel something at my back entrance. It's too big to be the nozzle of an enema bottle, thank God. She presses, and my muscles give in quickly. "Ohhhh," I moan as a small anal dildo goes in. I moan again as she pushes in slowly. "Sir," I purr.

"Color?"

"Green plus, Sir."

She chuckles. "You *are* an anal slut, aren't you?" She grips my other hip. I feel so much right now. I offered my body, so I have to trust her with it.

She pushes in slow and steady until the harness presses against my spread ass cheeks. She pulls out just as slowly, and I am in heaven. One simply cannot rush anal fucking. She applies more lube. She pushes in again, this time more quickly. It isn't long before she thrusts in and out in a steady rhythm. "Put your forearms on the floor again. Hold yourself up while I get to work."

Thank God. My neck was starting to ache, not to mention the rice embedding itself into my forehead.

Her thrusts increase in intensity, and I am in heaven despite the rice. "Yes, Daddy," I say in encouragement. "Fuck me, Daddy. Oh, God," I moan in pre-orgasm. I have no idea if I have permission, but I may cum from this. "Oh, Daddy. Yes, yes!" I lower my torso, allowing her to go deeper inside. I wish I could touch my clit because I would supernova.

She moans low behind me, and her breathing is heavy. She's going to cum. "Cum, Daddy. Soak me. Cum inside me, Daddy."

She grunts her approval at my words and bucks in and out of my ass. She's cumming. And I am so close but can't get there. She thrusts a few more times and leans over my body. Her weight on top of mine is agony.

"Daddy," I say, my voice clearly indicating discomfort.

She micro thrusts inside me, basically humping me. She is enjoying her afterglow despite my discomfort. Okay, whatever, but you're freakin' heavy. She takes a big breath, pulls out of me, and stands up. I can't see with the blindfold on, but I hear her moving behind me. Without warning, she feeds the anal beads into my body. She commands me to count. When we get to seven, I think there is no way I can do one more bead, but just as I'm finishing the thought, she shoves the eighth and final one inside me.

"Yep. Definitely an anal slut," she says. "Get up."

I lift my knees off the rice and then walk my hands back toward my feet. It would be nice if she would lend me an arm or something, but I guess that's not going to happen. I brush the rice off my knees as I stand and then wince at the rice embedding themselves into my bare feet under my full body weight.

Next time make it Legos, Daddy Vic, I think sarcastically. C'mon, where's your creativity?

She pulls the blindfold off, and I blink in the dim lighting. "Go check that string now. Change it if you have to."

"Yes, Sir," I say and head to my coat to grab a fresh tampon, just in case.

"Meet me in the playroom," she calls back. "And don't make me wait. I don't like to wait."

Once I finish cleaning up in the restroom and attempt to get some relief for my knees using cool water, I find her in the playroom adjusting some kind of contraption. I groan. Now what?

"Come here," she says tersely. "Kneel on the platform. It's padded. Your knees will be happy."

Thank you?

"Lean forward, hips against the lower bar. Yes, good. Lean forward and rest your shoulders and chest on the upper bar." Thank goodness both are padded. My breasts fall straight down like cow udders. They sway back and forth as I adjust myself in the contraption.

The bars remind me of those uneven parallel bars that gymnasts use, but these are torso height apart and close to the ground. She adjusts the lower bar because, apparently, I am a little taller than the last woman draped over it.

"Rest your chin here." She taps an obvious chin rest and then proceeds to Velcro my neck in place. "No worries, IC, you can pull yourself out of all these restraints if you need to." She velcroes my wrists to the bar. "Comfy?" she asks, and I almost burst out laughing.

"Um, I guess, Sir," I say tentatively. "What's about to happen?"

"You're going to love it," she says, not even remotely answering my question. I hear her turn some kind of crank, and once again, of course, my legs are opening wider. Slowly she pulls out the anal beads, applies more lube, and pushes something at my back entrance. Ahh, it's a dildo. It fills me.

"Oh, Sir," I moan. "So good." God, I really am an anal slut, aren't I?

"We'll start at the lowest speed, of course. Until you get used to it, and then we'll speed it up." She flicks a switch, and the dildo moves in and out of me at a snail's pace, but it is heavenly. I can't believe she has me hooked up to a real-life fucking machine. I'd heard about them but never been strapped to one. The thought makes me clench up, and the machine whines.

"Don't tighten. Relax. Enjoy it. Imagine my hands grasping your hips, my cock thrusting in and out of your ass."

I'm not sure why I need to be velcroed to the machine until she shows me three vacuum tubes connected to clear hoses of some kind. She flicks another switch, and I hear the distinct sound of an air compressor. My eyes grow wide. "Sir! What are those for?" I know full well what she intends to do with them, and the fact that she's holding three of them in her hand makes me squirm.

She reaches around and swats my behind. "Don't make me tie you down for real, now. You won't like that." She takes one of the vacuum tubes and places it against my forearm. "It's on the lowest sucking setting. You'll be fine. You have to get used to the machine before we increase the intensity." The vacuuming is not steady but pulses as if someone is sucking. Oh, God, she really does have a nipple fetish. "But first, you need a bit." She puts a bit-gag in my mouth and tightens it behind my head. I know all about bit gags through Mama_Luvs, thank you very much. Then, the blindfold goes back on. Great, just great. She places something over both of my ears and then I realize they are noise-canceling headphones. I've never had complete sensory deprivation like this. One thing I cannot do is freak out while hooked up to this weird machine.

Daddy Vic uses both hands to rub my breasts and pull them longer. She gently pinches and pulls my nipples hard, and I shiver, which makes them even harder. I gasp around the gag when she attaches one of the vacuum tubes to my right nipple. Ahh, yes. I moan my approval. I settle into the sensations, which only heighten after she attaches the other tube. Both nipples are sucked at the same even cadence. My ass is fucked oh so slowly but rhythmically. This is heaven. Her rough, warm hands caress my back and ass cheeks. She must like what she sees. I risk another ass swatting and arch my back into her hands. She doesn't swat me, so that must be okay.

She pats my ass cheeks two times, and then the dildo speeds up. "Oh," I moan. I cannot form words around the bit. If I could, I would say, "Fuck yes, Daddy Vic."

Her hands are on the fleshy part of my breasts again, massaging them, pulling them downward. The hands go away, and the suction increases on my nipples. I am flooded with sensation and feel my core, neck, and face flush.

I'm not quite overloading, but I will. Soon.

My senses reach out to find her, but she doesn't touch me again, and I don't even know if she is still in the room. I relax and let myself feel everything, even down to my toes. I have no idea how long I have been attached to these machines when I feel her near me. She uses two fingers to split my furrow and expose my clit. Oh, yes, Daddy Vic, touch me. Make me cum. My clit is hard as she strokes me. I moan encouragement. Yes, yes, yes, I telegraph mentally. Two fingers stroke my clit along the sides, and I can't help my bucking hips.

I jump when she attaches the third vacuum tube. My clit gets sucked in deep. The regular sucking motion on my clit is almost more than I can take, and I buck my hips again, this time in rhythm to the driving dildo. Pleasure coils low in my belly and spreads upward and outward. I'm going to cum. These machines are going to make me cum.

The pleasure spreads to my pussy, and pre-orgasmic spasms hit me. I moan in exhale as my orgasm builds and then gasp when it hits. My entire body spasms. My whole body orgasms. It's too much, too much, too much, and I scream behind the bit in panic. I can't take it.

I wave my hands and try to snap my fingers. Oh, Daddy Vic, let me out! And just like that, the dildo and suction tubes stop. My entire body droops in relief, and I struggle to catch my breath as aftershocks torture my body. The network of nerves from my ass to my clit to my breasts is short-circuiting all at once.

She releases my neck first and then my arms. The bit gag, headphones, and blindfold remain in place as she guides me off the machine and down to the mat. A pillow goes under my head, and a light blanket goes over me. Maybe it's a sheet, but I don't know. Daddy Vic lays down and spoons me from behind. She lifts the sheet, and then the tip of her dildo enters my ass. She fucks me gently. I have one last thought before I pass out – holy shit, she just milked me like a cow, a human cow.

~~~

On Monday morning, I sit in my office after my Calculus 1 lecture. I have no idea how I got through it coherently because Daddy Vic had me up late both Saturday and Sunday nights until 2 a.m. She didn't seem to care that I had classes this morning. And I dutifully wore my skirt to the coffee house Sunday afternoon and then to her apartment. I am also wearing another one of my new skirt outfits at work today. Oddly, but thankfully, no one has said a word to me about my sudden penchant for wearing skirts and feminine blouses, which I'm grateful for because I wouldn't know what to say. Uh, my Daddy Domme requires me to be femme for her? Nah.

After my hours, despite having a ton of work to do, I am heading home. I am exhausted and will see Daddy Vic again in a few short hours, precisely at 8 p.m., so I'll nap at home to rest up. She told me to take care of myself better, but, God, I wish I could eat real food. "A light breakfast and then protein shakes only" is the rule every day during anal week. I have the morning reminder texts to prove it. I wish my gosh-darn period would finish already, and that way, anal week would be over. It sounds like I'm complaining, but I'm not. Okay, maybe a little because I'm exhausted and because Daddy Vic has some weird fetishes.

I mean, she gave me a mind-blowing top-ten orgasm on the milking machine. But, c'mon, a milking machine? After that, I vaguely remembered her fucking my ass while I was on the floor, but that part is a blur. To revive me, she gave me some water and a small protein shake. There was more blow-job training with a longer dildo when I became sufficiently coherent, but I gagged every freakin' time. She got so frustrated that she strapped me down to the spanking horse and beat my body with a small whip. It wasn't fun at all, especially because she'd said she wasn't good with a whip yet. It sure felt like she knew how to handle it. And I didn't call red because, well, I kind of deserved it for gagging so much.

Sunday was pretty much a repeat of Saturday, complete with coffee shop nipple sucking, but thankfully minus the rice on her kitchen floor. And I'm proud to say that I was able to relax enough to swallow the five-inch dildo down my throat this time. Yay. She seemed unaffected by my accomplishment, though. And I had another orgasm on the milking machine, but this one was not as intense. Probably because my ass kind of didn't and still doesn't want to play anal week anymore. But I didn't tell her that. I mean, c'mon, she might leave me if I refuse to play.

I am grateful that she didn't ask for a daily picture of my aroused pussy at work today. Maybe she's afraid she'll see a tampon string or something. Who knows? But she still wants me to keep myself aroused at my desk as usual. So here I sit in my office, rubbing my nipples discretely as instructed. I refuse to use any of the vacuum tubes in my office and instead use them in the restroom. My legs are spread wide by my desk, wider than I've ever gotten them, and my hand is slipped through the one open button in my shirt. My fingers push the top of my bra out of the way so I can reach my nipples. The unbidden memory of Daddy Vic in the kitchen, slowly pushing her dildo into my ass, heats me up immeasurably, and my hips start bucking slightly. I want to get off so bad, but I can't. I'm not allowed. She owns my orgasms now, too, son of a gun.

Fuck it. I pull my hand out of my shirt, button up, and stand up. I need to get off. I am about to head to the restroom again when there is a knock on my office door.

"Shit," I mutter. I hope it doesn't smell like my arousal. No, no, I have that heated wax thing spewing hints of vanilla all around. "Come in," I say and clear my throat. I take a sip of water to cool my ardor and then clamp my legs together tightly.

"Professor Garneau?" One of the graduate students that I'd helped with ring theory the week before walks in shyly. "Are you available? I saw you had office hours."

"Sure, sure," I say. "C'mon in." I point to the only other chair in the room.

"Thank you," she says and sits down. She is no longer wearing a Reds cap, and her dark hair is pulled back into a loose ponytail. She is quite attractive. I hadn't noticed that last time.

I take another sip of water. I have to cool my furnace down. Holy moly. "What's up? Oh, and remind me what your name is so I know who I'm talking to."

"Oh, sorry," she says. "My name is Bianca. Bianca Lopez."

"Nice to meet you, Bianca. So, tell me what's up."

"Well, not that I want to rat, but Professor Baxter is never available for his office hours, and we need help with this stuff."

My blood boils, but I try not to let it show. "Do you want me to mention something to Dr. Wainwright?"

"I don't know," she says, obviously frustrated. "Baxter will just take it out on us. You know?"

I shrug, not knowing how else I can help her.

"I mean," she continues. "We just want to learn the material, and he's not a good teacher. He's just not. I'm not trying to be disrespectful, but no one understands. I wish you would teach this class, Dr. Garneau."

"I'm flattered, but I've got my hands full." I gesture to the student problem sets that have been piling up higher than usual ever since my new kinky lifestyle took over.

"Can you …"

When she doesn't finish, I encourage her. "Can I what?"

"I mean, I hate to ask, but can you help me understand Galois Theory? I'm meeting the guys tonight for a study session, and I will be the hero if I can explain it to them."

I laugh. "That's a tall order. I took an entire course on Galois Theory in my fourth year."

She grins. "So, you can help me?"

"Listen, yes, I'll help you. But if any of my own students are here, then you'll have to go to the back of the line. Deal?"

She sits up taller. "Oh, absolutely, Professor. Thank you. What's your favorite kind of cookie? You now have a lifetime supply coming to you."

"Not necessary," I say, "but if you must know, I like chocolate chip."

She laughs.

"Pull your chair over here." I waste no time and start the impromptu lesson. "So, as you know, one of the most fundamental problems in algebra is how to solve polynomial equations, right?" She nods, and then I joyfully spend the rest of my office hours helping Bianca understand the mathematics I love.

Chapter 11
Stop!

I place my hand in Daddy Vic's as she helps me out of her pickup truck. I link my hand around the offered elbow, and we head into the BBQ place. She says she will "finger me silly" here, but I don't see how because there are several rows of picnic tables inside with no private booths or any dark corners. We sit, and she orders for me. I love it when a Domme takes charge like that. Well, except when Mama_Luvs ordered fish for me at that restaurant. Yuck. But Daddy Vic gets it right, and I have stars in my eyes for her. I pull off a few paper towels and lay them down as placemats for each of us. I fold a few more as napkins.

"I'm going to suck your bare nipples now, IC," she says with a lecherous grin.

I look around. Here? Is she going to do that here?

She reaches over and yanks off my shirt. The whole thing comes off with one pull. I'm not wearing anything underneath. I try to cover myself, but she latches on to the closest nipple and sucks. It hurts, and I tell her so. She lifts her head. Barbecue sauce drips from her lips. I look down and see it oozing from both nipples. I also see that I am completely naked now. A buzz of people has gathered around, primarily women. Most are licking their lips. They want a taste. Daddy Vic scoops me up and throws me face up on the table. She yanks my legs apart.

"Dinner is served," she says to the crowd, and they descend on me.

I wake up with a start. My heart is pounding. Oh, my God. What the fuck kind of bizarre dream was that? I sit up and put my feet on the floor to ground myself and wipe the sweat off my forehead.

"What time is it?" Five o'clock in the afternoon. I had an hour-and-a-half nap. I take a deep breath and exhale slowly, trying to slow down my rampaging heart. What a stupid dream. The first part was nice, but Daddy Vic hasn't taken me out to dinner since that first impromptu date precisely one week ago today. I guess one week isn't a long time, but it seems we moved really, really fast in the sex department but really, really slow in the get-to-know-each-other department. And I want that part, too.

I will need to shower and shave before heading over to Daddy Vic's, but I need a protein shake first. I'm starving. I open up one of the supplement packets and dump it into one of the ready-made protein shakes that I now keep in the fridge. Blah, it tastes awful. I drink a large glass of water afterward to wash the taste out of my mouth. I only have one supplement packet left, so I'll have to remember to ask for more when I get there.

I'm still a little shaky from the dream, so I kneel on my pillow in an attempt to ground myself. Head down, eyes shut, palms up this morning. I try to capture that feeling of opening myself up for my Domme, for Daddy Vic. I try to get to that place where the world goes away, and Daddy Vic is my only focus. I offer her my body. I fulfill her needs with no regard to my own. That is my duty and obligation as a submissive. But, no, I've got that wrong somehow. It's not an *obligation*. That makes it sound like a chore or something. It's more than that. Fulfilling her needs should fulfill mine.

I can usually get into a calm space fairly quickly, but I can't shake the stupid dream. I don't know what's bothering me. I mean, sex with Daddy Vic is the best I've ever had. It's what I was hoping for with my first-ever Domme, Mistress Ciara. But she didn't want me. And forget about Mama_Luvs. Being sexually abused isn't my cup of tea, thank you. And we're not even going to mention the ridiculousness that was Goddess Julie. Thank God it never got beyond that one online liaison with her.

Daddy Vic likes me, doesn't she? I think she does. It would be nice if we could talk like normal people or something. Discuss the weather, maybe? She says I'm a good fuck. That's something, right?

Kneeling submissively is doing nothing for me but making my head spin with thoughts I have no control over. I leap to my feet and head to the bathroom, where the lovely enemas are waiting for me. For not the first time, I wonder if giving myself so many enemas every day like this is safe. But I trust Daddy Vic and go for it. She freaked out when she saw my tampon string. I can only imagine what would happen if she found anything brownish on her condom-covered cock. She'd probably tie me up and throw darts at me.

Speaking of darts, I noticed that Rikki had a few of those electronic dartboards in the coffee shop. I used to play a lot in college to make extra cash. Maybe I'll leave early and stop by for a coffee and a dart game.

That decided, I enema it up, shower, shave, and do the unthinkable. I put on underwear and a panty shield in addition to the tampon. I also put on pants. Yes, I'm wearing pants. Ha. Just to the coffee shop, though. I stuff a skirt into a bag to change in the car at her condo complex.

I pull my car onto the road heading for Denton Heights, and my phone rings. Is it Daddy Vic? Inviting me to dinner, maybe? I look to see who it is. Oh, wow, even better.

"Hey, Lisa," I say, answering the phone. "I'm driving, but I have you on speakerphone. How are you, woman?"

"Hi, B," she says in her cheery lilt. "Are you headed to see your new butch hottie? I need updates." The cheery lilt turns into a whine. "You're keeping me way too much in the dark on this one."

I laugh and give her the briefest of updates and then tell her about my new condom trick with my mouth.

"Oh, my God, B. That is so awesome." It sounds like she genuinely means that. "And, hey, if you can get past that initial gag reflex on your deep throat lessons, then you're in. I never could get past that."

"Hey, I don't know if I'm going to get much further, to be honest," I say. I turn onto Market Street in Denton Heights and look for a place to park. Too bad the lot next to Rikki's Coffee Shop isn't a parking lot. It would constantly be full.

"Well, do whatever feels comfortable," Lisa says. "But I want to ask you something about your girlfriend's nipple fetish."

"She's not really my girlfriend, Lisa," I say, kind of embarrassed.

"Hmm, she's not the tell-me-all-your-troubles type?"

"She's not even the how-was-your-day type."

"That sucks," she says. "At least the sex is amazing, isn't it?"

"No complaints."

"B, listen, I don't want to intrude, but are you guys getting into lactation or something? It just sounds like when I did that for Rachel a few years ago. I mean, you have to pump and suck to stimulate the milk ducts constantly. And the drugs, too. The really good ones are illegal in the United States. Ridiculously hard to get."

"She's just heavy into nipple sucking, I guess. Lactation is something I would have to be privy to, don't you think?" I can't help thinking about the supplements Daddy Vic is making me take three times a day. Could she be …

"Hey, B? Are you there? Oh, shoot. Stupid phone. I think I lost you."

"No, no, no. I'm here," I say. "I'm looking for a parking spot."

"Oh, I'll let you go then. And, by the way, you don't seem like the hucow type to me."

"What the hell is a hucow?" I ask. She is constantly expanding my BDSM vocabulary.

"A human cow. Tell me you've never heard of it." She laughs and adds, "It is a huge fetish, and not just for the hets. Let me tell you. Did you know with the right cocktail of hormones, even transgender females can lactate? I've seen it. And I hear there's this huge black market for the milk."

Was Daddy Vic trying to milk me with that machine? Was she going to sell my milk? My *milk*? A wave of nausea passes through me. "Oh, God," I say, feeling woozy.

"I know, right?" Lisa says.

"I have to go." I am feeling sick to my stomach.

"Okay, friend," she says. "Don't be such a stranger, okay?"

"Talk to you later." I hit the end call button, hoping I wasn't too rude, but holy shit. I don't want to be a human cow. Oh, God. Do Daddy Vic's supplements have that illegal medication in them? "Fuck," I say out loud in the quiet car. "I took them *willingly*."

I am so naïve. Oh, my God. I close my eyes and picture myself kneeling on my pillow. I breathe in and out purposefully, and it isn't long before the nausea dissipates. I decide to confront Daddy Vic tonight. I will tell her that I will no longer be taking the supplements and that I call *red* on the milking machine if that's even what it is.

But it might not be a milking machine, part of me argues. And maybe those supplements are just vitamins or something.

"No, fuck that line of thought," I say out loud and unbuckle my seatbelt.

I need air, and I need coffee. And if they have pastries, I'm getting one. Maybe three. As if I would have the nerve to defy Daddy Vic. Ha.

The coffee shop is packed. I stand in line to place my order and realize that a darts tournament or something is going on. How cool is that? Guess I won't be playing tonight. Oh, well. I just wanted to play for fun by myself and not in front of a bunch of people, especially because I haven't played in forever.

Brittany's face lights up when she sees me, and she takes my order. She won't let me pay, and I am really confused as to why.

After a few minutes, one of the baristas calls for me, "Professor."

"Here," I call back with a shake of my head. Brittany wrote that down as my name. Oh, well. That's what she calls me, I guess.

Seeing no one that I know besides Brittany, who is busy working, I stroll over toward the dart action. Three boards are going with six teams competing in this round. Every Monday evening, the sign says. How cool. Everything is electronic, including the scoring. I haven't played seriously since college, but that was only to earn beer money. Not that I drank beer, but they didn't need to know that. I probably bought mechanical pencils at the student union or something nerdy like that.

I take a sip of my hot vanilla latte with cinnamon and check out the action for a while. One guy is racking up points against his opponent. "Point whore," I mutter under my breath.

The man standing next to me bursts out laughing. He is an older man, and frankly, it looks like he belongs on a barstool in an Irish pub rather than sipping coffee in a coffee shop. His white caterpillar eyebrows totally complement his round, jovial face. "And, what, pray tell, young lady, would you have her do to combat this 'point whore'?" he asks with crisp pronunciation.

I grin and say, "Well, she needs to do a combination of things. Obviously, she needs to point up. I'd try to hit those nineteens to score on him and bridge the gap a bit. But she also needs to close out her twenties because that's where he's making his points."

He nods and calls to the woman who is about to throw. "Jaleesa, two throws to close out your twenties. One to score on the nineteens. Swap that next go if you don't close."

She gives him a thumbs-up, and then he looks at me and says, "Thank you, young lady. May I have your number?"

My eyes grow wide.

"Oh, goodness." His belly laugh turns heads and also turns my face red. "Not for that, darlin'. I need you on my team."

"Oh, no, no," I say and put a hand up in defense. "I'm just watching."

"At least tell me your name then."

What's the harm? "Bernadette," I say succinctly.

"I'm Seamus," he says. "It's nice to meet you, Bernadette. One day, I'll get you to play with us."

A cheer goes up in the crowd as Jaleesa successfully closes out the twenties, so the point whore can't run up the score anymore. And then another cheer goes up as soon as she nails a nineteen, gaining ground on him. Her opponent scowls and harrumphs his way back to the line for his go.

I take my cue and turn to see my usual hangout spot has opened up, and no one seems to be making a beeline there. I head over to claim a seat and hear someone call me. "Professor! Professor!"

"Hey, kiddo," I call back to Madison. She and Shasti are in line to order. "Join me?" I point to the empty seats around me.

"Yes," Madison says gleefully. She is such a ray of sunshine. I am so glad I decided to come out this evening. I've missed interacting with people on a social level.

It isn't long before Shasti and Madison join me in our lovely, isolated section in the corner of Rikki's coffee shop.

Shasti sits down with a sigh.

"Been a long week already?" I offer.

She chuckles. "Yes, and it's only Monday."

"Don't I know it," I say.

Shasti totally gets mom-face on me and says, "You look a bit tired, Professor."

"I haven't been getting enough sleep, I think."

"Too much ooh-la-la time with Daddy Vic," Madison singsongs.

"Madison," Shasti warns.

Madison's face falls. "You promised," she whines softly.

Shasti rolls her eyes at me and then looks back to her submissive. "Little

Bear, do *not* tease the professor."

Madison bounces on the sofa, obviously pleased with her Mistress.

I shrug my shoulders and shoot Shasti a questioning look.

Shasti sighs again. "She's reading a book about a submissive woman called Little Bear, and now that's what she wants me to call her from now on."

"Exactly," Madison chimes in. "The story's called, 'C'mere, Little Bear.' I can lend it to you if you want." She pulls out her phone, and her thumbs fly across the small screen. "There, Professor, I just loaned it to you."

"Oh, electronically?"

"Yes, when you click on it, you'll have to download the app if you don't already have it," she says through a monstrous grin.

I lean forward and say, "Little Bear, that is the kindest thing anyone has done for me in a long time."

"Welcome," she says, beaming. Her attention rockets to the dart players when another cheer goes up in the crowd.

Shasti leans closer and stage whispers, "One time, I had to call her Bucko." She rolls her eyes again. "That one lasted quite a while. About three months."

I laugh with her and then take a sip of my coffee. I feel the sting of tears in my eyes and blink them back. I want what they have. I want a Domme who knows me like Shasti knows her little. I want a Domme who lets me try new things within her safety net. I want a Domme who accepts me for me and doesn't try to change me. "Like skirts and long hair," I mutter.

"How's that?" Shasti says.

I wipe my eyes and say, "Oh, nothing. Just muttering nonsense."

She gives me the concerned mom face again, and I look down at my coffee. I check the big clock on Rikki's wall. Plenty of time before heading to Daddy Vic's.

"Hey, Bucko," someone says, and I look up. It's the dart player named Jaleesa.

Madison has stars in her eyes when she looks up at the incredibly pretty bronze-skinned black woman making her way over. Her skin is so smooth. She looks like a supermodel. So tall. Her dark curls are pulled back into a tight ponytail. I look down because it's not polite to drool at the local dart players.

"Hi, Miss Jaleesa," Madison says breathlessly and bounces on the couch.

Madison sure has a lot of girl crushes.

"How's my special girl?" Jaleesa asks and tousles Madison's hair. Jaleesa winks at Shasti, who beams at the attention her little is getting.

"Good," Madison answers, suddenly shy.

"Just 'good'?" Jaleesa echoes. "Not fabulous or stupendous?"

Madison shakes her head.

"Aww, too bad. Personally, I am stoked because I finally beat that…" she leans in and lowers her voice, "full-of-himself a-hole."

Madison gasps and covers her mouth. "You said a bad word, Miss Jaleesa." She shoots a look at Shasti, who presses her lips together, trying not to laugh.

"I *almost* said a bad word, Bucko," Jaleesa says. "I know how sensitive your ears are." She looks over at me. "A-and," she draws out the word making it two-syllables, "I have you to thank."

"Me? For you saying a bad word?" I smile so she knows I'm teasing.

She laughs, and the sound fills my heart. "Seamus pointed you out. He told me you came up with that strategy. The jerk just couldn't close out his nineteens, and that's how I got him."

"Turnabout is fair play. I'm stoked you caught him with that." I laugh along with her. "That is fantastic."

Jaleesa makes her way around the furniture and sits on the couch next to my chair. She is strikingly pretty, which makes me instantly nervous. The confident way she carries herself, could she be a Domme? I mean, she seems to know that Madison is a little. Oh, God. No. I have to stop this line of thinking. Daddy Vic is my Domme, and I'm not going to do anything to compromise that.

Jaleesa reaches into her back pocket and pulls out a business card. "Please don't think me forward, but I do hair." She runs her fingers through the ends of my wild and untamed locks. "But you seem to be, er, in between hairstyles?"

"Something like that," I say. I am a little taken aback by her touching me so intimately. I don't know her. She is a stranger to me. But she is friends with Shasti and Madison, so I decide it's okay.

"I totally see the perfect cut for you. You have such a pretty face, and those dimples are to die for. I can give you a cut to frame your face artfully. I see a lob cut coming a bit below your chin. Layered angular cuts. Oh, it'll be perfect. And a change in product will give it a healthier sheen. Maybe a change in diet, too? You'll be beating the girls away with a stick. But I'm sure you're doing that already."

I am a bit overwhelmed by her attention, but thank her for the suggestions. Maybe Daddy Vic will be pleased that I found somebody. She'll have to okay it, of course. My hair seems to be important to her. "Um, thank you. I'll give you a call when I'm ready."

"Good." She pats my knee once. She turns back to Shasti and Madison and says, "Okay, time for me to head home. "Got a sub locked in a cage, and I bet she's dying to be released."

"Ohh," I say way too loudly. The shock of her statement hit me viscerally.

"Mistress," Madison whines, "I want a cage."

Shasti sighs and says in an exasperated tone, "Thank you so much, Jaleesa. You are such a *big* help."

Jaleesa simply laughs and stands up. She leans down next to Madison. "What do you think, Bucko? Should I let Tina out of her cage when I get home?"

Madison shakes her head no.

"Ooh." Jaleesa recoils. "You are a harsh Mistress."

"Rawr," Madison roars, making everyone laugh.

"Gotta go," Jaleesa says.

We say our goodbyes, and then I say to Shasti, "She seems nice."

"She is a good soul."

"Does she really have a person named Tina locked in a cage?"

"Probably," Shasti says with a nod.

We chat amiably for a while, and I think it's strange that I don't see Rikki anywhere. I guess it's hard for her to be here every minute of the day. You'd have no life. Shasti and Madison eventually take their leave, much to Madison's dismay, and cries that she doesn't have much homework. Shasti remains unmoved and mentions a Biology lab report that seems to be due tomorrow.

The darts crowd is dying down, and I know it's getting close to my own departure time. I am just about to stand up and check my period situation in

114

the restroom when Brittany bounds over, perpetual phone in hand, and plops down next to me.

Brittany turns and calls over her shoulder, "I'm on a sanctioned break."

I look up and see Rikki nod at her. She also sees me and smiles. My insides turn to goo at the smile, so I look down quickly.

"So, how's Daddy Vic?" Brittany asks.

"Good," I say. I am distracted, though, because I can see Rikki behind the counter, and she is wearing a tight turtleneck sweater that is leaving nothing to my imagination. Her breasts are high and perky. Her nipples are hard. I wonder what she's doing. She has a clipboard in hand and seems to be taking inventory, maybe?

Brittany laughs. "That good, hmm?"

"Sorry," I say in apology. I feel my face flush in embarrassment. I was ogling her girlfriend. Not cool, Bernadette. Totally not cool. "I'm a bit tired. I haven't been sleeping well. I'm going over to Daddy Vic's in a few minutes, actually."

"The old eight o'clock, no sooner, no later thing?"

"Yes," I say. "How did you –"

"One of my friends was a Daddy Vic sub for a little while."

"Oh, interesting."

"Has she put you on the hassock yet? Oh, wait, better question. Did she make you masturbate in front of her? Rumor has it that Daddy Vic always makes new girls rub themselves to orgasm at least once."

"Brittany." My tone warns that I clearly don't want to talk about it.

"Okay, okay," she says. "My bad."

"Brittany," Rikki calls from behind the counter. Her clipboard is still in hand. "Where's the top to this blender. Mark says he assigned you to clean it."

"Be right there." She sighs heavily and stands up.

Once again, she leaves her phone on the table in between us. The ding of a text rings out. Again, I know I shouldn't, but I do. Out of the corner of my eye, I read the texts as they come in.

MISTRESS: When I get my hands on you, know that I'll tie your hands behind you. You'll be shoved down on your knees to worship my feet.

MISTRESS: After I've had my fill, I'll kick you away to sprawl on the floor where all slaves belong. My foot will hold your head down as I beat your bare back, ass, and legs. I'll beat you until you cry, slave, and then I'll –

I look up and watch as Rikki scolds Brittany about responsibility. Rikki does not have her phone out. Rikki is not the one texting Brittany right now.

MISTRESS: Where's my slave tonight? Working hard for that redheaded boss of yours?

My chest constricts when I realize that, oh, my God, Brittany is cheating on Rikki. And right in front of her. I stand up, and before I can stop myself, I snatch up Brittany's phone and march it over to her.

I shake the phone at her. "You can't do this." My voice is loud, but I don't care. "That's not fair. How can you do this?" The burn of tears prickles behind my eyes as I toss the phone on the counter. It bounces once and lays still.

I've made a spectacle of myself, and I know it, so I run for the front door. Tears threaten to become more. I have to get out of here.

The cold January air revives me a little, but my heart is pounding. I am hopping mad. How can that brat cheat on someone as nice as Rikki? And Rikki doesn't even know it. And those disgusting texts about scat? Probably not from Rikki, either.

"Stop!" someone behind me commands.

My feet root themselves to the sidewalk instantly. Even without turning around, I know who has spoken. My tears start up again instantly.

Chapter 12
Respect

A strong arm goes around my shoulders and pulls me to her. I fall into Rikki's chest and cry against her warm body. She is so comforting, and when I think about Brittany cheating on this nurturing soul, my tears turn into sobs.

"Shh, shh, shh," she shushes me gently. Her gentle hand strokes my back.

It takes me a minute, but I finally get the sobs under control. Not my tears, just my sobs.

"Come with me, Professor." She drapes my forgotten coat over my shoulders.

I silently let myself be led back toward the coffee shop, but instead of going in the front door, she veers down a narrow pathway along the side of the building. She unlocks an outside door, and I find myself in a small room. It's an office. And a messy one at that.

She leads me toward a couch, but I have different ideas and kneel in a clear spot on the floor.

"Oh, okay," she says in a surprised voice.

I lower my head, close my eyes, and place my hands face down on my thighs. I focus on breathing to get my tears under control. Embarrassment pushes against the sudden sadness filling my chest.

Rikki seems to respect my need for a moment to gather myself, and I hear the couch springs squeak under her weight. "Professor?" she asks tentatively after a few minutes.

"Yes, Sir?" I don't look up or open my eyes.

"I'm not a ..." She clears her throat and then squats down in front of me. She lifts my chin with her fingers and says, "Open your eyes, please." I do. "Professor, what happened in there?" She nods toward a door opposite the one we came in. It must be the door to the actual coffee shop.

Her compassionate green eyes are diving into my soul, and I am so empty that I start crying again. I hold my head in my hands and rock. "I'm so sorry, Sir. I can't be the one to tell you. You have to ask her."

"Who?"

"Brittany. Ask her."

"I will." She is quiet for a moment but then says, "I will, but I want to know why you are so obviously upset." She shifts position and sits on the floor in front of me. With the way she is sitting, she is now below me.

"No, Sir," I say. "Please. I should be below you. Always."

"Sit up." I am putty to her commanding voice and comply. "I am not your Domme, Professor. You can show me respect in the same way that I show you respect, but you are not lower than me. Ever."

I don't respond. I don't know what to say.

She clears her throat and asks, "Who makes you feel lower?"

The gaping hole in my chest blows wide open, and my waterworks begin again.

"Are you speaking out, Professor? Are you talking to her? Telling her how you feel?"

"I don't know what she's doing to me," I say. "I like the sex, Sir, but I don't know. I don't know."

"What don't you know?" She lifts my chin again.

And then comes the deluge. I tell her everything about Daddy Vic. I tell her how I am an object on display, how we never talk about our personal lives, and how she makes me touch myself at work and about the machine and giving me drugs to make me a hucow. My sadness turns into hiccupping sobs as I say, "Sir, I don't want to be a hucow."

"A hucow," Rikki repeats, her words singeing with anger. "When are you seeing her next?"

"Right now," I say and start to get up. "I have to go. I can't be late."

"Stay," she says. God, there is no denying that voice. "You're canceling tonight."

"I am?"

"Yes. You can't go there in your current state. Give me your phone."

I fumble for it in my pocket and hand it over without question. The sadness squeezing my chest is back. Okay, it never left, but I feel it more keenly now.

"First of all," she says, "you will put a six-digit passcode on this phone ASAP."

"Yes, Sir."

She types in a text to Daddy Vic saying that I am ill and cannot meet her this evening. She hands me the phone, and I nod my approval at the message. She makes me hit the send button, and I close my eyes, wondering what future train wreck I have just put into motion.

"Up," she says.

Her voice has wrapped itself around my free will, and I say, "Yes, Sir." I shake my head. "I mean, Ma'am. I'm sorry, Rikki. I'm just kind of tired." I stand up as gracefully as I can.

"Professor, please take your coat off and lay down on the couch for a while. Don't leave until I finish closing up out there."

"Okay. Thank you."

She reaches into a mini-fridge and hands me a bottle of water. I drink about half of it, and then exhaustion overtakes me. My eyes are swirling closed, and I lay down on the couch. She puts a pillow under my head. The last thing I remember is Rikki pulling a blanket over me.

I wake up to find Rikki sitting at her desk in the dimly lit office. I tell her that I need to go home, but she doesn't want me to. She invites me to sleep upstairs in her apartment over the coffee shop so she can make sure I'm okay. There is no way I will get in between her and Brittany, so I lie and say I am okay to drive home. It's only twenty minutes, I tell her, and she reluctantly acquiesces but makes me promise to text her the moment I am home. She tells me that she took the liberty of programming her name and number in my phone but promises that she didn't snoop anywhere else. I didn't even think that, but that's good to know.

Once I'm home, I text Rikki, and she replies instantly as if she had her phone in hand waiting for me. Knowing someone was out there worried about me, even briefly, feels good.

And then I read the two-word return text from Daddy Vic.

DADDY VIC: Feel better

That's it? She didn't ask what was wrong or how I was feeling or even make suggestions for getting better? Whatever. I throw my phone on my desk and take a shower. As the water runs over me, I rehash all the drama that unfolded in only a few hours. Rikki knows all my fears and worries about Daddy Vic, but she doesn't seem to know that her bratty girlfriend is majorly cheating on her with some skank behind her back. And that is so not fair of Brittany. Add to that my embarrassment of publicly calling Brittany out in front of Rikki's customers. I will not be surprised if Rikki politely suggests that I take a permanent break from visiting her coffee shop.

To distract myself after my shower, I decide to find a famous mathematical curve for Wednesday's Calculus 1 class on implicit differentiation. I settle on one of my favorites - the mathematically elegant Witch of Agnesi curve. Two diametrically opposite points of a circle form the curve made famous by the Italian mathematician Maria Agnesi in the mid-1770s. Of course, I'll throw in the fact that she was appointed a professorship at the University of Bologna, Italy – an extremely rare feat for a woman in her time. It's good for students to learn a little history of the subject I love so much.

That settled, I head to bed and fall asleep thinking about someday visiting Italy to walk where she walked.

~~~

The following day at work, I wear pants and reasonable protection for my period. What Daddy Vic doesn't know won't hurt her, right? But as quitting time rolls around, I realize that I'm just not up for her objectification of my body, milking machines, or anal week. And I am genuinely having a bout of bad cramps today and would rather go home, take a nap, maybe, and regroup. I text her that I am still not feeling well and won't be able to see her tonight. I don't get a response until I step back into my apartment.

Only after I hang up my coat and set my briefcase down on my desk do I read the text.

DADDY VIC: Feel better. Tomorrow, 8 p.m.

I sigh and glance at her message again. "Really? You can't even ask me what's wrong?" I shake my head. "When I pass out on one of your contraptions, you take care of me, but outside of your sex dungeon ... nothing." I sigh and roll my eyes. How much longer can I keep this up? I need to talk to her tomorrow night about the whole hucow thing and find out exactly what's in these supplements. Definitely.

That decided, I place the phone face down on the counter and go about heating some frozen enchiladas in the microwave. "I could have a salad with this," I say and then break down laughing. There is no salad in this apartment. Never has been and probably never will be.

While my dinner is heating, I head in and take a quick shower. My period flow has slowed down considerably, and I can tell that I am pretty much done. Maybe that means that anal week is over. That would be just fine with me. My ass and rectum are sore beyond a reasonable doubt, as are my nipples. My body needs to recover, and having these couple of days off has helped.

"You wouldn't have these days off if it wasn't for Rikki," I singsong. Oh, shut up. "You like her." She's taken, moron, and then I roll my eyes while throwing on some sweats. My apartment is chilly. I head to the kitchen to pull my enchiladas out of the microwave, turning up the heat as I go by the thermostat.

I sit at my thrift-store kitchen table and take a moment to mentally thank Rikki for helping me last night. I would have brought that weird mood to Daddy Vic's with me and, who knows, probably ruined everything with her.

I need a distraction. Oh, shoot, I never looked at the link Madison sent me. I reach for my phone on the counter and tap the link. The story opens to the cover page. On top of the screen, it says that the book is on loan and that I have two weeks to read it. "No pressure there," I say to my phone. Okay, let's see who this Little Bear character is. Oh, it's a collection of short stories. Cool. I swipe a few pages and find the first story.

Little Bear's Twilight Dream
There's that moment between wakefulness and sleep that is luxurious. It is a giving in, a surrendering to the

twilight. I was in that state moments ago but became fully awake and aware of what she was doing to my body. But let me back up so I can relive it myself.

I am in her bedroom, but not her bed. There are certain times she requests my presence in her room while she sleeps. Other times I am in a smaller bedroom in the back of the house. I know how lucky I am that she allows me my own space. She is an extremely thoughtful owner. But this night, I am sleeping on the daybed in the corner of her Master bedroom. I do not call her Master, though; I call her Mistress. And I have given myself freely to her for whatever she desires.

I listen as she settles into her bed. She is quiet for some time, and I can finally let myself relax because she does not need me right now. I lay on my side, facing the wall. My muscles relax, and I let out a contented sigh as I breathe in the freshly laundered pillowcase beneath my cheek. My eyes close, and I drift toward sleep. The dream begins quickly, or so I think. In my dream, Mistress's hand lifts the thin cotton sheet from my naked body. I am used to being nude around her. She requires it. I am only to be clothed if working in the yard or out in public. Perhaps it is her way of reminding me of my place, reminding me of my submissive role, subservient to her wants and needs. A role that I finally let myself embrace after leaving a high-stress computer analyst job at a well-known Fortune 500 company three weeks ago today.

Cool air caresses my skin as the sheet is lifted. What a wonderful dream this is. Fingertips touch my hip. This tangible sensation shoots me into wakefulness. "Miss," I say and struggle to sit up, "are you all right?"

A finger lands on my lips, and a "Shh" whispers in my ear. "Settle back down, Little Bear." I do as I'm told. I am quiet, but I am definitely no longer asleep.

The three fingers on my hip trace a pattern known only to her. Her fingers begin a path higher, up my side. I tighten up as she hits a ticklish spot. I squirm a little, and she murmurs, "Hmm," as if taking inventory of my body's reactions.

The pads of her fingers trace a meandering path up my torso. Another tickle spot appears near my armpit, but this time she says nothing. She runs her fingers up and over my shoulder and then lovingly across my cheek and jawline. She traces my lips. She lingers at my lips and says, "Open." I open my mouth, and she slides her index finger in. "Wet my finger, please." I moan as her command sends an arousing jolt through me. I suck her finger gently, feeling her long nail on my tongue, and swirl my tongue around the tip. Abruptly, she pulls it out and thrusts her thumb in. I do the same to that digit. I do not question why. That is not my purpose. My only purpose is to do as she asks.

Her wet fingers latch onto my right nipple without warning, making it even more erect than it was.

"You like this," she says. "Don't you?"

"Yes –" I choke out as she tweaks my nipple between her fingers. "Yes, Miss," I finally get out.

"Hmm," she says again. She must be adding information to her database.

"You'd like me to put some clamps on those erect nipples, wouldn't you? Let them bite down hard? Make you wet with desire?"

I moan at her words instead of answering directly. The increasing pressure from her thumb and index finger on my captured nipple shoots delicious pain straight to my clit. Pain translates to desire along its journey south, and I am on fire. Too soon, she lets go, and I moan at the loss.

She chuckles. She knows how to play with me.

I am still lying on my side when she nudges my top leg forward toward the wall. I am not entirely lying face down, but almost. The cool air tickles my wet sex.

Her fingers trail down my side, through the ticklish spot, and back to my hip. They continue over my right ass cheek to the notch between my legs.

"What's this?" she says as if in wonder. "You are very wet, Little Bear. How did this happen?"

I try to stammer something, but she cuts me off.

"Did I give you permission to become wet?" Her fingers dip into my slickness, and then she holds them up in the dark room for me to see them glisten in the glow of the streetlights. "Did I?" Her fingers return to the source and trace my swollen outer lips, slick with my tribute to her. She carefully avoids my clit. A sharp smack on my ass from her left hand jolts me into awareness.

"Yes, Miss," I say instinctively. "I mean, no, Miss. You did not permit me to become aroused."

Another hard smack. "Then why did you?" Her fingers continue their exploration. She pinches my sensitive inner lips between her fingers and then gives them a pull and a twist. I moan. The pain is exquisite. "I bet you'd like me to go in. Wouldn't you?" As she says these words, her thumb and middle finger deftly open my lips wide. Her index finger circles the opening.

"Yes, Miss. Yes, yes," I say breathlessly, my voice high and tight.

"Why should I give you what you want, Little Bear? Why should I fuck you with my fingers?"

"Because … because I've been good. I've been *your* good girl."

"Hmm," is all she says as her index finger slowly makes its way inside me. She swirls the finger around my inner walls as if measuring the surface area.

Another finger joins the index finger as she slowly slides them both in. Then out. Agonizingly slowly, she pushes in and then pulls out. A third finger joins the others as she plunges in harder and harder. I can't help but lift my ass higher as if to draw her fingers in deeper.

"Mistress? I'm going to —" I can't finish as a pre-orgasmic wave hits me.

"No, Little Bear," she says calmly, "there will be no cumming. Not yet. Maybe not even tonight. Your Mistress is simply enjoying her property. This pussy I'm sliding my fingers in and out of? It belongs to me. And I will do with it what I wish."

I moan as she continues pumping me. "Yes." It's all I can get out.

Another sharp smack on my ass. "Yes, what?"

"Yes, Mistress," I say in pure agony. "Yes, you –" A wave of pre-orgasmic bliss spikes through my inner core again.

"Go on, my pet."

"You own my body, Miss." I moan as I ride my arousal. "Use me as you wish, Miss. You own all of me."

Another smack, this one softer. "Good. As long as that is understood." With the hand that smacked me, she rubs my burning ass cheek. "You can touch yourself, Little Bear."

"But Miss–"

"You can cum. Let me feel you tighten around my fingers. Let me feel your body thank me for rewarding you this way."

My fingers zip to my swollen clit. It doesn't take but five strokes. My soul caves in on itself and then hurtles me outward into the universe as I explode. I gush my tribute all over her hand. My inner walls grip her fingers tightly as my body spasms around them.

"That's my good girl. Cum for me, Little Bear." She continues to pump me.

"Cum hard for me."

Her continuous thrusting inside my body makes my orgasm last longer. The waves keep coming. Too soon, she slows her pace. "That's it, little one. You came hard, didn't you? To please me?"

I nod and say breathlessly, "Yes, Miss." It's the best I can do as I try to catch my breath.

Slowly, she pulls her fingers out of my slit and trails wetness up my body. She presents them to my mouth. I smell my scent on her fingers, which causes me to moan.

"Open," she says. I open my mouth and lick my arousal from her fingers.

"Ahh, my little toy likes to cum," my Mistress says. "Doesn't she?"

I nod, her fingers still inside my mouth. She pulls them out and then rests her hand on my hip. I feel their wetness on my skin.

She leans down and kisses my temple. "Sleep now, Little Bear. Your Mistress has a special task for you first thing tomorrow morning. Maybe even before breakfast."

"Thank you, Miss." I can't help the smile creeping across my face. "Thank you. Is there anything I can do for you right now?"

"So eager," she says to the room. "You were a good purchase." She taps my ass lightly with her hand. "Sleep now. You need your rest. I plan on making use of that tongue of yours tomorrow."

I moan in gratitude. "Thank you, Miss. It will be my honor."

She chuckles, and then my skin grows cold when her hand leaves me. I hear her wash up in the bathroom and then get back into her bed. All I can think is that my Mistress wants me. Oh, I hope I fall asleep quickly so that tomorrow will come faster.

"What a sweet story," I say and close the e-reader. I am aroused but way too tired to touch myself. I can totally see why Madison likes the stories. I think she must be attracted to the obvious power differential between the two characters. The new sub and the experienced Domme seem to respect each other. However, the issue of mutual respect hits a little too close to home in light of recent events. Brittany's betrayal of Rikki. Daddy Vic's possible non-disclosure about the true nature of those supplements, not to mention her detached and almost stone-hearted demeanor toward me. Those don't seem respectful. At all.

I will go to Daddy Vic's tomorrow at 8 p.m., no sooner, no later, I decide firmly. And I will make sure that my voice is heard. Coming up with *what* I'm going to say keeps me awake longer than I would like. Still, I eventually nod off, hopeful that my relationship with Daddy Vic will become a little warmer and a little fuzzier tomorrow evening after I've had my say.

Chapter 13
Gentle but Firm

"**D**o *not* make me repeat myself, slut."

This is not how I pictured this evening going. I want to talk, but Daddy Vic has other ideas, so I do as I'm told and roll over on the hassock face down. She yanks my legs wide apart and secures my feet with the Velcro straps.

"Show me that you're done menstruating."

Oh, God. Seriously? With a sigh, I pull up on my knees, reach underneath, and dip two fingers deep inside. I pull them out and show her.

"Put them in your mouth," she says. "Clean them." Her tone is cold. I think she is displeased that I bailed on her two nights in a row and showed up in pants tonight. "On all fours."

While I'm doing what she asks, she straps down my left wrist and then yanks my fingers out of my mouth to strap down the right. She walks behind me, and I hear the distinct sound of a condom foil packet opening. And then she opens a second. I groan. What is about to happen?

She thrusts a dildo inside my vagina, and I am told to keep it inside. She walks back to the other side of the hassock and jams a ball gag in my mouth. Crap, I don't like the way this is headed.

She steps behind me again and wordlessly applies lube to my tiny hole. Ahh, it is still anal week, I see. "Lift your ass, whore."

The lubed anal dildo slides into me slowly, and I can't help but moan at the pleasurable intrusion. With the dildo still lodged in my pussy, I feel so full. God, my body likes penetration. Of all kinds. She yanks the vaginal dildo out, and I hear her clothes rustling. She must be attaching it to a harness or something.

"Yesh," I say in encouragement around the ball gag in my mouth when the dildo is jammed back inside me, and a hand grabs one of my hips. The other hand has taken hold of the anal dildo and is guiding it in and out. "Oh, yesh." God, how much I love being fucked by Daddy Vic. She increases her pace, and I feel sub-spacy already. But then she stops and pulls both of them out.

I feel something drape across my back. Oh, shit. It's the flogger. Without a word, she flicks it at my ass, causing me to cry out at the sudden sting. She hits me again and again and again. She moves to my thighs. And then to my back. I cry out with each new strike. My skin is burning. She mumbles something under her breath, and I make out a couple of words. Something about somebody minding their own fucking business. So why am I getting punished because someone else stuck their nose where it doesn't belong? I don't know.

Both dildos return. Pressing against my sore ass as she thrusts creates the duality of pain and pleasure. I'm not sure which sensation is more real at the moment. I rock my hips to her rhythm until she abruptly stops again.

This time, she uses the crop on my already hot and inflamed skin. It stings, and I try to move away from her strikes. She laughs, but it is an evil laugh. There is no escaping. Ahh, but there is a way. I can't call red because my mouth is gagged, but I can pull out of these Velcro restraints at any time, and she knows it. The problem? I don't want to.

Both dildos are reinserted, and it isn't long before she slams into me so hard that she cums and then falls on top of my body. I simply can't hold her weight and fall flat on the hassock. She falls with me. She thrusts gently into my body with her phalluses for a bit longer, probably milking out her orgasm.

I am so friggin' turned on that I am ready to cum. My orgasm is hovering right there in the near distance. But, damn, I can't reach my clit. I yank my arm back to escape the Velcro, but it doesn't budge. I can't get the right angle on it or something. I try the other arm. What kind of freaking super Gorilla glue Velcro is this? My heart, which is already beating fast from my body being beaten, goes on overload. I'm starting to panic. I snap my fingers to get Daddy Vic's attention.

She lifts herself up and off of me, managing to keep the dildos lodged in my body. "Relax, slut. Stop fighting." She slaps one of my already sore ass cheeks five times, which stops me from moving. I have no idea what she's doing behind me, but then I hear the distinct sounds of pictures being taken.

"Mmph, mmph, mmph," I mumble around the gag. She doesn't have my permission. Holy shit. She pulls out of my body and slaps my ass cheeks again. "I said to stop moving, bitch."

That is a tone I have never heard. I stop struggling. This is such a Mama_Luvs moment that I hate myself right now for thinking I could ever have anything with Daddy Vic. She's as much a narcissistic, sadistic bully as Mama_Luvs is.

"I'm not getting your head or face in any of these shots, so relax. I'll show you the ones I'm going to keep, and you can watch me delete the others. And besides, how many pictures of your seeping wet cunt have you sent me in the past week? So don't play all high and mighty now."

I have to admit that she's right. She takes several more pictures and then moves around to show me closeups of both dildos inside my body and shots of my swollen pussy and ass. She makes a show of deleting a few of them. I try to say, "Delete them all," behind the gag, but it only comes out as "Mmph, mmph, mmph."

"These are good," Daddy Vic says and then moves out of sight. "Perfect for the wall of pussies I have in my bedroom. Oh, that's right, you never made it to my bedroom, did you, whore? Too bad." She undoes the restraints on my ankles, and I pull myself up into as much of a sitting position as my bound wrists allow. "Now," she says, "I am going to release your hands, and you are going to walk over to your clothes and get dressed calmly. After that, you're going to leave and never come back."

Her words surprise me. I don't know what to say, but I can't say anything anyway because I am still gagged.

"I know you're wondering why, but it is my prerogative to take on subs or let them go whenever I want. Sometimes on a whim." She's still standing behind me, probably posting my pussy all over the Internet. "You're not right for me, Bernadette. Do me a favor, and don't embarrass yourself by begging me to take you back. That won't look good on you, and it just won't happen."

She releases my left wrist, and I shoot over and free my right before she has a chance to. I bolt to the door where I lay my clothes, undo the strap on the ball gag, and throw it on the floor. I work my tongue until I have enough saliva to say, "What you were trying to do to me was wrong, Victoria. I was naïve and didn't catch on to your whole lactation thing. You could have asked, but no. You took advantage of me instead. Shame on you." Tears sting my eyes. I pull on my pants and my shirt and stuff my bra and boi shorts in my pockets while she calmly sits in her command chair watching me, her fingers steepled. Seriously, she has nothing to say? She's not even trying to defend herself.

I pat my pockets – phone, wallet, keys. Got them all. I grab my coat off the peg. "You could have been special to me, Victoria," I say with as much calm as I can muster. I purposely use her full name so that she understands that I see her as a real person and not her Daddy Vic Domme persona. "I honestly hope you find someone who will be able to break that self-absorbed shell of a heart of yours and find the real you inside." I unlock her front door and twist the knob. "That person isn't me, and we both know it." I open the door and say, "Goodnight, Victoria."

~~~

I keep the world at bay for the next day and a half and focus on teaching my classes, updating my lesson plans, answering work emails, and grading problem sets. Thursday, during lunch, I go back to Planned Parenthood and get another STD/STI test. I thought they might protest my coming back so soon, but they took me right in. Now that I'm in the system, I'll be getting my results faster. God, they must think I am a big slut. Maybe I am, but a clean set of results will put a ribbon on my breakup with Daddy Vic. I can figuratively wash my hands of her.

On Thursday evening, I end up paying my bills and then going to bed early. By Friday afternoon, I am crawling up the walls and text Shasti and Madison to see if they want to meet me at Rikki's Coffee Shop after dinner. Shasti suggests we meet earlier, and she'll bring a pizza for us to share. I tell her that is a wonderful idea and that I only like plain cheese if that's okay. She sends a laughing emoji and says that Madison and I are two peas in a pod in this regard. Then it's my turn to laugh when Madison's only contribution to the texted conversation is the word "YaaaaaY!"

Madison and Shasti are already in our favored spot at the coffee shop, and Shasti holds up a bottled water, indicating that I don't need to get anything at the counter.

"Hi, you guys." I plop down in one of the comfy chairs. "So good to see friends."

"Hi, Professor," Madison says, bouncing on the couch.

"Hey, kiddo," I say and then amend it when she pouts. "Hey, Little Bear." Her face brightens. "Thank you for the book loan. I started reading the stories. They're cute."

"Told you." She bounces her empty paper plate on her knee, trying to catch Shasti's eye.

I chuckle at her antics. She truly is a little, and Shasti is her perfect partner. I sigh.

"What's up, Professor?" Shasti asks.

I shake my head almost imperceptibly and wave away her question. She hands me a plate with a plain cheese slice, and I thank her.

"You know," I say and cringe at my tone. I have been in a self-reflective mood for the last few days, and they are about to get dragged into my musings. "I think I learn something new from every relationship. But do you think my Dommes have learned anything from me?"

"Undoubtedly," Madison says, and I am surprised at her grown-up response. "You teach them what class is all about. Don't you think, Professor?" Her grin is slow to spread, but I laugh once I get it.

"Class?" I roll my eyes. "Oh, you are too funny, Little Bear."

Shasti grins at her charge and says, "Power exchange, if done right, almost guarantees that partners learn from each other. And power exchange is just that. An exchange. Victoria can't help but be affected and influenced by you."

"Make that past tense," I say.

Madison's eyes grow wide. "Oh, no. You and Daddy Vic broke up?"

I nod and then shrug.

Madison sighs and looks down, dejected.

"No, no, no, Little Bear," I say. "It's okay. We, uh, enjoyed each other's company for a nice while, but we both realized that we weren't suited to be a forever-after D/s combination."

"I'm sorry, Professor," she says.

"No need," I say. "Seriously. I learned some things from her, like how

133

she practices safe sex when my other Dommes didn't. And, um, she gave good aftercare following impact play."

"Impact play?" Rikki says as she walks up. "Yes, please." Her eyes look hungry, and I figure Brittany is in for it later on. That is, if they're still together. I am not going to be the one to ask or bring it up. At least Rikki isn't showing me the door right now, so maybe my outburst has been forgiven.

"They broke up," Madison blurts and receives an immediate scolding from Shasti about boundaries.

"Oh, I, uh, hadn't heard," Rikki says coolly. Almost too coolly.

"Yes," I say but don't elaborate. Maybe she's thinking about Brittany's infidelity and considering her own breakup. I can't read her.

Rikki clears her throat and asks, "Did I hear the words power exchange?"

"Yes," Shasti says. "The professor was wondering if Dommes learn from their subs."

"Absolutely." Rikki sits on the couch next to Madison. "The Domme's first job is to learn as much about her sub as she can. Wants and needs from both sides are discussed and agreed upon. And if something feels off, I have to trust a sub to tell me. If she doesn't tell me, then she isn't holding up her end of the exchange. Trust is lost," Rikki says quietly. "The relationship is then on shaky and unequal ground."

Something heavy has overtaken our little group, and I'm sure it's because I confronted Brittany. In fact, I don't see her here this evening. Maybe they already broke up. Oh, my God. I'm to blame.

Shasti clears her throat and says, "D/s relationships have an agreed-upon power imbalance, but truth be told, we have equal power. Sometimes, I think subs have more."

"We do?" Madison perks up.

"Yes, indeed, peanut. If you decide you don't like wearing the onesies I pick out for you anymore, then, well, I have to adjust according to your needs."

Madison pats Shasti's forearm. "You always get it right, Mistress. And you know how much I *love* shopping." It's clear by her eye-roll that Madison loathes shopping.

"Except maybe the toy aisle, eh, Little Bear?" Rikki teases.

Madison beams.

"Now," Rikki continues, "the Domme has to find out what the sub needs and then tries to supply that. Sometimes, I try so hard to make sure my sub is satisfied that my own needs don't get met."

Shasti nods her agreement but stays silent.

"It all comes down to communication, doesn't it?" I say, having an epiphany. "Like, I have no idea if Daddy Vic's needs were met. We never talked. I know that mine were not." Madison shoots me a skeptical look. "Okay, okay, certain needs were met gloriously, but not others. But I didn't think she wanted to talk about my other needs, so I never mentioned anything."

"And that," Rikki says, slapping her open palm on the arm of the couch, "is completely unacceptable." Her eyes are storming. "Open and honest communication builds trust." She roots me to the couch when her fiery eyes meet mine. I swallow. Hard. She notices and then visibly relaxes. "Sorry. Sorry," Rikki apologizes. "Just a pet peeve of mine in this blasted community."

"Professor, who was that pretty Latina girl in your office the other day?" Madison asks shyly.

"Oh, kiddo, I didn't know you were there. You should have knocked and said hello."

"I know, but you guys sounded so happy talking about your weird math." Madison shrugs.

I thanked Madison silently for changing the subject. I gave a broad-strokes explanation as to who Bianca was and why I was helping her with her course when she wasn't even my student. "It's a shame these graduate students are going into top-level courses woefully unprepared." I shake my head. "And I can't get Wainwright –" I clear my throat. "Excuse me. I can't get *Dr.* Wainwright to understand that these graduate students are floundering and need help."

"Sounds like they need something like a review course before moving on," Rikki says.

Her words jolt my brain. It makes perfect sense. "Yes, that's it! A foundations course." I lean forward in my seat. "A course geared toward Masters' and Doctoral degree candidates who need an intensive review of the basics in calculus, linear algebra, group theory, proofs, induction, and other good stuff before moving on."

"Sounds like you are just the one to create this course, Professor," Rikki says, beaming.

The wheels in my head are turning. "It could also be a course that weeds out those that won't find success, thus saving everyone's time and effort." I grimace. "I'm trying to say that nicely."

"I'm sure you'll be gentle but firm," Rikki says.

"Gentle but firm," I repeat in an almost whisper. That is precisely what I want from a Domme. Rikki's expression conveys a mixture of encouragement and pride and is just too intense for me right now. I look away because my mind is going places it shouldn't. "Dr. Wainwright won't give me the time of day about a course like that, though."

"You won't know until you try, right?" Rikki says. "What would motivate you to sit down and develop a plan for this new course, Professor? You seem passionate about it."

The question surprises me. "I'm not sure," I say. "I have so much work to do." I think about the endless stacks of problem sets I have to grade.

"That sounds like an excuse," Rikki says. "How about this? You are not allowed to come back here until you show me a course outline or plan that you've developed to present to this Dr. Wainwright."

I search her face, wondering if there is some hidden agenda underneath her words. Is she blaming me for Brittany's unfaithfulness?

"Ooh, harsh, Miss Rikki," Madison says.

"Hey," Rikki says with a shrug, "it was just a thought. Something to motivate the good professor here."

I sit there stunned. Is she …? Is she guiding me to tackle something I find intimidating? Is she helping me find a way to succeed? Is she using her voodoo Domme powers on me?

"I'll be back with it tomorrow afternoon," I say confidently.

"Actions have consequences, Professor," Rikki says, one eyebrow raised in question. "What will be the consequences if it's not done?"

Keeping firm eye contact with her, I say, "Then I will bus tables for however long you deem appropriate." Oh, God, what am I doing? I don't even know what kind of bear I'm poking.

Rikki and Shasti exchange a look that I can't interpret, and Madison groans while hiding her face in her hands. "Oh, Professor, you don't know what you're getting yourself into."

Rikki bursts out laughing. "Hush, Little Bear. Don't give away my secrets."

~~~

That night, alone in my apartment, I research the university's graduate course catalog and jot down the fundamentals and prerequisites needed for success in each of the courses required for Masters' and Ph.D. candidates. Two in the morning hits, and I realize that this is when I typically get home from Daddy Vic's. Instead, I've got something I think is a worthy proposal for a 7000-level course that I tentatively call "Foundations for Graduate Mathematics." Guess who won't be busing tables tomorrow?

I decide to one-up the challenge Rikki gave me and send Dr. Wainwright a clear and concise email explaining my new course proposal and why I feel the university needs this course. I also explain why I should be the one to teach it because the last thing I want is for him to accept the course but let someone like Baxter ruin it.

Saturday morning comes quickly, and I've barely gotten enough sleep, but my mind is going a million miles an hour. I'm stoked to show Rikki that not only did I accept her challenge, but Dr. Wainwright returned my email this morning telling me that my proposal looked good. He wants to see me at 7 a.m. in his office on Monday to discuss it.

I draft a text to Rikki asking if it would be okay for me to come by the coffee shop around noonish. I don't want to bother her in any way, but I am chomping at the bit to show her the proposal. For some reason, I hesitate before hitting the send button. Maybe I shouldn't bother her. I mean, she has that whole Brittany mess to deal with.

My excitement overrules my head, and I hit send, reasoning that Rikki is a straight shooter and will tell me if a visit is inconvenient. I print out a copy of my proposal just in case she wants to see it.

I am astonished when I get a reply almost immediately.

RIKKI: Can't wait to see you! Come by the side entrance. I'll be in my office.

I throw on a black pair of jeans, a green flannel shirt, and my black Timberland boots. I'm feeling fabulous and free because I no longer have to wear skirts that I hate. I'm just going to be me. Who else can I be?

Although it's almost noon when I leave, the skies are dark and stormy. Well, it is the end of January, and snow is always a possibility. I find myself whistling as I drive and thank the parking gods when I get a spot right in front of the path leading to Rikki's office. After I show her the proposal, I'll probably stay for a coffee and maybe try my hand at one of the dartboards. I brought a stack of singles just in case I feel brave enough to try.

I take a deep breath outside of Rikki's office door and then knock four times in a rhythmic sequence. I thought about doing the shave-and-a-haircut knock, but I don't want to seem dorkier than I already am.

The door opens, and I lose my breath. Rikki is stunning. Her ginger hair is pulled up on her head in a loose bun. Loose tendrils hang down, and I just want to brush them off her neck. The top two buttons of her cobalt blue blouse are unbuttoned, and the shirt is tucked into neatly pressed black slacks. God, I feel so underdressed.

"Come in, come in, Professor," she says and steps back.

"Thank you, Rikki." I take a surreptitious breath to calm myself. I came here for one thing and one thing only, and that is to show her that I met her challenge. That's it.

"Here, let me take your coat." She hangs it on an overloaded set of hooks near the door. It looks like every single coat and sweater she and Brittany own are hanging on those hooks.

At least a dozen pairs of shoes sit jumbled on a landing leading to a staircase that obviously goes somewhere. An attic, maybe? An apartment? The lone window near the front door, along with two matching lamps on her oversized and overcluttered desk, creates a homey glow. "Are those the stairs to your apartment?"

"Yes. Convenient, don't you think?" She gestures for me to sit on the couch, so I do.

"Very convenient," I say. "But I might feel a little claustrophobic if I worked and lived in the same place." I shrug. "But that's just me."

She doesn't respond. Instead, she goes into her mini-fridge and offers me water, which I take. She pulls one out for herself. Maybe she's one of those Dommes, like most Dommes, that only likes to talk about the things they want to talk about. That's okay. Everyone has their quirks.

"It does get a bit suffocating sometimes," she answers, totally blowing my Domme theory. "I, uh, have trouble giving control over to the assistant managers sometimes. Not that they are incompetent or anything. I just, eh, you know. But I promise, I do get out on occasion."

"Good, because everyone needs a break sometimes. Maybe that's my challenge for you." I raise my eyebrows and challenge her with a smirk.

She purses her lips together and smiles back at me. "I'll think about it." Ahh, there's the Domme in her. Never relinquishing control. "Speaking of challenges. You said you finished that new course proposal?"

"I did." I hand her the printout.

She reads my printout silently—all of it. I look down at the spot on the floor where I knelt and had my mini-meltdown five days ago, hoping I wasn't a complete idiot.

She glances back at me. "I have no idea what a lot of these words mean," she says with a chuckle, "but this looks thorough and well put together." She scowls. "Darn."

"Uh oh. What's wrong?"

"I thought I had some free labor today." She laughs, and I do, too, but my laughter is because I am relieved. I thought I had disappointed her or something.

I then fill her in on my late-night email and the fact that I have a meeting with Dr. Wainwright first thing Monday morning.

"Professor, I'm so pleased." Rikki leans toward me. "Truly. That is great news."

"Thanks. I hope something will come of it." Rikki has a way of making me feel seen and heard. It feels good.

She leans back and says, "Would it be okay if we talk about what happened last Monday evening? The thing with Brittany?"

My heart clenches. "Okay." I glance down at my kneeling spot again. Oh, God, I know she saw me.

Her voice is gentle when she says, "Do you want to, um, kneel there, Bernadette? It's okay."

"Yes, Ma'am. May I?"

"Of course." Rikki hands me a pillow for my knees and waits until I get settled. I look up at her, and she says, "Brittany asked me to apologize to you if you found anything offensive on her phone. She never meant for anyone to see those messages."

"I bet she didn't," I say sarcastically, but then feel bad instantly. "I shouldn't have snooped."

"No, you shouldn't have," she says, and I feel instant shame. "I'm sorry the two of you haven't hit it off."

"It's not that." I look down at my hands resting face down on my thighs. "I like her free spirit very much, actually."

Rikki quietly moves to sit on the floor in front of me. Oh, no, I cannot let her be lower than me. I adjust and sit cross-legged so we are at least the same height when sitting. "Tell me."

"Rikki…" I can't do it. I can't be the one to tell her.

"Bernadette," she says quietly, but it is a clear and gentle command.

My face scrunches as I try to hold back my tears. Mission failure.

"Bernadette," she says again and pulls me into an embrace, "you're breaking my heart. Tell me what's wrong." She rubs my back, and I cry into the swell of her neck.

I do my best to suppress my sorrow at having to be the one to tell her. "I …"

"It's okay. You're doing great." She continues to rub my back.

"Brittany is cheating on you," I blurt.

She pulls away, and I cringe, waiting for her to call me a liar or go into a rage. "Brittany is not my girlfriend, Bernadette."

"What?"

"You thought that she and I?" Rikki chuckles. "Brittany is not and never has been my girlfriend or my lover."

"But isn't she your submissive?"

"My submissive?" Rikki shakes her head. "I can understand why you would think that. Brittany's Domme is overseas for a couple of months on assignment, and she asked me to keep an eye on her."

140

"Brittany doesn't live upstairs with you?" I look toward the stairs. I had been thinking that Brittany was upstairs in their shared apartment, maybe even listening to the conversation.

"Nope," Rikki reaches over and lifts my chin. "She lives with her parents in the room she grew up in."

"How did I get that so wrong?" I ask. "Ma'am, I am so sorry." My hand covers my mouth. "I made such a fool out of myself the other day."

"No, you didn't," Rikki says. "We've all been concerned about you. Especially that little one who has a major crush on you."

"Madison?"

"No," she says with a laugh. "I believe she goes by Little Bear these days." I let myself laugh, too. "And, you know what, Professor?"

"What's that?"

"I think I'm going to take you up on your challenge to get out of here more often."

"Oh, yeah?" I say, grateful for a change in subject. "And how are you going to do that?"

"By asking you out for lunch." Before I can respond, she says, "Bernadette, would you like to have lunch with me?"

"As in a date?"

"Yes."

"Yes," I say so fast that I almost pull a muscle. "Rikki?"

"Yes, Professor?"

"Can we please *not* go to Mamma Mia's?"

"Ahh, yes." She nods knowingly. "Absolutely. Mamma Mia's is officially off limits." She holds her hand out to help me up.

Chapter 14
Little Bee

Rikki pulls her Subaru Outback from behind the coffee shop. The car itself looks like it's seen better days, but who am I to judge? I get in after she cleans off the seat for me. Apparently, she uses the passenger seat as a second office and trash receptacle. Usually, that kind of thing bugs the heck out of me, but I'm going on a date with Rikki. That's the only thing my brain can handle right now.

She takes me to the Indigo Café several blocks from the coffee shop. It's nearly empty, thank goodness. I'm not great in crowds, and I want to focus on getting to know her. Knowing she is single is a complete game changer. Hopefully, I won't make a fool of myself. Again.

"So," Rikki says as we wait for our soup and sandwiches to arrive at our table, "the story about this place is that the owner of the café was a bit restless and went on an extended bird-watching trek for several months. She vowed that when she spotted an indigo bunting, a bird she'd never seen, that would be the place she would settle down and stay."

The waitress sidles up to our table with our order and adds, "And it was right here in Denton Heights that she happened on an entire field of indigo buntings as they were migrating back to their northern breeding grounds. She took that as a sign, settled down here, and opened the cafe."

"What a sweet story," I say to the waitress and then include Rikki with my smile. "They are beautiful birds." I point to the stunning photograph on the wall at our table.

The waitress smiles and asks Rikki, "Will there be anything else?"

Rikki looks over at me with raised eyebrows.

"I'm fine, thanks," I say, finding it interesting that the waitress only addressed Rikki.

"I guess we're good," Rikki says. "Thank you."

We make small talk while we eat, but then Rikki says, "I have to be honest, Professor. I'm glad you're done with Victoria." I look up at her with a questioning look. "You got out of there a lot faster than most."

"She was a big mistake," I say. I take a sip of water, thinking I'd like to order a hot cup of coffee, but don't dare. I'll get one at Rikki's when we get back.

"Don't think of it that way. Your relationship with Victoria was a learning experience for you. It's only a mistake if you don't learn from it."

Rikki looks like she's struggling to explain herself better, but I cut her off. "I totally get that. She's a very one-sided person, though. She never wanted to know the real me. I was –" I sigh and shake my head. "I was the next piece of meat on her slab, if I can be blunt. That's not what I want in a relationship."

Rikki's green eyes do that whole soul-searching thing again, and I am melting. She reaches across the table and puts her hand over mine. "I want to know you, Bernadette. The real you. All of you."

Oh, God. This is happening so fast. What do I say?

I must have hesitated too long because she pulls her hand back and says, "But you need time, obviously."

Before I can stop it, my hand flies across the table and grabs hers. "Yes."

She narrows one eye as if trying to decipher what my one-word response means, and I feel the blush creeping up my neck.

"I mean, *yes*, I want to get to know you, too, Rikki. I don't need more time."

"I'm glad." She squeezes my hand and then lets go. An adorable pink blush flushes her cheeks. "So, um, tell me one beautiful thing you saw or experienced today."

Is she changing the subject? She's changing the subject. She's nervous. So am I. I clear my throat and repeat, "A beautiful thing I've seen today?" *Besides you?* I bite my lower lip. Her gaze moves from my eyes to my lips. Oh, God, she is turning me on with that expression. "Umm, please don't think me cheesy, but all I can think to say is *you*." I look down at my food. I think we've both kind of forgotten about our lunch.

"Bernadette," she says in a serious tone, "I wasn't searching for a compliment."

"Can't help it, Ma'am," I say without wavering and look up. "It's the truth. In the short time I've known you, you have done a million things that make me feel seen and heard. I've not felt that in a long, long time."

She searches my eyes for an overlong moment and then clears her throat. "May I ask you a few pointed questions?"

"Yes, Ma'am," I say. The way she carries herself, holds her head, looks at me – all of it is sending me into full-on submissive mode. The fact that I've switched to addressing her as *Ma'am* is a dead giveaway, and she must be picking up on that.

"What do you, as a submissive woman, desire? What do you get out of the experience of being submissive?"

"Oh, umm, well," I hesitate, wondering where the waitress is, but I have to trust that Rikki will keep us both safe from prying ears. "Can I back up a bit? I am what I like to call a soft butch. I've been told that I walk with confidence, although I don't feel it most of the time. I played sports and did well in school and basically went after what I wanted."

"And have a very impressive degree and career to show for it," Rikki says.

"Thank you." Now, it's my turn to feel the blush creep up *my* neck. "Because I am somewhat masculine or butch or whatever you want to call it, my girlfriends expected me to be the aggressor or the top. And Rikki," I look up at her, "I hated every minute of that. I hated making the decisions. I hated their expectation that I had all the answers."

"I get that. Completely," Rikki says with a gentle smile.

"And then," I say in a low voice, "I accidentally discovered a porn video with a female Domme and her female submissive." I nervously clear my throat because I can't believe I just admitted to watching porn. "Umm, I was riveted. I mean, I pictured myself as that bottom. After further research and joining *Kinks.com* –"

"You're on *Kinks?*" Rikki interrupts. I nod. "Excellent. We're all on *Kinks*. You have to see Madison's page. It is so cute."

"Aww," I gush. "I can't wait."

"She is going to be so excited to add you as a friend. I'm surprised she hasn't asked you yet."

"Shasti probably has something to do with that," I say.

"No kidding," Rikki says. "So, although the world seemed to expect you to be a top, you weren't feeling that?"

"I was not. The more I read, the more I felt there was finally something out there to describe how I had been feeling for thirty-two years. I am submissive. It explains so much."

"You're thirty-two?" Rikki asks.

I nod. "Thirty-three in June."

"You're ageless, Professor. Youthful, yet so wise and authoritative."

I scoff. "Me? Authoritative?"

Rikki nods. "I've seen it. You don't seem to suffer fools, Bernadette. And before we met, Madison painted this total Domme picture of you. I had no idea what kind of person we were going to meet that day at Rocco's Diner."

"That was the first time I met you."

"It was." She smiles, and the blush in her cheeks deepens. "Shasti and I weren't sure if you'd be there. I knew Madison's heart would be broken if you weren't. But there you were, sitting by yourself."

There was no way I would admit that I hadn't gone to Rocco's explicitly to meet up with Madison and her friends. No, that secret would go with me to the grave. "I'm glad I met you all. You, Shasti, Brittany."

Rikki rolls her eyes. "Brittany was extra bratty that morning. She didn't want to go out in the snow. Too cold, she said."

"I remember she was a bit of a handful. And you reprimanded her. That's why I thought you guys were a couple."

"I get that. I have basically been babysitting." She laughs, and it is the most wonderful sound in the world. I can't help the grin on my face. This beautiful woman wants to get to know *me*. I think she knows more about me at this point than Daddy Vic ever will.

"How old are you, Rikki? If I can ask."

"Thirty-six last month. December."

"Oh, I missed your birthday."

"No worries. I downplayed it big time. Madison insisted we have a chocolate chip cookie cake, though."

"I bet. That one loves her sweets," I say. "So, to finish up my thought about being submissive, I had a few liaisons and fell in love with the

Dominance I felt from these women. It was so fulfilling for a while. But then I realized that they weren't interested in the *me* part of me. The thinking/feeling me. It was so cliché. But giving up my power to someone else, if only for a little while, is intoxicating."

Rikki nods. "You like someone caring for you. Making decisions for you."

"If it's genuine and in my best interest, then yes," I say simply.

Rikki nods again and seems to be lost in thought.

I clear my throat and ask, "So what do you, as a Domme, get out of the experience?"

Rikki's expression softens. "I am a nurturer. I like to help people, but many of the women I've been with claim to want help, but they don't. Not really. They want an interesting and exciting fuck, and then they're done." She narrows her eyes and adds, "My ideal relationship is to have a strong partner who is like a first mate to my captainship. We agree that I am the captain steering the ship, but I will seek her insight and advice. She understands that I am human, too, and that I also have needs." She looks up at me and seems to be about to add something, but then presses her lips together.

"Just the fact that you asked me what I need speaks volumes about you, Rikki," I say and reach for her hand again. "I already know what a caring person you are."

She lowers her voice and says, "I also have, err, certain appetites in the bedroom."

"Don't we all," I say back.

She searches my face again for something, but I don't know what. I am having difficulty reading her.

"Ladies," a voice says behind me, "I think you'd better head out. This storm is here and only getting stronger." The waitress hands Rikki the check.

We both look out the window and to our surprise, it is snowing so thickly that you can't see across the street. "Oh, shoot," Rikki says. "C'mon, Bernadette. We'd better go."

We got so lost in our conversation that we never noticed the weather. No wonder the café was empty.

"You, too, Sandy," Rikki says. "Close up and go home."

Sandy gives Rikki a military salute, and Rikki chuckles. Rikki drops some cash on the table and then holds out her elbow for me to take. Oh, wow, this is just like the Daddy Vic dream I had. Luckily, it won't end up the same way.

Rikki's car supposedly has good traction, but we slip and slide the couple of blocks back to the coffee shop, thankfully making it there safely. We go into her office, dump our coats, and head into the shop. She says to the few remaining customers, "Time to get home, everybody. We're closing up."

She totally controls the situation and tops off the customers' beverages, apologizing for any inconvenience. I shake my head. It's not as if she has any control over the weather. I dive in, grab a bussing tray and a clean, wet rag, and work my way around the tables, picking up cups, glasses, and trash. A quick wipe, and I'm on to the next table. I've never bussed tables before in my life, but I get the hang of it pretty quickly. I take the dishes over to the kitchen window and send them through. The woman washing dishes thanks me, and I ask her if she needs help.

"Sure, come on in and separate out the trash for me."

I introduce myself and get to work. Rikki comes in and says, "Marta, I'll take over. Go home. Everyone else is gone."

"But, Boss," she protests and keeps spraying the cups.

"Out," Rikki says and takes the sprayer from her.

"Okay, Okay," Marta says and takes off her apron. "See you tomorrow, Boss."

Rikki nods. "Be safe and give that little girl of yours a hug from Miss RiRi."

Marta chuckles and says, "I will."

Once Marta leaves the kitchen, we are completely alone in the coffee shop. Rikki turns to me. "You need to go now, too."

I look at the mess surrounding us and say, "Nope. I'm not leaving you with all of this."

"If you don't go home now, I won't let you drive later. The snow is sticking out there."

"Okay by me," I say and don't look up. I can't. I'm too afraid she'll push me out the door and make me leave. Leaving is the last thing I want to do.

The sprayer stops spraying. She turns to face me.

"On your knees, please," she says, and my heart clenches.

I put down the coffee mug I am washing and grab onto the edge of the large sink to ease myself down to the wet and dirty mat. I put my hands face up on my thighs, expressing my openness and desire to please her. I keep my head and eyes down. Arousal blooms in my chest and spreads lower. I don't want her to send me home, but I'll go if she commands it.

"This is quite an act of defiance, little bee."

I swallow hard. She has a nickname for me already.

"What are we going to do about this?" She lifts my chin. "Eyes open, please."

I melt when I see the intensity in her eyes. She is as aroused as I am and steps closer to run her fingers through my hair. She's practically petting me. She squats down and looks at me eye to eye. "Consent is important. Do you understand that?"

"Yes, Ma'am." I nod.

"I hate to bring it up, but I have to. I have tested clean for STDs and STIs. I can show you the paperwork."

"No need, Ma'am," I say, getting lost in her eyes. "I just got my results from the test I took Thursday, post-Victoria. I can show you. They came in on my phone when we were at the café."

"No need, little bee. Trust has to start somewhere." She cups my chin possessively. "I would like for you to go upstairs to my apartment, get two towels out, and get ready to shower with me." She does that soul-sweeping thing she does with her overpowering green eyes as if wondering if we should embark on this new journey together. I soften my somewhat frightened expression and smile. She smiles back as if we have now sealed a deal. "Bernadette, if anything I suggest or do is unacceptable, you will tell me immediately. Or use your stoplight safe words."

"Oh, yes, Ma'am. Yes." I can't help my enthusiasm. I want her to know that I am on board with this whole liaison. I grab one of her hands and kiss the back of it. I will myself not to tear up. Her touch feels so right.

She reaches for my hands, and we stand up together. She pulls me into a full-body embrace. Somehow, our bodies seem to fit together perfectly. Oh, God, how I want her to kiss me. She pulls out of the embrace, and I groan at the loss.

She chuckles and says, "Brighten up, little bee. I'll be right up. Go now."

I nod and turn from her. My core is shaking as I find my way through her office and up the stairs toward the apartment. I open the door and fumble for a light switch. It's only mid-afternoon, but the storm makes it dark inside. The entryway light illuminates a large studio apartment. There is a kitchenette off to one side, a cozy living room area with a couch, and two overstuffed chairs, but the room's most prominent feature is the king-sized bed set up on a platform. The bed is immaculately made with an inviting gray and teal satin comforter. I see the door to the left of the bed and assume that is my goal. Inside the spacious bathroom, I find a linen closet and pull out two fluffy towels. I lay them on the oversized countertop near the shower. A washer and a dryer occupy the large bathroom, too. Yikes. Rikki needs to do laundry, judging by the mountain of clothes on the floor in front of the washing machine.

I sneak a peek in the shower, intending to clean it before she arrives, but it is immaculate. I am not sure what else she intended me to do, so I use the restroom and then kneel at the foot of her bed, fully clothed, waiting for her.

Rikki thunders up the stairs but then comes to an abrupt stop upon entering the apartment. She makes a funny noise that I cannot interpret, and I decide not to look up. I hear the door shut and soft footsteps approach. She cups my chin to lift my head. "Stand for me, little bee," she says. I stand, and her gaze meets mine as she steps closer. She reaches for the top button of my flannel shirt and pauses as if asking permission. I nod almost imperceptibly, and she begins to undress me. Once I am nude, she pulls me in her arms and presses her lips to mine. Oh, God, yes. I love kissing. Her lips are soft yet insistent. She pushes her tongue gently through my lips, and I suck lightly. She moans her approval. We break apart breathlessly.

"You are a beautiful woman, Bernadette," she says to me reverently. I think my entire body blushes at her words. "Go warm up the water."

I do as she tells me, my core quaking with a mixture of nerves and desire. I'm not sure if I should kneel, but she takes that decision away when she enters the bathroom fully nude. Her body is perfection. Curvy in all the right places. She is fair-skinned, and her breasts are so inviting. She has a smattering of freckles on her body, and I plan on getting to know each one of them intimately.

She takes my hand and then pulls me into the stream of water after her.

She backs me up against the shower tile and presses her body against mine. She sears me with kisses, and I am positively putty in her hands. She pulls away and says, "That ought to hold you for a minute."

"As long as there will be more like that."

"Absolutely." She opens a new mesh shower puff. It is dark purple, and I love it. She pours lovely-smelling body wash on the scrubby and proceeds to wash me luxuriously, getting to know my body. I am practically purring. No one has ever washed me like this before. When she is finished, she grabs her own green scrubby and starts washing herself, but I intervene and take it out of her hand. She protests at first, but I am insistent. She seems unused to this kind of attention, but I persist and love the small moment of power I have, making her raise an arm or spread her legs so I can wash her as thoroughly as she did me.

I linger longer than necessary between her legs because I'm waiting to see if she will pull me in to service her. She does the opposite, pulls me back to a standing position, and kisses me again. Doesn't she know how much I melt when she does that? She must. We both decide to wash our hair, and it is an incredible sensory experience when she washes mine. She quickly does her own, but maybe next time, I'll be able to do it for her. I want to learn how to be of full service to her.

When we step out of the shower, she wraps a towel around herself and then proceeds to dry me from head to toe with the fluffiest towel I have ever felt. I feel so pampered. No lover has ever done this for me. She blow-dries my hair so I don't "catch a chill" and then instructs me to kneel at the foot of the bed.

I am brazen and grab a throw pillow from the couch to kneel on as I wait for her. Hopefully, this small move for relief won't get me in trouble. The white noise of the blow dryer as she dries her hair is comforting somehow. Calming. I have no idea what is about to happen. And seriously, I have no idea how in the world I came to be kneeling by Rikki's bed this evening, but I do know one thing. I want this. I want her, and if I think about it, I've wanted her since the moment I met her.

She stands in front of me, and I look up. I can't help but see the smile growing on my face. A similar smile sprouts on hers, and I wonder what she's thinking. She reaches for my hand to help me up. She leans in, and I think she will kiss me, but then she pushes me back on the bed and tells me to move back so my head rests on one of the pillows. The satin comforter underneath me is soft and luxurious. She crawls from the bottom of the bed and hovers over me. Her thighs straddle mine, and her hands fall on either side of my head.

"I'm going to kiss you now, Bernadette." She strokes my face with her fingers. "Will that be okay?"

"More than okay," I say huskily, put my arms around her neck, and pull her to me. I hope this bold move is okay with her.

She doesn't balk, and I gasp when our bodies touch. She is so lovely. Her breasts press against me at the same time her lips find mine. Her touch is soft at first but heats up quickly. It isn't long before her knee pushes my legs apart, and her thigh presses against my already wet center. She moves her thigh up and down, and I moan into her mouth as I arch up against her.

Abruptly she leaves my lips and starts a trail of kisses down my neck, finding that sensitive spot just behind my earlobe. She brushes her lips across my collarbone and makes her way to my breasts. She licks the peaks hard, and I moan encouragement. My nipples have had several days to recover from Daddy Vic and are wonderfully sensitive again. Much too soon, she moves lower, and I realize that she is going to go down on me. "Ma'am," I say, "I should be servicing you." I struggle to sit up.

"Lay back, little bee," she commands gently. There is no defying that tone. A surge of adrenaline hits me, and I shudder and give in to her wishes.

She dips a finger into my center and parts my labia. She runs her fingers up and down as if petting me. Not accidentally, her fingertip caresses my swollen clit, and I arch up to meet her touch. "So responsive," she says and looks up at me with a lustful hunger. Her sensual energy fills me.

She leans down and kisses my clit. I moan softly, which causes her to moan in response. Making love to me is turning her on, too. She runs her tongue down through my labia and back up again, pausing to kiss my clit. She pushes a finger inside my well. My body arches up for her. A second finger enters, and they begin to move.

"Oh, yes, Rikki. Yes." I undulate my hips to her rhythm. Amazingly, I already feel an orgasm building in the distance.

She sucks my clit hard and then flicks her tongue over the sensitive peak.

She pumps me and then turns her fingers around to caress my G-spot. Holy fucking shit that feels amazing.

I am quaking as my orgasm slowly builds its way toward its peak. I am panting like I've never panted before. The orgasm is right there, but she's keeping me on the edge. Holy fuck. My body trembles. I am not in control. She sucks me hard and rips the orgasm from my body. I wail as I cum and buck like a bronco, my thighs clamping her fingers inside me. She hangs on and continues to rub my G-spot from within. Wave after orgasmic wave travel through my body, and I gasp for air. My thighs finally release their grip, and she pulls her fingers out gently.

She crawls up my body and lies next to me on her back. She nudges me gently, and I roll over to lay in her arms, my head on her chest. The kiss she plants on my forehead seals the deal. I must find a way to keep this amazing woman in my life. I cannot mess this one up.

"Thank you," I say, still a little breathless.

"I think you're the first person ever to thank me," she says, sounding perplexed.

I take a deep breath and let it out slowly. "Top ten," I say.

"Oh? Only top ten?" I can hear the smile in her voice. "I'll have to keep working on that. Won't I?"

"You might kill me in the process," I say and nuzzle against her. She chuckles, but I am surprised that she is not pushing my head down for me to pleasure her. Instead, after a moment, I take the initiative and kiss my way down her body. I have a few interesting places in mind for stops along the way.

She protests and tries to pull me back up, but I sense that these are half-hearted efforts, so I continue my trek. Once I reach my ultimate goal, I moan at how wonderfully sweet she tastes. I love the scent of an aroused woman and do my best to find what pleases her. I am a quick study, and before long, she grabs my head and bucks into my face as she cums. When she is finished, I clean her up with my tongue until she earnestly pulls me up to her and kisses me hard. She must taste her salty yet sweet essence on my lips, her tribute to me.

"You have an intuitive touch, Bernadette," she says when she lets us come up for air. "You found all the right ways to touch me." I smile against her skin. "I'm going to keep you around for a while, little bee. If that's okay."

"Yes," is my simple answer.

Her arms go around me, and we cuddle. From out of nowhere, she throws a blanket on top of us, and I am content. I have never had a Domme cuddle me after sex. Even Jen never did. I push thoughts about my exes away and fall asleep in the circle of Rikki's strong, protective arms.

Chapter 15
Best Snow Day Ever

"I've never felt this way about anyone before, Shasti," Rikki says.

My eyes blink open, and I am momentarily confused as to where I am. And then it all comes flooding back. I'm in *her* bed. Rikki's bed. Oh, God, we made love last night. The feel of her skin against mine, nestling against her, my hand on her chest – it was heaven.

"I thought you were going to take it slow," Shasti says in a tinny voice. "Movies, dinners, game nights."

I sit up and realize that the door to the apartment is open, and Rikki is downstairs in her office on the phone. Oh, God, I shouldn't be overhearing this.

"I was," Rikki says, "but then she looked at me with those blue eyes, and I was gone."

"You've liked her since the moment you met her, Rikki. I am not surprised."

"She is so sexy, Shasti."

"And this has nothing to do with the whole Victoria thing?" Shasti clears her throat as if to say she does not really want an answer. "Did you talk limits?"

"Not yet. Not in so many words," Rikki says. "But last night, we had the best vanilla sex I've ever had. And let me just say this. She is not a pillow princess."

Shasti laughs. "Unlike Sarah and Emily and Jessica and Eil–"

"Stop," Rikki says and inhales through her teeth. "Don't say that last name. I don't ever want to hear it again. And, besides, you make me sound like a whore."

"I'm just saying these women were attracted to you but never gave you anything back."

There is silence for a few moments, and I wonder if I should close the apartment door or maybe hide in the bathroom.

"Rikki, are you there?"

"Yes, I just ... she's different, Shasti. More mature. A newbie in the world of BDSM, for sure, but she's her own person and ..."

"And what?"

"I felt so fulfilled last night."

"Looks like this snowstorm came at the perfect time."

Rikki laughs. "Yes, indeed. We're not opening today. I put a sign on the door and updated the website. I called the staff to let them know they're getting a paid day off. Not a single one complained."

"You have always been generous with your employees, Rikki," Shasti says. "I have a question for you. Cotton or Jute?"

"Ahh, rope play on a snow day. Madison's school is closed?"

"Mm hmm," Shasti says. "Oh, you should tell the professor that the university is shut down, and she can sleep in."

Upstairs, I breathe a sigh of relief. Unbelievably, I hadn't even thought about my responsibilities and the fact that I had a calculus class to teach this morning. Oh, shoot, and that meeting with Dr. Wainwright. Surely, he wouldn't expect me to come in during this snowstorm. I'll check my phone later if I can find it.

Downstairs, Rikki says, "So you're tying the little one today?"

"Absolutely! She's been bugging me for weeks to do a full Shibari session with her."

"With suspension?"

"Yes, yes," Shasti says with enthusiasm. I'll post some pics on *Kinks* if it's any good."

"Excellent," Rikki says. "We'll look for them later. And go with cotton today. She'll last longer."

"That's the way I was leaning," Shasti says. "Rikki, be safe, and don't rush things with the professor. She's had a few relationships that have bitten her in the behind if you know what I mean."

"I know. I know," Rikki says. "Listen, I'm going to head upstairs and see if my beautiful blue-eyed bee is awake yet."

They say their goodbyes, and I dive under the covers, pretending to be asleep. I hear her soft footsteps come up the stairs and then sense her near me. I stir, open my eyes, and smile at her. She smiles back and sits on the edge of the bed. She is wearing a forest green satin robe tied at the waist and looks like a Goddess.

"School is canceled today, little bee." She points to the window. It is still snowing.

"A snow day?" I sit up on my elbows.

"Mm hmm." She brushes a lock of hair off my forehead. "You are so beautiful, Bernadette."

I blush and look down. "Thank you."

She reaches for my chin and pulls my head up so I can look at her. "Coffee?"

"I thought you'd never ask."

"Let's shower first."

"Is that a good idea, *Ma'am*?" I emphasize the word Ma'am, not because I am feeling submissive but because the last time we showered, we ended up making love in her bed.

She puts both hands up in defense. "Strictly washing. Okay, maybe a little kissing."

"May I, uh, …"

"Oh, yes, yes, yes. Sorry. Go use the facilities. I'll get the coffee set up."

Once we're in the shower, I'm afraid we'll never leave because she has the best kisses I have ever experienced. It's as if she puts her entire soul into that point of contact. Rikki is strong-willed and in charge, and we stop just short of things escalating. She commands me to step out while she finishes up. I towel off, and then she turns off the shower and hands me a robe similar in style to hers, but mine is a lush, deep purple, and I absolutely love it. My purple robe completely complements her green. I have a feeling that she has a great eye for color and design.

As she fixes the coffees for us from her fancy-looking machine in the kitchenette, I feel so content. I also feel a bit unworthy, having never experienced this before, but I bask in its essence anyway. We sit on the couch, me practically in her lap, and watch the snow fall outside the big window.

"We need to talk limits, little bee," she says and takes a sip of her coffee.

"I know," I say. It almost feels like a mood spoiler.

"Sometimes I have subs fill in a checklist. I don't want to do that with you because it feels too much like a business arrangement, and I don't want it to feel like that with you."

"Neither do I," I say succinctly and let her lead. I have a feeling I will be doing a lot of this.

"First and foremost, I am not a FinDomme. Do you know what that is?"

"Yes, Ma'am." Ahh, I am feeling submissive. It is incredible how she can send me to a submissive headspace so quickly. "It means you don't expect money or gifts from a wish list. And Ma'am?"

"Yes, little bee?" She leans down and kisses the top of my head.

Oh, I am swooning from her affection. I clear my throat and say, "Nor am I a leach. I do not expect you to pay for everything. In fact, I owe you my share for the café yesterday."

"I appreciate that, but I asked you to lunch, so it was on me." She wraps an arm around me and squeezes. "But thank you for offering. And I'm glad you mentioned the 'leach' thing. I have been, um, burned before." She gestures to the studio apartment.

"What do you mean, Ma'am?"

"I used to own a house. It was my aunt's house that I inherited after she passed. I had to sell it to pay off many debts that weren't mine. I almost lost the shop." She sighs deeply, and I know not to ask her about it. "I, uh, also do not have toilet or bodily function fetishes, nor do I want to experiment with those. So, if you –"

"I don't have those fetishes either, Ma'am," I interrupt. "I am just beginning to figure out my pain tolerances if that helps."

"Yes, yes," she says. I hear the unmistakable sound of a snowplow scraping away the snow on the street below. But the falling snow doesn't seem to be anywhere near stopping. They are just going to have to come back and plow Market Street again.

"I know about your restraint issues, and we'll find workarounds for that." She maneuvers so she can look me in the eyes. "I am going to restrain you today, Bernadette. But there will be a valid reason for it. It will be okay, I promise. I am going to make you feel good, little bee. Is that okay with you?"

I have no voice at the moment. She segued so quickly into playtime that

I am taken off guard. "Yes, Ma'am," I finally peep. "I, um, also have hard limits against breath play, forced orgasms, and men."

"Noted," she says.

We finish our coffees, and she moves our cups off the coffee table. Something is about to happen, I think. She tosses an overlarge pillow on the floor. "On your knees before me, please."

I slide off the couch and lower myself onto the pillow, thinking how wonderfully thoughtful she is. Before I can get my hands adequately positioned, she says, "Robe off, please."

I try to hide my growing grin. She says "please" a lot. That's nice. I disrobe and toss it on the couch. She does not reprimand me for not folding it. Good. I hate having to stop the momentum to do that. God, I am so turned on now that she is clothed and I am not. This must be a new fetish for me— CFnf—Clothed Female, naked female. Who knows? All I know is that I feel wonderfully vulnerable right now.

"Thank you, Ma'am," I blurt, risking a reprimand for speaking out of turn.

"For?"

I put my palms up and lower my head. I'll close my eyes if she tells me to. "Thank you for giving me your attention. For allowing me to serve you."

"Mm hmm," is all she says.

"Spread your legs, please. Wider. That's it." She stands up and pulls her robe tighter around her. "Beautiful, little bee. Just gorgeous. Look how wet you are already." I feel another surge of wetness hit my center as she says that. "Pleasure-ready pose, please."

"Ma'am?" I don't know what that is.

She chuckles. "Hands behind your back. That's it. Stick out your tongue and keep your eyes on me." She is in Domme mode. It's funny how I can tell. I wonder if she can tell when I feel submissive. "You know what's about to happen, don't you, little bee?"

I nod and flick my tongue. I can't help the smile creeping up my face. I love taking instructions from her.

"Rigid," she instructs, meaning my tongue. She moves in front of me and opens her robe. She lifts a leg on the couch behind me. Using two fingers, she spreads her labia, revealing a swollen clit. My Rikki is aroused. She maneuvers so her clit touches my tongue dead on. I sigh involuntarily. "Good girl," she says and pets my head. She tilts her hips back and forth and rubs herself on my tongue. "Swallow," she says. Oh, she tastes so good.

"Pleasure pose." I stick my tongue out. "Flat," she instructs. "Head back." She rubs her vulva over my flattened tongue and sighs contentedly. "Good, good little bee. Ohhh," she moans and increases her pace. "Swallow." God, she knows just the right times to let me swallow and regroup. "Rigid." My tongue goes out hard. She positions herself in such a manner that my tongue is centered at the entrance to her vagina. She pushes against my face. I moan as her essence covers my nose, cheeks, and chin. "Swirl," she commands, and I do so, whirling my tongue around and cleaning anything I can get to.

I pull my tongue in and swallow. She grabs my chin and puts her face in mine. "Did I tell you to swallow?"

I shake my head as best I can, but she has my chin held fast. "Words. Use them." Her grip intensifies.

"No, Ma'am. I'm sorry, Ma'am." I've disappointed her.

"We'll try again. I expect any sub of mine to follow rules, learn commands, and anticipate them. Will you do better?"

"Yes, Ma'am," I say.

"Good answer." She starts me over again with pleasure pose, and we progress through rigid, flat, swirl, and swallow. She adds in kiss, suck, flick left/right, flick up/down, and light switch. These were easy enough, and it is right in the middle of lightswitching her clit that she grabs the back of my head and bucks against me. Her moans spur me on. Her cum is thick and luscious on my face. "Hold," she commands breathlessly. Her spasms feel wonderful against my face. And you know what? *I* did that. Me! I was the one that made her cum while on my knees. I swell with pride.

"Clean," she says, still holding the back of my head. "Oh, good girl." She sighs. "Flat." I react instantly. She rubs her clit over my tongue and says, "Kneel back, please. Hands behind your back. Yes, yes. That lifts your breasts, making you very enticing."

I look down and close my eyes. She is done using me for now. I will be still and content until my services are needed again.

She breathes through her recovery and then gets up without a word, leaving me right where I am. I am a puddling mess of arousal and know that

I am ruining her pillow. I hear her fussing with the coffee cups in the kitchen area. She blows out a sigh, betraying the intensity of our session. I feel it, too, Ma'am, I say inside my head.

She walks past me, her bare feet barely making a sound on the hardwood floors, but I am tuned in to her whereabouts. She closes the door to the restroom, and eventually, I hear the toilet flush, the water in the sink run, and she comes out.

"Go freshen up," she says. "I put out a new razor for you. Use the hand mirror to make sure you get everything."

"Yes, Ma'am. Thank you, Ma'am." I open my eyes, stand up, and move to the bathroom.

I use the facilities and then assess myself in the mirror as I wash my hands. "Is this what you want, Bernadette?" I whisper out loud. An evil grin creeps up my face. "Yes," I mouth to my reflection. Although I want to leave her essence on my face, she didn't tell me to, so I wash my face and hands and then rinse out my mouth. And then I rewash my hands. I do my best to fix my hair into something other than Monday morning snow day bedhead and then focus on shaving quickly but thoroughly down below.

"Kneel," she says when I emerge, and this time, I see a folded towel laid out at the foot of the bed. I kneel as instructed. "You follow directions well, don't you?"

"I try my best to please you, Ma'am," I say and look up at her. And I mean every word. She has an intoxicating power, especially now in full-Domme mode. I will do whatever she wants. My gaze falls to her breasts. They are the perfect C-cup. I feel like a starving baby bird and want to wrap my lips around her nipples, one, then the other, and back again.

She raises an eyebrow at my gaze and then clears her throat. "And that's all I can ask, isn't it? That you try your best?"

"Yes, Ma'am." I shudder as adrenaline rushes through me. She notices and seems to know that I am hyper-aroused.

"I'm going to try something with you." The purr of her voice has me, one part melting and one part shaking. "You can stop things at any point, little bee. I will check in, and I expect an honest answer. I can't be with you if I can't trust you. Understood?" Her hand is on my chin, forcing me to look up at her.

"Yes, Ma'am. I understand." Now, whether or not I'll be able to tell her to stop is another matter entirely.

She reaches behind me, and I hear the distinct sound of a lighter flicking. My eyes widen. Fire play? Oh, no, no, no. I'm not sure about this. She comes back around so I can see her, and I relax visibly, exhaling my relief. If she sees my nervousness, she doesn't react.

"This is not an ordinary candle, little bee," she says. "It's made of a certain type of wax that doesn't burn as hot as most store-bought candles. It's relatively safe for wax play. I will not touch the fire to your skin at any time. Understood?"

"Yes, Ma'am."

"Keep your hands behind your back. In a moment, I'm going to let a drop of hot wax fall on your thigh. It will hurt. I'll drop another and blow out the candle. You'll then tell me if we can continue."

"Yes, Ma'am. I've never done this, but I'm willing to try."

"That's my good, good girl." Her words make me shudder. Being called a "good girl" always seems to hit me at my core. She leans down and kisses me softly on the lips. The kiss heats up, and I am powerless. I love kissing. She pulls away abruptly and laughs when I groan. "Eyes up and open. I want you to watch."

She raises the white candle and then tips it sideways. I hold my breath as a drip of wax forms at the edge. It falls, and I am completely unprepared and gasp at the white-hot pain. She doesn't hit me with another drip right away because she's watching my reaction closely. The pain transforms into arousal, and I tilt my head back and shudder. She beams at my response.

"Ready?"

"No. Yes."

"Which is it?"

"Yes," I say. I'm ready. I think.

But she doesn't move. Is she hesitating to make me anticipate the tilt of the candle? She clears her throat. She's waiting for me to do something. Oh, God, I never learn, do I?

"Yes, *Ma'am*," I say. "I'm ready."

"Tsk tsk, little bee," she says. "You've earned yourself a third drop."

"I'm sorry, Ma'am," I say. "I know better than to forget to address you properly."

"I would hope so." She tilts the candle and lets one and then another drop fall toward my thigh. I hiss as they hit me, and both hands shoot forward reflexively to guard my skin. I moan through the pain as it turns to pleasure. I move my hands behind my back.

"Color, little bee?" She blows out the candle.

I moan. "I didn't know it would feel like this, Rikki." I moan again, remembering the sensations. She clears her throat, and I know she wants an answer to the question she asked. "Green, Ma'am. Green."

"Thank you," she says. "May we continue with this activity?"

"Oh, yes, Ma'am," I say. "Yes, please. I like this activity very much."

She instructs me to remove the comforter from the bed and to put down a canvas-looking drop cloth. She says it is flame-retardant. Good thinking. She has me lie down in the middle of the bed.

"Remember when you disobeyed me and brought your hands out front?"

"Oh, yes, Ma'am," I say, ashamed. "I'm sorry, Ma'am."

"Don't be. I figured you would do that. It was a way for me to show you why I need to restrain you. We're literally playing with fire, and I can't risk an accident. She reaches under the bed and brings up a strap. She puts my left wrist in a smooth, satiny-feeling fabric and attaches the strap to it. She asks me to pull. It doesn't budge for a moment, but then it slides free. "Will this work?"

"Yes, Ma'am," I say. "Thank you." She sears me with another one of her amazing kisses. God, how I love kissing her.

She secures my other wrist and moves on to both ankles. The lighter flicks. She lights the candle. She watches the flame as it burns and then drips it onto my breast. I gasp. "Hurts so good, Ma'am." She nods and sends another drop my way. I moan on impact.

"Relax, little bee," she says evenly. "You're tensing up."

She's right, I am.

She blows out the candle and then opens a drawer in the bedside stand. Oh, great. A blindfold. My favorite. I hope there are no headphones. I may call yellow. I need to hear her.

She secures the blindfold silently, and I hear the lighter flick on again. "I will not drop wax on your face, head, or neck."

Does that mean all the other parts of my body are fair game? My brain is screaming yellow.

Hot wax hits my other breast, and I writhe and cry out at the pain it brings. The drops come at a faster pace now. I am breathing hard. I am so aroused that I will need her to touch me soon. Wax makes a direct hit to my right nipple, and I hiss. Another direct hit on my left.

"Ma'am, I need –" I moan as another drip of wax hits my stomach.

"Yes, little bee? What is it that you think you need?"

I arch my pelvis up at her words. "Touch me, Ma'am. Please, for the love of everything good, will you touch me?" I cringe at the neediness in my voice.

She responds by leaving a slow trail of hot wax directly down my stomach and abdomen, heading right for my lower region. Oh, crap, she said she would not drop wax on my head or neck. She never mentioned my lower region. Holy shit. Wax hits my mound.

I gasp. Adrenaline surges. "Yellow." I hear no movement from the wax bearer. "Sorry, Ma'am," I say. "Sorry."

"Never be sorry for using your safe words," she says gently. "I expect it, and I'm proud of you."

My pelvis arches on its own. Oh, God, my body needs to be touched, and I tell her. I beg her to touch me. It's unbecoming, but I can't help it.

"Green then?" She asks calmly, ignoring my pleas.

"Yes, yes, yes, yes, yes," I say. "Ma'am," I throw in at the last second.

Another drop hits my mound, and another and another. She moves down in between my legs, and I can feel her breath on me. A drop hits my labia, and I gasp, arching up toward her. Another drop hits. Oh, God, is she going to hit my clit with that hot mess?

"Yellow. Yellow. Yellow," I say again, frustrating the ever-loving life out of myself. I take a moment to catch my breath. "Green, Ma'am."

The wax hits my clit dead center, and I arch up and howl. "Oh, God, Rikki. Holy fuck." My whole body shudders as the wax drips down over my most sensitive parts.

Her lips surround my clit and suck off the wax. She must have blown out the candle because she wraps her hands around both legs and dives into me. She licks my clit, and I buck my hips. I wish I could hold her head where I want it. Before I can even think to ask permission, my orgasm hits me. I arch up, and she stays with me as I flood her face with wetness. She keeps licking and sucking and flicking and pulls a second orgasm out of me.

I wake when I feel the restraints being removed. Rikki crawls into the bed next to me, and I shimmy so I can lay my head on her chest. I hope she doesn't mind that I am covered with wax. Heck, she put it there. Her strong, protective arms go around me, and she kisses the top of my head.

"Best snow day ever," I say. I almost tell her I love her, but I snuggle closer instead.

I'm not sure if I'm asleep and dreaming, but I think I hear her whisper softly, "What, oh, what are you doing to me, little bee?"

Chapter 16
Free

"We should go back to bed."

"Do your work, little bee."

I pout and sigh loud enough for her to hear, but she is unaffected. Of course, she isn't. She knows me pretty well by now. We've been together for over two months, and it's the end of March, the last day of my spring break, so she knows my many moods by this point. Including my somewhat bratty, I-don't-want-to-do-this mood, which is the current one I am in as I sit in front of my computer slogging through school emails. She is on my couch reading a Little Bear story, a loaner from Madison.

"How's your book?" I ask. "Is Little Bear getting flogged by the Domme?" Hint, hint. Maybe we can do that later? Rikki takes me to heights I have never experienced before during impact play. She is truly gifted in that regard. She is becoming my drug.

"Do your work."

Oh, she is relentless, but she has been, oh, so good for me. Being with her makes me feel grounded. And the sex? Holy moly. It's beyond any of my other experiences combined. Except for that foursome orgasm when I passed out at Mistress Ciara's, Rikki can now claim nine of my top ten orgasms. Hands down. Probably because, in addition to her skills, there is a lot of love and affection between us. Yes, I've told her that I love her, and yes, she has said the words back to me. But we're only two months or so into this thing, and I don't want to push.

I mean, we've shared so much with each other. We know all about each other's families. She knows about my mom's losing battle with cancer and that Dad now lives with my brother and sister-in-law back home in California. She doesn't have family nearby. Her father, brother, and sister still live in Wilkes-Barre, Pennsylvania, where she grew up. Her mother died in an incredibly horrific way, and it's clear to me that she still hasn't gotten over it. A whacked-out right-to-lifer put a homemade bomb in a women's health center where Rikki's mother volunteered. Four people were killed. Rikki's mother was one of them. Rikki was about twenty-four at the time. She told me she had become a little lost after that, so at the urging of her father, she agreed to take her Great Aunt Tilda up on the offer to live with and care for her. She speaks about her Aunt Tilda with reverence, but unfortunately, Aunt Tilda passed away several years ago. Rikki decided to stay in Denton Heights, though, having inherited the house and became well-entrenched in the local BDSM scene. And even though she lost her mother twelve years ago, she says it still feels like it was yesterday. She gets many hugs from me whenever I think about that, and she doesn't know why. That's okay. It's my way of letting her know that I love her.

Resigned, I click on the next email in the long list. "Eureka," I say and bolt out of my chair.

Rikki bursts out laughing. "Did you just say, 'eureka'?"

"I got it. I got it!"

"You got what?" Rikki gets up and embraces me from behind. I point to the email message from Dr. Wainwright. "Oh, wow. You got the Foundations course you designed?"

"Yes, yes, yes." I turn and nestle my face into her shoulder. It's one of my favorite places to be. "Oh, this is so great." I turn around and scan the rest of the email. "The Board approved my course as a 7000 level. See? I told them that was the appropriate level. Dr. Wainwright says graduate students are very interested. And, and, and I'm getting extra compensation for teaching a third prep. And, oh, my God, Rikki, look at this. He's giving me a research stipend to develop the course." I grin. "It's because of you that all of this happened."

"Me?"

"Yes. You took an interest when I was frustrated with those graduate students. You listened and challenged me to do something about it. I never would have done that without your push. You are truly the captain of my ship, my love."

She kisses me, and my knees go weak like they always do. I still can't believe that this beautiful woman chose me to be with. Sometimes I think it's a dream.

"We could, uh, go back to my bedroom," I suggest. "I could show you my deepthroating skills again."

She whacks me affectionately on the behind. "As impressive as those skills are, sweetie, we've already showered from this morning's playtime, and you need to finish your work. You have school tomorrow, and I don't want schoolwork hanging over your head this evening. I have other plans for you."

"Oh, really?" I ask. "Does it involve flogging?"

"Nope."

My face falls.

"All good things must wait, little bee." She kisses my forehead. "I want you to sleep at my place tonight."

"Oh?"

She nods again. "Bring work clothes with you. And don't forget shoes this time."

"Yes, Ma'am," I say.

"Do your work." She maneuvers me back into my desk chair.

I spend another half-hour reading and dealing with various work emails, saving some to deal with during the week, making notes on others, and resolving several issues from students. Of course, most of my emails back to the students contain a stand-alone sentence reminding them of my office hours. Too often, they want me to email them the answers. That is not a good way to learn, in my opinion.

Satisfied that my work emails and lesson plans are in good shape, I switch over to my personal emails. Oh, no. There's a message from Jen.

"Eureka!" I shout again and bolt out of my chair, this time knocking it over. "She's moving out. I get my freakin' house back." I read more of the email. "She wants me to come by and pick up April's rent, but they'll be out as of May first. My house is going to be all mine again!"

Rikki is back up and pulls me into a hug. "That is exceptional. I know how much you've been chomping at the bit to get your house back. Does it say why she's moving out early? She's breaking the lease, right?"

I read the entire email. "Oh, this is not good. She says Cassidy has an auto-immune disease and can't take the cold winters anymore. They're moving to Albuquerque, New Mexico." I look back at Rikki. "Wow, that's going to be a big change. Jen says Cassidy got a job transfer." I think about the lease question Rikki asked. "Yes, she's breaking the lease, so I will also collect the lease-breaking fee."

"Maybe you shouldn't be so hasty," Rikki says and picks up my desk chair from the floor. She sits down and pats her lap for me to sit. I love sitting on her lap. Oh, my God.

"What do you mean?" I wrap my arms around her neck and lay my head on her shoulder.

"You told me once before that as long as you give your apartment manager one month's notice, you can break your lease without penalty, right?"

"Yes."

"So, if you give them notice this week," Rikki said, tightening her arms around me, "then that's no penalty for you. Perhaps, in light of Jen and Cassidy's situation, you could extend that same courtesy to them."

I nuzzle into her neck. "You're wonderful," I tell her.

"Why do you say that?"

"I wouldn't have thought of that. Sometimes, I'm too focused on the rules to step back and think what the best approach should be." I look her in the eye and then give her a quick kiss on the lips. "You help me see and understand things, Rikki. And that's one of the million reasons I love you."

She smiles and pulls me into a kiss that heats up quickly. I'm ready to move back into my bedroom, but she has other ideas. "See if we can come by today." She releases me.

Deflated, I say, "Okay." Instead of emailing Jen, I send her a text, and she responds fairly quickly. "Jen said it's okay to stop by this morning. I'm all done with work stuff, so we could go over now."

"I'm looking forward to meeting your ex," Rikki says with a smile and kisses me on the forehead. Oh, no. I don't like the way she said that. I have yet to meet any of her exes. "I would love to see this house of yours finally. But first. On your knees, little bee."

Those five words put together in that exact order always flush me with arousal. Does she know that? She sometimes commands me with those words when I'm in the middle of doing the dishes, grading problem sets, or even when we're watching movies in her apartment. I am to drop everything and go down on my knees immediately. Nothing is more important than pleasing her, she tells me.

She has made me understand that when she wants to use my body, she can and will. One night, she woke me by kissing my face. It was such a gentle way to wake up. She kissed her way down to my mound and planted a kiss there. I hoped she would kiss lower, but she didn't. Instead, she jerked my legs apart, impaled me on a lubed dildo, and fucked me until she came. She tossed the dildo off the side of the bed, lay down, snuggled me tight, and went to sleep. I think it was her way of showing me that I was hers and that she could use me any way and any time she wanted to. I lay awake a while that night, making comparisons to the time Mistress Ciara woke me with a hand over my mouth and a dildo thrusting inside me before I even knew what was happening. At least Rikki had the decency to kiss me awake before using my body. And at least Rikki had the decency to snuggle me afterward. Mistress Ciara did neither. With Mistress Ciara, I felt used. With Rikki, I felt loved.

Rikki tilts my chin up and says, "You will be civil to your ex and her new girlfriend."

"Yes, Ma'am," I say, looking up at her from my knees. I am getting used to looking up at her from this position.

"You will be assertive, not aggressive, and make sure you don't get the short end of the stick. This is business."

"Yes, Ma'am."

"I'll be right there with you, but this is your situation. And you, little bee, are going to handle it."

"Yes, Ma'am. I will. Thank you for the reminders."

She strokes my face with the back of her hand, and I lean into it. Again, this showing of affection is one of the many things I love about her.

"Pants and panties down," she says. "Ass up."

I know better than to question my Domme. I am learning this particular lesson the hard way. One time, I was in her office at the shop, sitting at her ridiculously cluttered desk grading papers, and she told me to strip. I didn't move and asked her if that was a good idea, you know, being in the office with only a thin door separating us from the shop. She almost lost her mind at the fact that I questioned her. I leaped to my feet and stripped. We did not play, though. Instead, she made me relieve Marta in the kitchen as soon as the shop was closed and everyone except Marta was gone. I was mortified that Rikki made me go into the kitchen nude, but Marta didn't bat an eye at my nakedness. I think I was blushing from head to toe in shame.

Apparently, Marta is also in the life, but I didn't know that. Marta went home, and Rikki left me by myself to finish the dishes and clean up the kitchen. I felt utterly alone. And then the real shame set in. Shame that I would question Rikki. After my punishment, we talked, and she told me that I had been on my own too long and I needed to trust that she will take care of me. She says I need to stop questioning her motives and her commands. "Do not question. Just do," she'd said. I need to trust implicitly that she will take care of me. I'm learning the lesson, but probably too slowly for her liking.

Another time, she pulled the blinds down in the shop's front windows and made me clean out the traps underneath all the sinks in the coffee shop, including the bathrooms. Then I did the same in her apartment, all totally in the nude. That job was particularly gnarly. But the message was sinking in that Rikki's commands were not to be questioned and were to be followed immediately and to the letter. And then there was the time I had to iron her clothes. I stood there naked and barefoot in her apartment, ironing for two solid hours, all because I had been engrossed in something on my computer and didn't hear her give me a command. Again, I am learning that her voice is the most important thing to pay attention to.

I unzip my jeans, pull them and my boi shorts down past my knees, and then get on all-fours. I bow my back, as she taught me so that she will have clear and easy access to my body. I didn't think we were going to play anymore this morning, but maybe she's changed her mind. I'm learning never to question what she does.

She walks behind me and strokes my ass cheeks. She pulls them apart, and I feel the cold tip of something enter my vagina. I moan encouragement. She slaps my ass but says nothing. I've learned that particular slap means to stop doing whatever it is I am doing. She pushes the object in, and I can tell that she is inserting a butt plug.

"You're wet," she says. "Very wet. Why?"

"I am in a perpetual state of arousal around you, Ma'am." It is the truth.

"We're going to see your ex," she says and pumps the plug inside me.

"Are you sure you're not aroused at seeing her today?"

"No, Ma'am. She does not arouse me."

"At one point, she did."

"A long time ago, Ma'am."

"Who fucked you this morning?"

"Mmm." I moan as a wave of adrenaline rushes over me. "You did, Ma'am."

"Did I ask permission to fuck you?" Her lips are now close to my ear.

"Oh, God." My pussy floods with arousal. "No, Ma'am. You don't need to. My body is yours to do with what you want."

"Mm hmm," she says, satisfied with my truthful answer. "Did you cum this morning?"

"No, Ma'am."

"And why didn't Bernadette cum this morning?"

"You didn't allow it."

"That's right," she says in a hoarse whisper. "Your body is mine." She pulls the plug out of my vagina, and I hear her open a bottle of lube. The plug pushes at my back door entrance. She applies constant pressure until the ring of muscles resisting her gives way. She slowly slides the plug in my ass and gives it a little twist. "You are to keep this in while we're out and about today. When you feel it, you will be reminded of who put that in your ass. You'll be reminded of who owns you. Is that clear?"

"Yes, Ma'am. Very clear." I want to tell her that I don't need reminding, but again, I've learned to go with her flow. I don't want to end up scraping gum and who knows what else off the bottoms of the tables in the coffee shop again. Honestly, I don't think our imminent visit with my ex threatens her. I think it is more of a possessive power thing.

She slaps my ass one more time and says, "Get up. Get ready to go."

I do as she tells me and pack my school bag, remembering to throw some work clothes together, including a pair of shoes, and we head over to my house. She used a smaller plug, so even though I can obviously feel it, it isn't that uncomfortable.

I'm excited to see my house. I haven't seen it in several months. And the nice thing is that the house is closer to Denton Heights and Rikki's apartment than my current apartment is, so that will be one of the many plusses about moving back in. It's closer to the university, too. Ahh, I can't wait.

We pull up the long dirt driveway, and Rikki taps my forearm. "Bernadette, this property is gorgeous. You said it was an old house, but you didn't say it was a three-story farmhouse. And the neighbors are so far away. How many acres?"

"Five." I am beaming. I have impressed Rikki. Yay. But what I'm not impressed with is the state of my house. It looks worn out and old. It needs love and attention. Maybe a new paint job? Oh, look, the crocuses are blooming. The daffodils and tulips should be next. I look up to see Jen coming out the front door. She walks down the porch steps and waits at the bottom.

"Cassidy's having a bad day," Jen says when we get out of the car. She has an envelope in her hand. "She's inside lying down."

"I'm so sorry to hear that," I say to her. "I didn't know she had that condition." Rikki walks up and stands by my side. She reaches for my hand. "Oh, sorry. Jen, this is my girlfriend, Rikki. Rikki, this is Jen."

"The *ex*-girlfriend," Jen says with a laugh and points to herself.

"Nice to meet you," Rikki says and extends her hand.

My stomach gets a little bit twisty as they touch hands. This is so awkward.

"Good luck with your new chapter that's about to start," Rikki says. "I hear New Mexico is an amazing place."

"Cassidy loves it there. Her uncle is going to let us stay with him until we can find our own place."

"That's great, Jen," I say.

She hands me the envelope. "This is for April's rent. I'm sure we'll be out before the end of the month, though. Our new address is in there, too."

"Thank you," I say. "So, uh, how have *you* been?"

"Hanging in there," she says noncommittally. Yep, that's exactly the way she was during our four-year relationship. I never could get a definitive answer out of her, except when she was opposed to something, and then her opinions came out loud and clear, whether I wanted to hear them or not.

"That's all you can do," Rikki says, "is hang in there." She must have sensed the awkwardness between us and jumped in.

We make small talk for a little while, but Jen never invites us in, probably because she doesn't want to disturb Cassidy. I could have, as the landlord, asked to go in, but I don't press it. I do, however, remind her that damage and cleaning fees will be taken out of the security deposit, and I will return the balance of her deposit within the guidelines of the lease. Business concluded, Rikki and I wish her luck on their move, and we head back to my car.

"Oh, that is so frustrating," I say as I back out onto the road.

"What is?" Rikki asks. She checks her watch, but I know we've got plenty of time before the art show.

"Being so close to my house but not being able to go in."

"Soon, sweetie. Soon." She stretches and says, "I need to make a note of protocol. You didn't know, so you won't be punished this time."

I remain silent, not sure what she's talking about.

"I am your Domme. Correct?"

"Yes, Ma'am. Yes." I keep my eyes on the road.

"Always address me first when introducing me to someone."

"I don't understand."

"You say, 'Rikki, this is Jen.' Not the other way around. Addressing Jen first makes me the lesser."

"You are not the lesser, Ma'am. Never." Oh, God, how quickly I go into submissive mode around her. I've noticed that it happens more and more. "I'm sorry I messed up."

"You're learning," she says and pats my thigh.

I am flooded with relief at her touch. She has forgiven me.

"Let's skip that art show this afternoon."

"Okay," I say and glance at her. "Are you okay? Do you feel sick?"

She pats my thigh again and says, "I'm fine. I just want to check on the shop. It can get pretty busy on Sundays."

"Aha, I knew you were anxious about Mark running things," I say, turning down a side street toward Denton Heights.

"Are you disappointed?" she asks.

"Not at all," I say honestly. "I'm just thrown off a little."

"By what?"

"You and Jen, you know, meeting."

She chuckles. It's her "Oh, you silly girl" chuckle. "It went fine."

"I know, but it was still weird."

We drive in silence for a while, and I think maybe I'll get a coffee and practice for tomorrow evening's dart tourney while Rikki checks on the shop. Seamus successfully recruited me for his team. Someone quit, so he replaced her with me. I'm a regular now, and I love it.

I find a parking spot down the street, and we walk to the shop. I pause at the overgrown lot next to the shop and say, "This would make a good parking lot, Rikki."

"Don't I know it," she says. "I, uh, haven't been able to find the owner." She shrugs. "One day, I'll dig deep enough and get hold of them."

I nod, thinking that maybe I should help her with that. Perhaps I'll do that as a side project. And then I can surprise her. We head to the side entrance to her office.

"I want to hit the bathroom before I go in the shop," she says. "Let's go upstairs." She gestures for me to go first.

"Okay." I have my school bag in one hand, but I pick up the lone pair of shoes on the landing with the other. I have been pretty successful training Rikki never to leave a room empty-handed, and the trip-hazard pile of shoes and the overgrown coat hooks are now managed to my satisfaction. Now, if she'll only let me clean her office, especially that cluttered desk. I smile. Yes, I am turning into a service sub. It suits me.

I head up the stairs and turn the knob. It's unlocked. Again. I turn to face her and say, "You know, Rikki, you really should keep this door—"

"Surprise!" a thousand people yell at once. I jump and fall back against Rikki. She laughs and holds me tight before nudging me inside.

Shasti and Madison greet me at the door. Jaleesa is here standing with a woman who must be her girlfriend, Tina, the woman she cages regularly. Brittany is here, too. She smiles at me, and I'm so glad I cleared up my misunderstanding with her. Marta winks at me, which somehow calms me minutely. There are many men and women from the darts club and several people I don't know, including a few scantily clad men and women.

I turn and say in a small voice, "Rikki, what's happening?"

"It's okay, Bernadette," she says in a volume meant for my ears only. I am so confused. What is she doing? Why are all these people here? Madison walks over and presents Rikki with a pillow with something on it.

"Rikki, what's happening?" I ask her again. My heart is pounding.

It's a collar. Rikki takes it off the pillow, and then Madison reaches for my bag and the shoes I'm still holding and relieves me of them. She places them off to the side and backs away.

"Bernadette," Rikki says again, "would you do me the honor of wearing my collar?"

Tears spring to my eyes immediately. "Me? You're collaring *me*?"

She nods, and I hear a series of "Awws" and "Oh, she didn't know" go up in the room.

"Yes, yes, yes," I say before she can change her mind. I fall on my hands and knees in front of her and lean forward to kiss her feet. I am sobbing and barely aware of the people witnessing my obeisance.

Rikki puts a hand on my shoulder and pulls me back up to a kneeling position. I am shocked to see her blinking back a sheen of tears. "I love you, little bee," she says softly as if she only wants me to hear. The leather collar she holds in her hands is gorgeous. It's about an inch wide and has been dyed green and purple—our colors. "Bernadette," she says a bit louder so all can hear, "I have been smitten with you since the very first moment we met at Rocco's diner. It didn't take long before I fell for you."

"About three minutes," Shasti says knowingly, causing the group to chuckle.

"Bernadette," Rikki continues. "You are the perfect blend of feminine masculinity. Something that turns me on mightily, I've discovered." The group chuckles at her intimate confession.

I know I shouldn't interrupt, but I can't help it. "Submissives are incredibly vulnerable," I say. "But you've always treated me with respect and not just a piece of meat." The group laughs again. "You've made it a point to get to know me for me. The real me. All my idiosyncrasies. My dreams. My fears." I should stop talking, but I don't. "You never demean me. You never humiliate me publicly or privately. Except maybe that one time." The group laughs again politely. "Correct me? Yes. Discipline me? Um, yes, on many occasions." I reach toward her face but can't reach. "And I have deserved the corrections every time. I trust you implicitly because you make me think about my actions. No matter what, I feel safe and protected with you. Something I haven't felt in a long time.

"Being with you, Rikki has made me a better person. I am more comfortable in my own skin these days. I'm learning how to stand up to opposition, speak my truth, and not get railroaded into doing something I don't want to do. You're teaching me that I am stronger than I ever knew." I pause for a moment, gathering my courage to say, "Rikki, your collar is a clear sign of ownership and control, and I welcome it. Because in my submission to you, I have never felt more free."

I am surprised when I hear a few people sniffling. Oh, gosh. I had kind of forgotten there was an audience.

"You are amazing, little bee." Rikki reaches around my head and places the collar on me. Her fingers work at the buckle, and she secures it around my neck. I run my fingers over the leather. Please kiss me, my eyes plead. She leans down and does just that. She kisses me as if no one is witnessing our intimate moment.

A cheer goes up, and applause breaks out in the apartment. I hide my face in the swell of her neck and burst into tears again.

"Shh, shh, little bee," Rikki says low so only I can hear. She strokes my hair. "You're okay."

"I know. This is all just so," I gesture to the collar and the friends witnessing the event, "overwhelming. I didn't know you were even thinking about collaring me."

"Since the moment I met you," she says and clips a leash on my new collar. She tugs on it and pulls me into a searing kiss.

Chapter 17
Becoming Bernadette

I run my fingers along my new collar and caress the D-ring in the front. I'm standing in front of the window watching the sharp blue March sky, stealing a moment from the already over two-hour celebration. I need a moment to try and make sense of what just happened.

Thank goodness Rikki let me take out that butt plug after about an hour into the party. Otherwise, I'd be one uncomfortable newly collared sub. Collared. Wow. To Rikki. My life is changing for real, isn't it? I mean, I was already committed to her, but this collar is a tangible way to remind me of that. To remind me that my one goal as her submissive is to fulfill her needs and desires and to obey her commands and requests. This is what I said yes to. I feel I've already been doing that. And she has been fulfilling my needs, too. We've had several conversations about Rikki's beliefs about collaring and how seriously she takes it, but I didn't think we were at that stage yet. And I certainly didn't think something like this was going to happen today.

I take a discrete selfie of the collar around my neck and send it off to Lisa. "Guess what? The hot redhead collared me today. I'll fill you in when I can. Tomorrow probably. Just know that I am very happy." I hear the ding of a return text within seconds. It has to be her. I can only imagine how exciting my first-ever *Kinks* friend is for me. I decide to read it later and tuck my phone into my pocket.

The apartment is small, so I can't help but overhear people talking about me.

"They are going to be such a power couple," someone says.

"Absolutely. And Bernadette is one of those pretty women who doesn't know they are. You know what I mean?"

"Exactly. She doesn't even wear makeup."

"She doesn't need to. Jaleesa herself did the hair, you know. It's a good style for her. Really brings out her feminine features."

"I know. Those cheekbones are to die for."

"And those dimples. Oh, my God."

"Right? And she's, like, a real person. Not the usual kind that goes after Rikki."

"Rikki found a gem in plain sight."

A third person groans and says, "And I can't believe she's so friggin' good at darts."

"She's a machine," the first speaker says.

My face is flaming hot, but I can't help the grin creeping up my face at the darts comments.

"She is going to kick my ass in tomorrow night's tournament."

"No kidding. You just have to last longer than seven minutes. That's the record so far."

My eyes grow wide. I didn't know people had taken that much interest in how I played. My face burns with embarrassment.

I jump when Madison appears at my side. "I knew Rikki was going to collar you, Professor."

"You did?" I turn toward her, my back now to the window.

"Yep. The minute I found out you were a sub and not a Domme," she gushes. "At Rocco's. I predicted it in January. Ask Mistress."

"I believe you," I say with a chuckle. "Why didn't you let *me* know?"

"You, uh, went for Daddy Vic, and at first I thought that was okay because, you know, Daddy Vic." She says it in a conspiratorial way and waggles her eyebrows.

I clear my throat. Daddy Vic is long gone from my memory. "To be fair, kiddo, I thought Rikki and Brittany were together."

"I know. Mistress told me you thought that." She had a bit of a scowl on her face as if that were the most preposterous thing she'd ever heard of.

"You know what else?" I say to her.

"What?"

"It's all your fault."

"What is?" Her confused expression is priceless.

"If you hadn't invited me to the friends' brunch, then I wouldn't have met Rikki."

She inhales sharply. "It *is* my fault!" She runs away, calling for her Mistress. "Mistress, guess what? Guess what?"

I laugh and shake my head at her antics, and then one of the male serving submissives wearing only a leather thong walks up to me with a tray. I reach for a mini-quiche and a napkin. The server bows his head to me and says, "Congratulations, Miss."

"Thank you. Um, but you shouldn't call me Miss, I don't think. I'm just a sub."

"Miss, if I may. You just got collared by Rikki Carmichael, one of the most beloved and powerful Dommes in this area. You will be called 'Miss' by many of us."

"Oh, gosh." I run a thumb across the side of my collar. It is comforting. "Um, thanks for letting me know."

"Yes, Miss." He genuflects and heads to the next guest.

My stomach is doing flips now, and again, I wonder what I've gotten myself into. I mean, seriously, "What am I becoming?" I murmur under my breath. "I'm becoming –"

"Bernadette!" Rikki calls for me by the front door.

I hustle over to her. The guests are starting to leave. I appreciate them being here, but I am getting tired. I follow Rikki's lead and thank each person for their good wishes. I make sure I remember their names because I will probably be seeing a lot of these people from now on, and I don't want to embarrass Rikki.

Rikki has her arm around my waist. I'm not sure if it's a possessive gesture or if she is just holding me up. Both probably. Once everyone is gone, she walks over and flops down on the bed. "Come lay with me."

I am quiet as I lay down next to her.

"You're overwhelmed," she says simply.

"How did you know?"

"This was a lot today." She rolls me over and spoons me from behind. "I should have prepared you better. I'm sorry."

"No, Rikki." I pet the arm holding me. "This was wonderful. And in time, I'll come to understand what it means to be collared to you."

"What do you think it means?"

"That you made a public commitment to me. And by accepting your collar, I made the same commitment to you." Oh, God, I am so sleepy. My eyes are closing. Did Rikki ask me something? "Mmm?" I say.

She chuckles and whispers, "We'll finish this later. Sleep now, little bee."

When I awaken, she is still lying next to me, but we are now face to face. She smiles. "Hello, collared submissive."

"Hi." I smile and blink my eyes a few times, trying to wake up. "How long did I sleep?"

"Not long." She brushes the hair out of my eyes. "About an hour."

"Oh, no," I sit up. "I'm so sorry. I need to clean up."

"Nope, nope, nope," Rikki says and slows my forward motion. "Jaleesa's subs – you know, the practically naked people here? They cleaned up while we were saying goodbye to everyone."

"She has that many subs?"

Rikki chuckles. "There is so much for you to learn, little bee. Jaleesa is a powerful and popular Domme."

"Wow. Does she have them all locked up in cages?"

Rikki laughs again. "I love you, little bee. And, no, she doesn't have all of them locked up. Just a few."

My jaw drops open. I can't tell if she's teasing me or not.

"C'mon, get up, collared girl," Rikki says. "Go get freshened up." She points to the bathroom. "Come out wearing only two things. That collar and a smile."

I wash up knowing that when she says, 'freshen up,' it means I am to clean all of my pieces and parts thoroughly and shave myself smooth. I had to write an essay one time as a punishment when I came out less than satisfactory. I hadn't shaved well enough. She was not pleased. All play stopped, and my essay about the history of shaving private parts became the priority. I discovered that pubic lice in the 1400s, bikinis in the 1940s, and miniskirts in the 1960s were the most likely culprits. I grunt at the memory as I toss my clothes in the hamper. I'll need to start a load tomorrow before I head out to school. Keeping on top of her laundry has become one of my many responsibilities.

When I come out of the bathroom, I am shocked at what I see. Rikki has strung up twinkling lights all around the apartment. Wait, come to think of it, the lights were there during the party but hadn't been turned on. This whole day has been a whirlwind of emotions for me ever since Rikki woke me this morning to have anal sex. I kind of had anxious flashbacks to Daddy Vic's anal week while she used me, but I didn't let on.

"So pretty, Rikki," I say, gesturing to the lights. There is a pillow on the floor at the foot of the bed. She points to it with two fingers. Lately, she's been using hand signals instead of verbal commands. It is clear what she wants, and I kneel. Kneeling also means not talking. It's funny how Dommes like silent subs. I will have to ask her later where the new pillow came from.

Rikki finds one of my hands and holds it. "Bernadette, there are three basic tenants to our relationship. Can you tell them to me?"

"Yes, Ma'am," I say. She has subtly and not-so-subtly drilled them into my head in the two and a half months we've been together. "Consent, honesty, and communication."

She points to a plaque hanging above the kitchenette with those three words on it. How long has that been there, and why haven't I seen it?

"I hung this plaque to remind both of us. If I break one of these rules, I will admit it and make amends. If you break one, then we'll have a discussion, and a punishment will soon follow."

"Yes, Ma'am," I say. "Have I broken –"

"No, you have not broken any of these rules that I know of, but I want to make sure you understand that I have rules in place for you, for me, and both of us for a reason. We have established good trust so far, I think." I nod. It's true. I have no reason not to trust her. "The only reason I will punish you is if I feel you have a lesson to learn. You have put faith and trust in me, and I promise to follow through, guide you, and mold you so that we can be the best individually and as partners. Understood?"

"Oh, yes, Ma'am," I say. My heart feels so full. It's as if she's pumping her very essence into my body with her words and the hand that she's still holding.

"As you've already experienced, I will use your body for my own needs. I also know and understand that you, my little bee, have needs as well. Not only sexual needs but emotional and even intellectual." She chuckles. "Yes, you have a real hunger for intellectual satisfaction, my love. It is completely refreshing, I must say."

I feel my face flush. Her eyes have never left mine. She never once looks away as if searching for words or ideas. The words are right there for her as she conveys her thoughts to me. It is uncanny how focused on me she is. She's always done this, and it is only at this very moment that I understand how unique and amazing she is.

"And," she continues, "you completely seem to understand that *I* also have emotional and intellectual needs. Most of my past partners have not understood that. That's what makes you so special and so well-suited to me. You follow instructions well, learn quickly, and are by no means passive in this relationship. You are like no one I've ever met before, Bernadette. I can understand why Madison thought you were a Domme at first. You are strong and confident in many areas of your life. Your consensual submission to me shows that you are strong enough to let me guide and protect you in the places where you are not strong and confident. Please understand that you never have to be alone with something that is difficult for you."

I can't help the tears welling up in my eyes. "Thank you, Rikki. I love you, you know."

Her face softens, and she strokes my cheek. "I know, little bee. I love you, too." Something clouds over her face, and she says, "Some say I collared you too soon. I wanted you to know that. Some are looking for us to fail – looking for *me* to fail."

"You?" I blurt. "Why?" My protective instincts are up.

"Another day, little bee. Another day."

"Yes, Ma'am." I can't think of a single reason why anyone would want to hurt Rikki.

"Do you trust me to take care of you?"

"Yes." I reach up and touch my new collar.

"And I trust you to take care of me," she says, her voice choked with emotion. She leans in and kisses me. It turns fervent instantly, and my arms go up around her.

She pulls back with a slight moan. "On the bed," she says. "Face up." I comply immediately, as I've been trained to do. "I'm tying you down for your own good, little bee." She raises an eyebrow to let me know she is serious. She makes quick work of it, and I cannot close my legs or do much of anything with my arms. From past experiences, I know that I can break free if I want or need to.

Rikki unties her robe and discards it. She climbs up and straddles my hips. Her sex is wet against my skin, and I moan my appreciation. She leans down and catches her weight on her hands. Her kiss is serious and heats up quickly. I moan into our combined passion but groan when her lips leave mine. She kisses the spot behind my earlobe. She knows by now this makes me shiver. But then she leaves much too quickly and kisses her way down my right arm. She stops at the inside of my elbow – I learned that it's called the elbow pit – and she licks that area. She places her entire mouth over the spot and sucks lightly while she licks.

Arousal shudders through me. "Rikki," I say. "Oh, my God. You're …" My head falls back, and I arch my pelvis as another wave of arousal hits my body. Who knew this was such an erogenous zone?

"Eyes on me, love."

I've been corrected. I will do better.

"I am the source of your pleasure, Bernadette," she says.

"Yes, Ma'am." I moan as she goes back to sucking my elbow pit.

She moves on and makes her way down my body. She reaches for something on the bedside table and holds up a handful of clothespins for me to see. "Mmm," I say, part moan and part acknowledgment. She peaks my nipples and encloses them gently with the clips. I writhe as the pain hits me, but then becomes pleasurable. She attaches several more clips to my breasts and then flicks them all. I watch her the entire time. *She* is the one inflicting this pain. *She* is also the one causing this pleasure.

She leaves my upper body and begins massaging my feet, something she's had me do for her on many occasions while she's watching television, reading a book, or in her office making business calls. I never realized how good it feels. "Rikki, this is wonderful," I say. "Thank you."

"I want you to feel good, little bee. It's a special day."

"Mmm, you always make me feel good."

She moves up my calves, kissing her way up to my inner thighs. She commands me to lift my pelvis and then places a pillow underneath me. She spreads my ass cheeks, and then I feel the flat of her tongue licking my rosebud, as she calls it.

"Mmm," I moan again. She is killing me with sensation.

She looks up from her ministrations, and I smile at her through half-lidded eyes. She smiles back and goes back to licking me. She stays there a long time, and I think I can orgasm from this. A layered sheen of arousal travels over my entire body. I hear myself moaning.

"Good girl," Rikki says. "Very good. Ride the feeling."

Her voice is my anchor, mainly because I am so focused on watching her as she requires.

She hardens her tongue and penetrates me. I moan in response. She pushes in as far as she can and fucks my tiny hole with her tongue.

"Oh, oh," I am in heaven.

She pulls out and sucks on my inner thigh for a while. I smile. There will be bruising there. She is leaving her mark. Claiming me. I arch my pelvis, instinctively requesting her to touch me there.

She moves on to nibble on my outer labia, and another wave of arousal hits me. She lifts her head, "Ride it, Bernadette. Ride it, my good girl. Do not cum without permission."

"Oh, God," I say. She has never had this rule. Why now? "Yes, Ma'am," I say breathlessly.

Her fingers enter my vagina and pump me slowly. "Good girl."

Her words make me shudder. I am floating on an ocean of stimulation. She is keeping me there knowingly. "Rikki," I say and draw out the last vowel of her name. It needs no response, and she doesn't give one.

She licks and nibbles around my entire pussy as she pumps me. Her fingers rake over my G-spot and send stars to my eyes. I spread my legs wider.

"Yes, that's it, my good girl."

Her words make me tremble. "Your good girl," I echo and moan.

She finally swipes her tongue over my clit, and I inhale sharply. "Yes, Ma'am. Yes."

She rakes her tongue through my labia and then pulls my clit in her mouth and sucks me. Her fingers continue to push in and out. My body shakes, and I am no longer in control of it.

"Hang on longer," she says. "That's my good girl."

"Rikki, please God, let me cum." Another wave makes my entire body shudder out of control. "I have to –"

"I'm going to count down from ten now," she interrupts. "When I get to one, I will tell you to cum. And you will. Isn't that right, my good girl?"

I moan my answer.

She raises an eyebrow at me. She wants actual words.

"Yes, yes, yes, Ma'am. I understand." I am riding the crest of sensations; how can I think straight right now?

She pulls her fingers out of me, making me cry out at their loss. She kisses my clit and then pulls away. She's not touching me anymore, anywhere. "Rikki," I cry. "Please, please, please." Oh, my God, I am a mess.

"Ten," she says while I die. "Nine," she says after an hour. "Eight."

I moan and almost close my eyes but don't. "Seven." She is the source of this ecstasy. "Six." I must focus on her. "Five."

"Please, please, please."

"Four." My pelvis arches on its own. "Three." I need her to touch me. "Two."

"Touch me, Rikki. Touch me."

"One! Cum for me, good girl," she urges.

My entire body seizes.

"Cum now!"

Her words rip the orgasm from me. I scream as it thunders through my entire body. My pussy spasms. My whole body spasms, and I writhe on the bed, restrained by her straps. Restrained by *her* will. Wave after wave hits me. I can't control anything. I gasp for air as I shudder and then, impossibly, lie still.

"Yes, yes, yes," Rikki says and climbs on the bed. She releases the straps, holding my arms, and pulls me into a hug. I turn and kiss her hard. I'm probably bruising her mouth, but she doesn't seem to care. Another wave hits me, and I moan into her mouth. I've barely had a moment to recover, and she straddles my hips. She thrusts against my hip bone. She finds my hand, shoves two, then three of my fingers inside herself, and grabs my wrist. She fucks herself with my hand and, in seconds, cries out as she cums. Her walls squeeze my fingers tight.

"Oh, Bernadette, I fucking love you." She continues fucking my fingers until she sighs and her breathing slows down. She lies by my side again, takes my fingers, and places them in my mouth to suck.

"Mmm," I moan. "My Goddess," I say around the fingers. I pull them out of my mouth and splay her hand over my heart. "My Mistress. My Queen. My Lover. My Dominant, Owner, Possessor, Counselor, Keeper. My Friend." I look her in the eye and say, "You are my everything. I am proud to wear your collar, Rikki. I am proud to serve you. And …"

"And what?"

"I'm proud to be your whore," I whisper and feel my entire body flush with embarrassment.

She kisses my forehead gently.

"Rikki," I say. I need her to understand. "I am so fulfilled. When I got scared about what I was becoming, you made me realize that I was becoming my truest self."

"You were becoming Bernadette, weren't you?"

I smile and snuggle into her open arms.

"Ma'am?"

"Mmm?" she says, rocking me gently.

"Did I see a flogger and a paddle laid out in the bathroom?"

"Mm, hmm. That will be your one-day anniversary gift tomorrow evening."

"Mmm," I moan and fall asleep, the happiest sub in Denton Heights.

~~~ The End ~~~

Newsletter Signup

Sign up for Danielle Grainger's newsletter to stay on top of new releases. She also likes to provide recommendations for books to read (other than her own, of course).

Sign Up Here:

https://mailchi.mp/32c278368547/danielle-grainger-newsletter

Reviews

Reviews help get my books into the hands of readers who enjoy books like mine. It's often difficult for readers of certain, err, tastes to find books they enjoy. Would you consider writing a review? Let's get the word out. Thank you for at least thinking about it.

About the Author
Danielle Grainger

Dani is an instructor who currently resides in the southeastern USA and has several pampered fur babies. She has always been an avid reader and ventured into writing after reading several novels she felt didn't accurately represent the BDSM lifestyle. With so many rampant misconceptions, she took a chance and crafted admittedly idealized versions of possible experiences. Dani hopes not only to entertain her readers but to enlighten and educate them as well.

Dani's Amazon Author Page:

www.amazon.com/stores/Danielle-Grainger

Dani's Facebook:

facebook.com/danielle.grainger.7777

Dani's Instagram:

DaniGrainger84

Dani's Goodreads Page:

www.goodreads.com/author/show/19699760.Danielle_Grainger

Books by Danielle Grainger

<u>THE DENTON HEIGHTS SERIES</u>

The Denton Heights Series is the series that comes BEFORE the Bernadette Series. This group of books tells the stories of the beloved characters who populate the Bernadette Series world and live the BDSM lifestyle. We learn more about the origin stories of Madison and Shasti; Jaleesa, Tina, Harriet, Dana, DeShawn, and Kari; Rowena and Minjung; and Rikki. Victoria (AKA Daddy Vic), Lydia, and Brittany also feature in this series. The Denton Heights Series is basically the "Prequel Series" to the Bernadette Series.

Under Her Wing (Denton Heights Book 1)
(The Shasti and Madison Story)
An age-gap lesbian MD/lg erotic romance with consensual light BDSM.

*** 2023 Finalist in the Golden Crown Literary Society Awards ***

Madison Kim finds herself on a bus headed to Denton Heights, Ohio, a suburb of Cincinnati. Her mother sent her there without notice to care for an elderly Korean woman Madison had never met. Madison is twenty-two-and-three-quarters years old and has a high school diploma, but she isn't smart enough to go to college...so they tell her. Now, she spends her time caring for Mrs. Park, going to the beloved Cincinnati Zoo, and watching movies on her outdated phone. She's not really sure why she's there, but she's taking it day by day. Then, she meets strong, nurturing Miss Shasti at a tea dance.

Shasti Balakrishnan has been looking for someone to call hers for more years than she cares to count. She wants a woman to love and care for in a nurturing Mommy Domme/*little-girl* scenario. She's thirty-two and already a partner in a thriving medical clinic in Denton Heights, but truth be told — she's lonely. She thought she'd found a companion in Amber back in D.C., but that fizzled out once they realized they weren't what each other wanted—or needed. And then she meets adorably precocious Madison at a tea dance.

ISBN: 978-1-953734-10-5 (e-Book)
ISBN: 978-1-953734-13-6 (Paperback)

In Her Cage (Denton Heights Book 2)
(The Jaleesa and Tina Story)
A lesbian interracial erotic romance with consensual light BDSM aspects.

Jaleesa Whitmore is a lesbian Domme in and out of fast relationships fueled by sex. She didn't understand addiction. Not yet, anyway. Although she had almost one full year sober, she was done with it. She was moments from heading down the familiar road of drinking that always made her feel good and filled that void. She was about to get her life back on its old track when a fateful encounter with a stranger, who would become a trusted friend, halted her downslide. She didn't know it then, but this encounter would not only lead her to a series of events and people that would change how she looked at life but how she approached it.

Tina Jenkins likes women but is asexual and afraid to try for another relationship. She does understand addiction. Just shy of eleven years clean of her opioid addiction following a dental procedure right out of high school, her parents carefully constructed and monitored everything in her world. It didn't matter that she was thirty-one years old and still living in the pink bedroom in her parents' house. It didn't matter that her mother now had to work from home, and her parents had to track her location and do routine searches of her bag, car, computer, phone, and room. None of it mattered because she was clean.

And then asexual Tina meets promiscuous Jaleesa. And everything changed for both of them.

ISBN: 978-1-953734-28-0 (e-Book)
ISBN: 978-1-953734-29-7 (Paperback)

Within Her Grasp (Denton Heights Book 3)
(The Marta and Shanice Story)
A lesbian age gap interracial erotic romance with consensual light BDSM
aspects.

"Within Her Grasp" is an age-gap interracial lesbian romance that tells the tale of two women who had settled for unhappy lives. And then they meet.

White, thirty-something Marta Ingersoll was done with people. She just wanted to be left alone at work and at home, thank you. Her inside cat and the outside stray were all she needed. And her sister, Nora, too, of course. But that was it. And then, one fateful afternoon, her instincts to save a woman in obvious distress kicked in, and her life was shoved onto a strange new course.

Black, twenty-something Shanice Ward never got a break. Life had thrown challenge after challenge at the young woman, and this latest thing was too much, but it wouldn't stop. Woken up from a sound sleep by someone trying to remove her clothing, she shrieked for him to leave her alone. He didn't, but then, the most amazing thing happened. She discovered that superheroes were real, and one had just flown into her room to save her, and her life was shoved onto a strange new course.

ISBN: 978-1-953734-30-3 (e-Book)
ISBN: 978-1-953734-31-0 (Paperback)

By Her Command (Denton Heights Book 4)
(The Rowena and Minjung Story)
A lesbian interracial erotic romance with consensual BDSM aspects.

"By Her Command" is an erotic interracial lesbian romance containing consensual aspects of BDSM. It finds Rowena Tate in need of a submissive who can also manage her household. It's also the tale of Minjung Lee, who is desperate to find a Domme so she won't find herself homeless again. Trust does not come easily for either of them.

Rowena is a white Domme in her late thirties. Through experience, she has come to believe that most, if not all, submissives are selfish creatures who only want what she can provide without considering the person behind the flogger and the paycheck.

Minjung is an East Asian submissive in her mid-thirties. Through experience, she has come to believe that most, if not all, Dominants are selfish creatures who go well beyond contracted limits because there is no one to tell them not to.

Despite their reservations, both are told by members of the Denton Heights BDSM community that they are a good match and lucky to have found each other. Rowena isn't so sure. Neither is Minjung. Time will tell, won't it?

ISBN: 978-1-953734-32-7 (e-Book)
ISBN: 978-1-953734-33-4 (Paperback)

Toward Her Passion (Denton Heights Book 5)
(A Rikki Carmichael Story)
A lesbian erotic reminiscence with consensual BDSM aspects

Rikki Carmichael is strong, stoic, and in charge. She does *not* need help from anyone. She can navigate her own life, thank you very much, and resents her friends' efforts to give her charity. She doesn't take charity; she gives it. Financial troubles threaten to topple her coffee shop business, her livelihood, and her sense of self-worth. Abruptly single and oddly uninterested in finding a new relationship, be it a long-term life partner or a short-term lover, she finds herself reminiscing about past loves and relationships: Hard Eileen, fun Emily, newbie Sarah, and young Jessica.

The anniversary of her mother's death all those years ago sends her into another bout of 'deep downs,' the code words her mother used for Rikki's bouts with depression growing up. Her bestie, Shasti, advises her to make room for someone, a new lover, or a life partner. Shasti wants Rikki to send a message to the universe that she is ready to receive someone into her life. And, lo and behold, in walks Esme, a blonde bombshell customer at the coffee shop. Rikki's hopes are lifted...until they aren't. With no biological family left to lean on, Rikki has to find the strength to become vulnerable and ask for help. Easier said than done. It's much easier to counsel others than to ask for help for herself. She discovers, however, that asking for help is where real strength lies.

ISBN: 978-1-953734-40-2 (e-Book)
ISBN: 978-1-953734-41-9 (Paperback

THE BERNADETTE SERIES

Dr. Bernadette Garneau holds a Ph.D. in Mathematics and has just gotten out of a four-year relationship. Shortly after the breakup, she began an exploration of her repressed sexual desires. One message from a beautiful and powerful online Mistress and Bernadette leaps into the world of BDSM. The Mistress takes charge, and Bernadette reels in the heady power this stranger has over her. She has gotten a taste of the life, and she wants more. She needs more. Several online and in-person experiences with BDSM and Power Exchange have led to cravings she doesn't quite understand. A brief sexual exchange with an online Goddess unleashes an incredible pain-to-pleasure connection that she hadn't understood before. As she sifts through the posers and one-night stands, she homes in on what her submissive nature needs from a Domme. The Bernadette Series follows Bernadette's journey into the world of BDSM and her search for love and sexual satisfaction. As she said, "I want a monogamous partner who wants to not only love and nurture me but who also wants to drape me over her lovely couch and have her way with me."

Wrecking Bernadette
(Book One in the Bernadette Series)
A lesbian's exploration of her sexuality with consensual aspects of BDSM.

Dr. Bernadette Garneau holds a Ph.D. in Mathematics and has been out of a four-year relationship for four months. One good thing about breaking up is that Bernadette is free to explore her repressed sexual desires. One message from a beautiful and powerful online Mistress, and Bernadette leaps into the world of BDSM. Mistress Ciara takes charge, and Bernadette reels in the heady power this stranger has over her. She has gotten a taste of the *life*, and she wants more. She *needs* more.

ISBN: 978-1-953734-00-6 (e-Book)
ISBN: 978-1-953734-14-3 (Paperback)

(S)mothering Bernadette
(Book Two in the Bernadette Series)
A lesbian's continuing exploration of her sexuality with aspects of BDSM.

Dr. Bernadette Garneau's universe is pushing her toward change. Her initial experiences with BDSM and Power Exchange have led to cravings she doesn't quite understand. A brief sexual exchange with an online Goddess unleashes an incredible pain-to-pleasure connection she hadn't understood until that encounter. But after sleeping on it, she clearly understands that this Goddess would never be the long-term relationship she sought.

Disappointed, she wonders if she should just give up and move back to California to be closer to her family. That is until she meets Mama_Luvs, an online Mommy Domme. The woman is nurturing yet stern from the start and is just ... perfect. And then Mama_Luvs wants to meet. Starry-eyed Bernadette packs for a New Year's Eve weekend, hoping that this time she's found *the one* – the one who wants to love and nurture her but who also wants to drape her over a couch and have her way with her.

ISBN: 978-1-953734-01-3 (e-Book)
ISBN: 978-1-953734-15-0 (Paperback)

Becoming Bernadette
(Book Three in the Bernadette Series)
A lesbian erotic romance with light consensual BDSM aspects.

University professor Dr. Bernadette Garneau has fallen in love with the world of BDSM. She has a nascent interest in the pain-to-pleasure connection, but she has yet to find partners interested in nurturing the soul within her body that they play with. Admittedly, she's had incredible sexual encounters with experienced Dommes, but all of them left her feeling cold for whatever reason. Most of them simply wanted a sadistic roll in the hay. Bernadette wants a strong Domme who will love and nurture her before flogging her on a St. Andrew's cross and afterward when her body is spent.

One afternoon, she finally musters the courage to venture out and meet some new friends in the local BDSM community. In walks a tall, handsome butch woman with fantastic hair and a confident stride. When this woman asks Bernadette, "Are you collared," Bernadette truthfully answers, "No," and accepts a dinner invitation for that very evening. She is walking on stars when she gets home at 2 a.m. after an ethereal sexual liaison. On the one hand, she wonders who she is becoming – she's never been this promiscuous. And on the other hand, she wonders if this strong butch woman could finally be the Domme of her dreams.

ISBN: 978-1-953734-02-0 (e-Book)
ISBN: 978-1-953734-12-9 (Paperback)

Desiring Bernadette
(Book Four in the Bernadette Series)
A lesbian erotic romance with light consensual BDSM aspects.

*** 2022 Finalist in the Golden Crown Literary Society Awards ***

Rikki Carmichael finally feels that deep D/s relationship she has been craving since her Aunt Tilda introduced her to *the life*. She embraced her dominant side early on, but finding a suitable submissive woman who wanted more than a quick roll in the dungeon proved elusive. That is until Professor Bernadette Garneau arrived on the scene. Now collared and committed to Rikki, will Bernadette prove to be different, or will she turn out like all the others — fickle and full of lies and deception?

And will this perfect sub stay with her when she realizes Rikki's ship is sinking? She'd almost lost the coffee shop she owns when creditors came knocking down her door en masse, seeking payment for debts that weren't hers. Rikki managed to keep her staff and most of her friends in the dark about it, but she has not been able to get out from under it. With high stakes all around, Rikki looks for the peace she is seeking within her relationship with Bernadette. If this one fails, it may be time to leave the life entirely and go live in a cabin somewhere isolated in the woods. But buying a cabin takes money — money she just doesn't have.

ISBN: 978-1-953734-03-7 (e-Book)
ISBN: 978-1-953734-09-9 (Paperback)

<u>Loving Bernadette</u>
(Book Five in the Bernadette Series)
A lesbian erotic romance with light consensual BDSM aspects.

Bernadette Garneau, a beloved professor of mathematics, is a natural submissive. She likes structure and rules and finally found a way of life and a woman who would provide those things for her. The BDSM community she stumbled upon in Denton Heights, Ohio, is where she found Rikki Carmichael, now her dominant partner and fiancée. Rikki is everything she's dreamed of. Yes, Bernadette found the captain of her ship. With Rikki's support and guidance, maybe other parts of her life can finally come together, too – like the respect she deserves but hasn't gotten at the university. Why won't anyone see that she deserves to teach those upper-level courses? And to move out of her closet of an office? What do they know that she does not?

Rikki Carmichael, the respected owner of Rikki's Coffee Shop in town, has finally found the woman of her dreams in super-smart and super-real Bernadette Garneau. Bernadette is a submissive who instinctively knows how to take care of Rikki and accepts Rikki's need to be in charge. Bernadette is the first submissive Rikki's ever had that wasn't solely out for her own gain. Once Rikki can climb out of the deep financial debt she's found herself in, she will finally make their engagement to be married public.

Miscommunication, faulty assumptions, and unmet expectations threaten this union seemingly made in heaven. When life comes at them hard and fast, they must rely on their bond and their loving, self-made family of friends.

ISBN: 978-1-953734-08-2 (e-Book)
ISBN: 978-1-953734-11-2 (Paperback)

www.ingramcontent.com/pod-product-compliance
Lightning Source LLC
Chambersburg PA
CBHW071200260626
47162CB00003B/1123